SUMMER LIGHT

CLOUD DANCER

THE SERIES

Linda McGinnis

For Janice,
an extraordinary friend,
an exceptional nurse,
and,
an excellent source of medical information.
Thank you for all your support.

..

Dear Reader,

Thank you for purchasing *Summer Light* and for your continued interest in the *Cloud Dancer Series*.

The characters in *Cloud Dancer* have evolved since *Pueblo Summer* was first written. I spent my vacations on the pueblo many years ago, but I'm sure that some things have changed there as well. I have continued to research pueblo life with each successive volume, but reliable sources are extremely limited.

I have done my best to portray with sensitivity, this culture which I admire and respect. If I have fallen short of the mark or offended anyone, I am truly sorry. Please feel free to contact me if I have misrepresented any of your traditions.

Sincerely,
Linda McGinnis

.

CHAPTER 1

Alonzo Herrera stood on the beach of the pueblo lake, holding the reins of two impatient horses and shading his eyes from the setting sun that swam on the far side of the water. His casual stance belied the pain that gripped his gut and hollowed his heart.

His brother, Paolo, was marrying Erin Fraser, the woman he loved.

The woman they both loved.

He turned to calm Paolo's restless horse, K'akana, who stamped his feet irritably. The two animals were as different as Alonzo and Paolo; Maasr'a, calm, patient, and pliant; and K'akana, high strung, short-tempered, and mercurial.

Alonzo gave K'akana all his attention, unable to watch his brother kiss Erin as the ceremony ended. More than anything, Alonzo wanted to swing up onto Maasr'a's back and escape the pomp and the pain.

Their cousin, Carlos, glanced around at him, questioning.

Carlos knew.

Actually, everyone knew.

Alonzo shrugged, feigning indifference.

The family crowded around the newly married couple, offering their congratulations. Alonzo was grateful that tending to the horses gave him an excuse to hang back.

When he and Paolo had made their peace the month before, Alonzo promised his brother that he would bless and support Paolo and Erin's marriage.

But, a promise couldn't change his feelings.

A promise couldn't erase a love that had lasted years.

Carlos stepped beside him. "You okay?"

"Yeah."

"Will they ride off into the sunset?"

"That's the plan."

Erin and Paolo walked over, hand in hand, smiling like children let loose for summer vacation.

"Congratulations," Carlos said, giving Erin a hug. "He'd better treat you right."

"No worries there," Paolo said.

But, Alonzo worried. He'd seen how Paolo had treated her the year before; seen the unnecessary games, testing Erin's love and commitment.

Erin turned to Alonzo with the soft smile he treasured. He took in the familiar fragrance of the Peace rose she carried; the rose they had planted for their Aunt Julia; the rose that was an experiment to see if the plant could survive a brutal pueblo summer in a self-watering pot.

The rose had survived the summer better than he had.

Carlos's sister, Neyse, had used the roses to make Erin's simple wedding bouquet.

"I hope you'll be happy." Alonzo turned his head when Erin leaned forward to kiss him, and sadness flashed in her eyes.

It couldn't be helped.

He'd promised.

Paolo hugged him fiercely. "*Hueh.*" The single word of thanks took in more territory than the land grant that had once surrounded their pueblo.

"Come and eat," their Aunt Julia urged, helping Erin's mother uncover the variety of dishes that sat on the picnic table. "It's going to be dark soon."

Erin and Paolo turned to join their families, who had gathered around the picnic table.

"Do you want something to eat?" Carlos asked.

Alonzo shook his head.

All he wanted was to leave.

*

The sun had long since set when Paolo told Alonzo that Erin wasn't prepared to ride a horse back to the pueblo. "Carlos can ride K'akana." He gave his horse a gentling pat. "I'm glad you were here, Lon. It wouldn't have been right without you."

Alonzo nodded, not trusting his voice.

"We'll see you soon." Paolo sounded unsure.

Alonzo seldom heard Paolo sound unsure about anything. But, their peace had been struck so recently that Alonzo wasn't confident about it either.

His brother had been furious when he learned that Alonzo and Erin had been meeting two nights a week in the spring, working on the watering system for a self-sustaining rose garden for their Aunt Julia.

Paolo objected to the project.

He objected even more to them meeting.

He objected most that they hadn't told him.

Erin assured Paolo she felt only friendship for Alonzo, but Paolo knew his brother felt something else entirely.

Erin had fallen for Paolo the first time she'd seen him, nearly a decade before. Being with her had never been even a remote possibility for Alonzo. However, his heedless heart had ignored the obvious, and it had belonged to Erin for years. She just hadn't known it.

Carlos joined them. "We should get going."

"Afraid you'll get lost?" Paolo asked, jostling Carlos. "The horses know the way, even if you two don't."

"We'll manage." Carlos mounted K'akana easily and

grinned down at Paolo. "Maybe better than you."

Alonzo's mother, Victoria, caught hold of his arm. "Don't stay away," she begged quietly. "We miss you."

Instead of an answer, he leaned over and kissed her cheek, then swung smoothly into the saddle. Pain mounted behind him, and held fast around his waist. There was no escape.

"Alonzo, wait!" His sister, Felicia, came running over. "When can I come spend the weekend? You said I could ages ago." The only girl among four children, Felicia was the youngest and everyone's favorite.

"Soon," he said.

"Promise?"

"Yes," he called over his shoulder. He felt his mother's hard stare, like an eagle's eyes boring into his head. She would not like fifteen-year-old Felicia spending a weekend out of her sight.

Being on Maasr'a's back comforted him, rocking gently as they made their way to the village. He'd ridden seldom recently. He missed it. He would do it more often if it didn't mean coming to the pueblo.

They rode to the barn in silence, unsaddled the horses, brushed them down, and fed them. Carlos had taken over the care of Mr. Montoya's animals when the old man had passed away in the spring.

"The horses don't get enough exercise," Carlos said. "You should come ride with me more often."

Alonzo opened the door to his car. "I will."

Carlos gave him a sharp look. "No, you won't."

"No. I won't."

Carlos wouldn't push. Alonzo was grateful that his cousin understood. Carlos was younger by two years, but had a wisdom that many his age lacked.

"See you, Dyaami," Carlos said.

Alonzo flinched at the sound of his pueblo name. "Yeah."

Driving south toward his apartment in Albuquerque,

Alonzo couldn't get his mother's sad face out of his mind. He'd moved to the city after he and Paolo had fought three months before, and she had been distraught ever since.

The pueblo no longer felt like home. Albuquerque didn't, either. How could anyone feel at home in a place where you couldn't feel the earth? Albuquerque was all asphalt and concrete and grass. Alonzo's feet hadn't touched the bare ground since he moved there.

He'd outgrown his job, or perhaps outlived his interest in it. As a water resource analyst for the New Mexico State Engineer's office, Alonzo spent much of his time at his desk. Working with Erin on water harvesting had been infinitely more interesting and challenging than anything he did at work.

Alonzo had spent hours researching their project. Now, he had a half-dozen ideas and nobody to share them with.

Especially not Erin.

The month before, he bought a self-watering pot like the one he'd purchased for the project with Erin. He planted a tomato, curious to see if he could grow food as successfully as roses. The patio outside his apartment wasn't the ideal spot, but so far, the plant was thriving.

He pulled into his complex parking lot, got out of the car, and locked the door. He looked around in misery. Asphalt and concrete and grass.

He needed to find his home.

*

Late Thursday night, Alonzo sat on his patio, enjoying a cold beer in the warm evening twilight. His decision to move to town had been made in haste, and he took the first apartment he'd seen. Within days, he was disappointed he hadn't waited for an opening on the second floor, where he could have seen the common area and swimming pool.

Now, he was grateful for the small private space with the

tall wooden fence. The tomato plant in the self-watering pot had seven steadily growing tomatoes. He checked them every day, gratified at how healthy they appeared. Roses for his aunt may have been Erin's aim, but Alonzo had hoped for a method to improve crop production on the pueblo.

He had ordered a second pot and was researching the best vegetable to plant that fall. Broad beans were at the top of his list, although winter cabbage and Brussels sprouts looked equally appealing.

When his phone rang, he put down the beer.

"Hey Carlos," he answered, seeing the name on his screen.

"Hi."

"What's up?"

"I got a call from PICC."

Alonzo had to think a moment before the letters registered: the Pueblo Indian Cultural Center.

"The Ramirez family was supposed to be dancing this month, but Mateo fell from a phone pole yesterday and busted his right leg."

"Ouch."

"I'll say. Anyway, they wanted to know if I could help out. I thought maybe we could do it together."

Alonzo hoped his silence would answer his cousin's question.

"What do you think?"

"No, thanks."

"Come on, Lon."

"No."

"Why not?"

"I don't know any dances."

"*Ma'a.*"

"Stop what?"

"Stop messing with me. You know plenty of dances."

"No."

"I'll pay you."

"How much?"

"How much do you want?"

"Nothing. I don't want to do it."

"I don't ask you for much, Dyaami."

True enough.

His heart wasn't in it when he asked, "When?"

"Saturday and Sunday, at eleven o'clock and two o'clock, for the next four weeks."

"Which dances?"

"Whichever ones we want."

Alonzo hesitated.

"Come on. It's no big deal. We know plenty of dances."

"What about clothes?"

"I can get them." He waited. "Well?"

"Oh, all right. I'll do it. *This* weekend. Find someone else for the rest of the month."

"*Hueh.* I knew you'd say yes."

"Like I had a choice?"

"Probably not."

"Are we going to practice?"

"What for? We've done the dances since we could walk. Do you need practice?"

"I suppose not."

"I'll pick you up Saturday morning."

"Don't bother. Bring my clothes here tomorrow. If they still fit, I'll meet you at the center on Saturday."

*

It was obvious that Alonzo's father, Ramon, had packed the simple white bag that Carlos brought to his apartment. The clothes were carefully folded, and every piece had been brushed clean.

He knew they would fit. He'd worn them for the spring dances. He dressed carefully on Saturday morning, making sure the black and green trim on his white kilt looked fresh, and the bells at his waist hung free.

He fastened the traditional green and yellow feathers in his hair, trying not to look himself in the eye. He seriously did not want to do this. But, Carlos didn't ask for much.

Alonzo walked from the parking lot into the Cultural Center, the bells on his moccasins heralding his arrival. Carlos wasn't there. Lacking anything better to do, he wandered into the gift shop.

Walking around, looking at nothing in particular, a photograph caught his attention. A lightning bolt of white streaked down the dark face of a horse, whose mouth nuzzled a woman's hand. It drew Alonzo in like a net cast around his heart.

He stood gazing at the picture, feeling Maasr'a's velvet soft nose in his palm. Maasr'a meant *light* in Keres, his native tongue, and Alonzo thought it perfectly described the horse's bright, easy spirit.

At first, Alonzo had been terrified of the giant animal, whose nostrils were big enough to swallow his small hand. But, Mr. Montoya had chosen the right horse for Alonzo, a gentle creature, the opposite of the fiery beast he'd selected for Paolo.

As Alonzo gazed at the photograph, an ache as heavy as the horse dragged at his heart. He missed the simple joys of his childhood, gone so long now that the memories had faded like a woven blanket left in the sun.

He couldn't help wondering if the horse belonged to the photographer. Her signature on the mat was as delicate as it was deliberate: Luz Fragua.

Luz.

Light.

"Hey," Carlos said, coming up beside him. "You ready?"

"Yeah."

His cousin pushed him toward the plaza.

"Who's drumming?" Alonzo asked.

"Frankie Cordero."

Alonzo didn't know Cordero, but he trusted Carlos. His cousin danced at PICC fairly regularly, and knew many of the other performers.

They walked out to the enclosed plaza, where a noisy crowd of visitors had already gathered. Carlos spoke to the M.C. and the drummer, and then the two cousins stood aside while the M.C. addressed the crowd and explained to them the dances Carlos and Alonzo would perform.

A flutter of movement caught Alonzo's attention. He turned. A beautiful young woman with long black hair and a big black camera moved closer. She tilted her head in greeting, but said nothing.

Carlos nudged him and motioned toward the center of the plaza. Alonzo heard the drum beat and his feet fell in with his cousin's, the rhythm so ingrained that they felt tied to the drum.

He was vaguely aware of the woman, who walked around the perimeter taking shots of him and Carlos as they danced. This would have been strictly forbidden on most of the pueblos, although some, like Taos, were open and tolerant of photographers.

When they finished their dances, many of the people in the audience wanted a picture taken with them. Some used cell phones, others, cameras. The two men posed genially, for the most part, without smiling.

Three young women, all white, gushed over them, asking questions, and exclaiming how much they enjoyed their performance.

"Have you been doing this for a long time?" one asked.

"We started dancing when we started walking," Carlos said. "It's in our blood."

Alonzo nodded in silent agreement, his attention still on the woman, who continued taking photos.

When all the tourists had finally left, Carlos said, "I knew that we could do it."

"Like you said, since we started walking."

"Right."

Alonzo's eyes followed the woman, who smiled at Carlos and went back inside the center. "Who is that?"

"Luz Fragua. She's from Jemez."

Alonzo bent and tightened the leather ties on his moccasins.

"Want to meet her?"

"No."

"You sure?"

"Yes."

"Okay. How about some lunch?"

Alonzo glanced down at his clothes. "Like this?"

"Mom packed some food for us."

"Great. I didn't have any breakfast."

"You're going to starve to death in that apartment."

Alonzo looked for the woman when they went inside. Apparently, she had left. He wondered about the pictures, but wasn't about to ask Carlos.

Sometimes silence was the only option.

*

The woman was back again when they danced that afternoon, hovering at the edge of the plaza, careful not to interfere with their dancing or obstruct anyone's view.

This time, she used a telephoto lens the size of Texas. Carlos seemed not to notice, but Alonzo felt self-conscious. Many in the audience were filming, but none of the cameras or cell phones seemed dangerous, like the one Luz wielded.

Alonzo felt the power of the lens pierce his skin and peer deep within him, into a darkness where insecurity and sadness and humiliation huddled. A darkness he did not want exposed. He turned his head, doing his best to avoid the intrusion.

She slipped away while Alonzo and Carlos were posing after the performance. When they walked back through the center, Alonzo wondered where she might have gone.

"You sure you don't want to meet her?" Carlos asked.

"Who?"

"Luz."

"Why would I want to meet her?" He pushed open the door toward the parking lot.

"No reason," Carlos said. He smiled and shook his head. "Sometimes you remind me of Paolo."

Alonzo felt his hair rise, sharp and prickly, on the back of his neck. "Don't say that."

Carlos considered his cousin's grimace. "Okay."

Once, the comparison would have pleased him; now, it stung like nettles.

CHAPTER 2

Alonzo arranged to meet Carlos at PICC again the next day. He arrived early, thinking he might see Luz, maybe even speak to her. But, she wasn't there.

When Carlos arrived, he gave Alonzo a strange look. "Why so early?"

"No reason." However he knew it wouldn't take much for Carlos to figure it out.

The dances went smoothly and when they'd finished the second set, Alonzo told Carlos he wanted to check out the gift shop.

"The gift shop?"

"Yeah."

"You haven't seen enough pueblo art in your life?"

"I want to see what they've got here."

A smile of understanding made its way slowly across Carlos's handsome face. "Whatever. So, I'll see you next Saturday."

"Next Saturday?"

"Yes. I told you they need us for a month."

"Didn't you find somebody else?"

"No."

"Seriously? Did you ask?"

"Yes. Nobody's interested. So, you'll be here, right?"

"I suppose."

"You know you love it...all that female attention." Carlos laughed as he headed toward the parking lot.

Several tourists were browsing in the gift shop. A few stopped him with questions about the dances. One woman asked to take a selfie with him, then insisted on showing it to him after she'd posted it on her web page.

He was about to leave when he saw a beautiful book, with her name at the top: Luz Fragua. The cover featured a sepia tone photograph of a ladder leaning against an adobe wall. Wooden ladders were commonly used to gain access to upper floors on the older pueblos. The book was entitled *Sunlight and Shadow: Taos Pueblo*.

He picked up the book and began leafing through the pages. The photos were all in warm sepia colors, lending a sense of age and history, while at the same time, revealing a more contemporary sensitivity. It was like walking through time with a modern master.

"Do you like it?"

The voice, intimate and curious, jolted him. He turned. "Yes."

Luz's smile was the essence of light. "I'm glad."

"You took a lot of pictures yesterday."

"I did. Unfortunately, none of them were what I wanted."

"What did you want?"

"Something that hits me like the ones in that book."

"Don't you know that when you take the shot?"

"Sometimes. More often, I think I've got something special, and then I'm disappointed. The best ones are when I'm completely surprised."

He looked down at the book in his hands. "Were these all surprises?"

"Some of them, yes."

"Nice surprises."

"Thank you. How did the dances go today?"

"Fine." He stood uncomfortably, wishing he could make the conversation last. It would have been easy for Paolo.

"Nice to see you again," she said, turning.

"You, too." He watched her walk away, light cascading down the sleek black braid that hung halfway to her waist.

He drove home chiding himself. He should have bought one of the books and asked her to autograph it. That would have made their encounter last.

Jerk.

He might not have the chance to see her alone again. He certainly wasn't going to ask her for an autograph in front of Carlos. Or anyone else, for that matter.

Back at his apartment, he endured the stares of other residents lounging around the community pool. He thought he heard one person mutter Tonto, but he might have misunderstood.

He showered and dressed, then checked in the kitchen for something to eat. Nothing. Glancing out the sliding glass door, he noticed the tomato plant on the patio, which seemed to have exploded overnight.

He discovered nine good-sized tomatoes, none of which had been ready the last time he'd looked. He picked six and ate three, sweet juice dripping down his chin and onto his recently clean shirt.

The experiment was turning into a success.

Would the beans do as well?

*

On Saturday morning, Alonzo picked the other three tomatoes off the vine. He'd ask Carlos to take them to Victoria, who loved fresh tomatoes as much as Alonzo did.

He was looking forward to being at PICC more than he'd anticipated anything in weeks. He had decided to go early, buy Luz's book, and wait for a quiet moment alone to ask her for an autograph.

But, Carlos was already in the parking lot when he pulled in, and his plan dissolved in an instant. He wasn't about to set himself up for his cousin's teasing.

"You're early," he said to Carlos as he got out of his car.

"I misread my clock. I thought it was an hour later. You're pretty early yourself."

"Words hardly heard at home," Alonzo said, grinning.

He handed Carlos the bag of tomatoes. "Will you give these to my mom?"

"Sure." Carlos opened the bag, held it to his face, and sniffed. "Are these from the self-watering pot?"

"Yeah."

"Impressive. I think maybe you're a farmer at heart."

"Maybe."

Tourists had already gathered in the plaza, many with questions and requests for photographs. The two men were busy until it was time for them to dance. During the break between performances, they drove through the line at McDonalds and bought burgers.

After the second performance, they both left. Alonzo didn't intend to buy Luz's book in front of Carlos and risk his ridicule. Carlos was never mean, but he did love to tease.

Best to wait.

*

A summer storm blew in that night. Carlos called early, to tell him that the dancing on Sunday had been canceled.

Alonzo checked the tomato plant, curious how it would fare in the downpour. If the system could not survive a heavy rain, it would never survive the pueblo.

All day, he fought the urge to visit the center. He needed distance from the pueblo, not more connection to it. With Luz, there was nowhere to go except back.

Early in the evening, his phone rang. When he saw the

name on the screen, he didn't want to answer. It stopped ringing for a while and then began again. There was no escaping the pueblo.

"Hello?"

"Hi, Alonzo. It's Julia."

"Hi, Auntie."

"We're having a birthday dinner for Neyse and Erin next Sunday, and I want you to come."

The response took only seconds. "I can't. I'm dancing at PICC."

"With Carlos. I know. You'll be done by four. You have plenty of time to be here for dinner."

More than enough time, he knew. There was no excuse.

"Alonzo?"

"Yes…"

"I expect you to be here."

Julia wasn't often pushy.

"I don't think…"

"The longer you stay away, the harder it's going to be to come back."

"What makes you think I want to come back?" he asked.

"This is your home. It's where you belong."

"It doesn't feel like I belong there."

"Come for dinner. Give it a chance."

"Let me think about it."

"Don't think too hard."

"No, I won't."

After they'd hung up, he wondered if his mother had put Julia up to it. Did they think he'd have a harder time saying no to his aunt than he would to his mother?

*

All week, Alonzo thought about Erin's birthday, and what he might give her. A reminder of the project they'd done together might please her, but he was certain it would not please his brother.

The thought of their estrangement hurt. The connection with his brother could never be what it had been. Erin was Paolo's wife now, and Alonzo had promised to honor that. Still, the tension remained.

Wednesday night, his phone rang after he'd gone to bed. He looked at the screen. Paolo.

He hesitated answering, but knew his brother would just keep calling. "Hello?"

"Lon?"

"Yeah."

"How are you?"

"Okay."

"I wanted to know—I was hoping—uh, are you coming on Sunday night?"

The new, uncertain Paolo. The one he didn't recognize.

"Yeah."

"I'm glad. I miss you, Lon."

He had no response.

After a sad silence Paolo said, "I guess I'll see you then."

"Yeah."

He hung up, tossed the phone on the dresser, and turned to the wall. Then, he tossed and turned all night, unable to find a comfortable spot in the uncomfortable bed.

*

He went to the mall early Saturday morning, looking for gifts for Erin and Neyse. He wandered from one store to another, perplexed by the chore and paralyzed by the choices. He hated this sort of thing.

After two hours, he was ready to give up. Nothing had caught his attention that he thought would suit either one of them. He went into the bookstore, bought a cup of coffee, and was ready to pray to Mother Earth for guidance, when he noticed a display of calendars.

Everybody needed a calendar. It was the perfect solution for both of them. He left the coffee sitting on a table and began considering the selections.

The options seemed endless. After half an hour, he picked one about Audubon Songbirds for Neyse; Juan would like it, too. He already knew a lot of bird calls.

Erin's wasn't so easy. There were several featuring roses. He poured over each calendar, finally selecting one that included a history of each month's rose.

When he went to check out, the salesclerk asked, "Do you need wrapping paper?"

Was he supposed to buy wrapping paper? His mom was in charge of that sort of thing.

What about a card?

He needed cards.

For the first time in weeks, moving back home sounded good. When the allure of his mother's cooking couldn't coax him, her dealing with life's daily demands, might.

He picked two simple cards, a roll of floral wrapping paper that he thought his mom might buy, and returned to the checkout counter.

Tape, he thought. And ribbon. Geez.

This was a pain.

Home had its advantages.

*

Heat pressed down on PICC that afternoon like the inside of an horno oven. By the end of the two o'clock performance, Alonzo and Carlos were both sweating freely. Despite the oppressive heat, tourists crowded around wanting photos.

Alonzo wanted a bottle of water and a shower.

They posed patiently for pictures, and then escaped into the air conditioned building. Alonzo had looked for Luz when he arrived, with no luck.

Yet now, there she was, carrying a stack of books into the gift shop. If Carlos hadn't been standing beside him, Alonzo would have hurried to help her.

Carlos nudged him and said quietly, "Now's your chance."

"For what?"

Carlos's smile said he knew his cousin well. "Nothing."

"I need a shower," Alonzo said. "I'll see you tomorrow."

The bells on his moccasins jangled loudly as he walked out with particular determination. When would he be able to get an autographed book if Carlos was always hanging around?

He showered, dressed, and hunted for something to eat. His refrigerator was as empty and bleak as the desert. He grabbed his car keys and left.

Half an hour later, he pulled into the parking lot at PICC, not sure if Luz would still be there, but very sure he could get an authentic pueblo meal at the Harvest Café. He walked into the gift shop first, hoping to find her.

"Can I help you?" an older woman asked.

"No, thank you."

"Let me know if I can show you anything."

"I will."

Near the back of the store, he saw a display of readily recognizable books. Like the other book, her name was at the top. Below a sepia tone photograph of the ancient Sky City, was the title, *Sunlight and Shadow: Acoma Pueblo*.

He picked up the book on the top of the stack and without even opening it, bought it. He stuck it under his arm and walked into the café.

He was seated near the front, and placed the book carefully on the table while he read the dinner menu. He was trying to decide between the Jemez enchilada and the Navajo taco when he heard her voice. He glanced up.

Her smile was as soft as down feathers in a baby bird's nest. "Do you like it?" she asked, nodding at the book.

"I haven't looked at it yet."

"Oh?"

"I was saving it."

"For what?"

"Until after I ordered."

The waitress approached the table. "Hi, Luz. Do you need a menu?"

"Have you eaten?" he asked.

She shook her head.

"Would you like to have dinner?"

She hesitated. "Am I intruding?"

"No."

She sat down across from him, and took the menu. "I'm Luz Fragua."

"I know. I'm Alonzo Herrera, Carlos's cousin."

"I know."

He wondered how, since they'd never been introduced. She must have asked someone, but whom?

"Do you know what you want for supper?" she asked.

"Yes. What about you?"

She smiled. "I always read the menu and then I always get the same thing."

"Tell me about the book."

"Not till you look at it."

After they'd ordered, Alonzo opened the book. The first photograph, that of a young pueblo boy whose father was adjusting his dance costume, took his breath away. He could feel his own father's presence, bent over, tying Alonzo's moccasins. The sense of alienation strangled his words.

She watched him as he pondered each photo.

When he'd paged through the entire book, she asked, "Do you like it?"

He nodded, afraid his voice would expose the unexpected emotion.

"I'm glad."

"Will you do more?" he asked when he thought his voice

would no longer betray him.

"As long as they keep selling."

They sat talking about the book long after they'd finished eating their dinner.

"I've always loved the old photographs of the pueblos," Luz said. "The sepia tones have been my favorite for as long as I can remember. When I see one in a book or a magazine, I can smell the heat, and the dust, and the struggle."

"Is anyone else in your family a photographer?"

"No. Jemez has some wonderful artists—potters, jewelry makers, and painters. But, I'm the only one who takes pictures. On this scale, anyway."

"Your folks must be proud."

"They think I'm crazy. They'd be happy if I'd get married. They'd be even happier if I'd have kids. They're afraid I'll end up an old maid."

"Old?"

"I'm well past thirty. I think it worries them."

Alonzo thought she looked closer to fifteen than thirty. Her smooth, hazel-hued skin was flawless, as if it had been painted with a brush of few bristles. Her hair was blacker than a raven's wings, with no trace of grey. And, he noticed, she certainly didn't dress like an old maid.

"Anyway, this is what I love, and I believe it's what I do best. My dream is to create a book for each pueblo."

"Nineteen books."

"Yes."

"Which one is next?"

"Laguna, I think."

"The biggest."

"Yes."

"Will that make it harder or easier?"

Her eyes focused in on him, as if his perception had captivated her thoughts. "Easier to photograph; harder to choose the ones to publish."

A man approached their table, nodded at Alonzo, and

spoke to Luz in a dialect Alonzo didn't understand. Then, he nodded to Alonzo again and walked out.

"I have to go." She pulled out her wallet.

"I'll get it," he said.

"Are you sure?"

"I am."

"Thanks."

She joined the man in the main hall, and they left together.

Was it his imagination or did a particular essence linger after she left? He couldn't name it. It wasn't perfume, it wasn't soap. It was bigger than an aroma. Bolder. Like she'd left a part of herself behind; left it there for him to enjoy.

It was then that Alonzo realized he hadn't asked her to autograph his book.

He put money for their meals with a tip on the table, picked up the book, and headed out to his car, smiling. Now he had the perfect excuse to talk to her again.

CHAPTER 3

Alonzo woke Sunday morning tangled in the bedding like a hook in a careless child's fishing line. On a day already hot and muggy, dancing would not be fun. He wondered if Luz would be at the center, then chided himself.

Why in the world was he interested in a pueblo woman, or any woman, for that matter? Hadn't he learned his lesson? No more women. No more pueblo. He'd left all that behind.

He showered, dressed, and drove to the center, unable to stop wondering about Luz. For better or worse, she wasn't there. Neither was his cousin.

Carlos rushed out to the plaza moments before the program was supposed to begin. "Sorry. I was helping Mom get ready for the party."

"It's okay. I could have done it alone."

"Yes, but you wouldn't have been as good."

The drummer started tapping, the beat ever stronger and louder, and the two men danced into the familiar world of their ancestors.

The heat didn't discourage spectators from asking the two men questions or requesting pictures. Much as he tried to keep his mind focused, part of Alonzo's attention was watching for Luz. Her name was aptly chosen, for she brought with her a particular light that he could hardly resist.

When they finished the second performance, Carlos said, "I've gotta go. I told Mom I'd do a few more things for her before dinner. I'll see you later, right?"

"Yeah."

They walked out to the parking lot together.

"Don't be late," Carlos said.

"What's late?"

"Late is when all the prune pie is gone."

Alonzo gave him a long look. "If you want me to dance again…"

Carlos held up his hand. "Point taken. I believe there's a pie with your name on it."

"That's more like it."

The truth was, Alonzo knew that in big things or small, Carlos would always have his back.

*

The day had cooled by the time Alonzo arrived at Julia's late in the afternoon; a storm front had rolled across the big desert sky and cloaked the world in a heavy grey mantle. He knew that by the time he drove home that night, it would be pouring.

He was not surprised that his mother was already there.

She greeted him as eagerly as if he were returning from a journey into space. "You're thin, Dyaami. You aren't eating enough. I have posole and bread for you at home. You can get it before you leave."

"Thanks, Mom. That'd be great."

The rest of the family straggled in over the next hour, welcoming Alonzo like a celebrity. Paolo and Erin were the last to arrive. Alonzo was surprised at how little Erin's brief hug affected him. He couldn't deny he'd missed her, but it felt like there had been a shift.

Was it her?

Or him?

"It's good to see you, Lon," she said. "I'm glad you came."

"I couldn't miss your birthday."

"What about mine?" Neyse asked, pushing at him.

"Yours either, little cousin."

"Little?" Juan said. "She's anything but."

"Careful, buddy," Paolo said. "You'll be divorced before dinner."

Juan put his arm around Neyse's waist. "Not a chance. She couldn't do without me."

"He's right," Neyse said. "Who'd do the dishes?"

Alonzo wondered if Juan had actually become that domesticated, although he knew he'd be smart not to comment.

"Could you girls come help?" Julia called from the kitchen.

"Anybody want a beer?" Paolo asked.

"Sure," Alonzo said.

"Not for me," Juan said, "but I'd take a soda."

Felicia took advantage of Paolo's exit to grab Alonzo. "I don't have any plans next weekend. Can I come visit?"

He smiled at her. "No."

"Why not?"

"Because I have plans."

"You're never going to let me come."

"Let's give Mom a little more time to get used to the idea, okay, K'ayama?"

Her Indian name, which meant chipmunk, brought a smile, accentuating the cheeks that had inspired it. "She won't ever get used to you being gone. You'll come back and I'll never get to visit."

He put his arm around her and whispered in her ear, "You can come sometime before Christmas."

"You mean it?"

25

"Yes."

Paolo brought the drinks. He took a long swig of his beer. "Nothing better on a hot day."

"I couldn't agree more," Alonzo said.

"Carlos says you've been dancing at PICC."

Alonzo nodded. "Yep."

"You like it?"

Alonzo heard the unmistakable disapproval. "It's okay."

"Are you tired of Albuquerque yet?"

"No."

"We miss you. Don't stay away too long."

"No. I won't."

He felt his brother's familiar hand on his shoulder; the hand that had hugged him, and hit him, and held him his entire life. Now, it brought an equal amount of pain and pleasure.

He missed his family, too. But, he couldn't come home.

Not after making such a fool of himself there.

*

Erin opened the calendar and gave Alonzo a smile that said he'd hit the mark. "Thank you, Lon." His nickname sounded completely different when she said it. She tore the cellophane off and began looking at each page. Her eyes lifted to his. "Peace. July is Peace."

He nodded. They'd always share that—the two of them.

"My turn," Neyse said, ripping the paper off her calendar. "Oh, Lon, it's perfect. Look, Juan. Bird calls. Maybe I can learn some, too."

Juan grinned. "You can't even whistle."

"Only because you won't teach me."

"How can anyone not know how to whistle?" Carlos asked. He leaned over his sister, whispering loudly, "You're a loser."

She punched him playfully. "Don't be mean."

26

Victoria and Julia came in from the kitchen, each carrying a cake ablaze with candles.

"You guys must be really old if they couldn't get all the candles on one cake," Alonzo's younger brother, Luis, teased.

Ramon looked at his youngest son. "If you want to have a happy life, never tell a woman she's old. Or fat."

"Or, that she's a bad driver," Tony added.

*

All that week Alonzo thought about the upcoming weekend, the last two days he would be performing with Carlos at PICC. The center scheduled dancers from different pueblos every month, and another group would take over in September.

That meant he wouldn't be seeing Luz again. He wanted to buy her other book and have her sign both of them, though he wouldn't be comfortable asking her unless they were alone. Carlos would make a big deal of it, and that was the last thing Alonzo wanted.

On Saturday, he was dressed and ready to go early. He drove to Starbucks, and got in line at the drive-thru window. Out of respect for his people and their traditions, he never went inside any public places in native dress.

Luz was at the cash register in the gift shop when he walked into the center.

"Hi," he said. "Are you working?"

Her dazzling smile hinted at dimples. "Yes. The artists take shifts on the weekends."

"How is the new book doing?"

"Better than I expected. A lot of folks are buying both at the same time." Her shy smile said she was pleased, though her heritage demanded humility.

"I wanted you to sign my copy."

"Sure."

27

"I don't have it with me."

"Really? You don't carry it around with you? How disappointing."

"Maybe we could meet sometime and have a cup of coffee or a soda. This is our last weekend dancing."

"Sure, we could do that."

"I should get your phone number." The uncertainty in his voice sounded juvenile and embarrassing.

"Hey, Lon."

He turned.

"Hi, Carlos," Luz said, giving him the same brilliant smile she'd given Alonzo.

"Hi, Luz. You working?"

"I am."

"So are we. Come on, cousin, we're late."

Alonzo turned regretful eyes on Luz. "I'll see you."

She nodded.

When they finished their first set, tourists flooded the gift shop, and Alonzo had no opportunity to talk to Luz. When they finished the second set, someone else was working at the counter.

"Your girlfriend is gone," Carlos said as they walked past the gift shop toward the parking lot.

"She's not my girlfriend."

"Looked like she was. She has eyes for you, Lon."

"She's looking for a sale."

"No, she's looking for a date."

"*Heem'e.*"

"Try not to be so much like your brother."

"Meaning?"

"It took him forever to admit what he wanted."

"I don't know what I want." The admission made him squirm. Stupid thing to think. Even worse to say.

When he opened the door to his car, a piece of paper fluttered to the ground. He bent and picked it up. No name. No message. Only a number.

She'd left it up to him, which made him suddenly unsure.

"See you tomorrow," Carlos said.

"I'll be here." He tossed the paper on the passenger's seat and started the engine. He resisted the urge to call her right then.

He resisted the urge when he got home.

He even resisted that night when he sat wondering if seeing her would be moving in the wrong direction.

*

The director of PICC spoke to them after the final performance on Sunday. "You two did a great job this month. I appreciate you filling in on such short notice."

"No problem," Carlos assured him.

"We've had lots of good comments from folks, and requests to have you back more often. I'd like to sign you up on our regular schedule for next year."

"Sure," Carlos said. "We'd like that, right Lon?"

"I guess." He still hadn't decided if hanging around there, and seeing Luz, was a smart idea.

"I'll contact you, Carlos. Thanks again."

"You bet."

They walked out to their cars.

"This has been good," Carlos said.

Alonzo looked at him with amusement.

"I was thinking. We should go fishing one day. Like we used to."

Like they used to with Paolo.

After a silence, Carlos added, "We could go somewhere different. It doesn't have to be our old spot."

"I don't have my gear."

"I can get it from your mom."

Alonzo felt a tug toward the pueblo, toward tradition, toward family.

"Sound good?"

"I suppose."

"Next weekend?"

"I guess."

"Saturday?"

"Yeah, okay."

"I'll meet you near the entrance to Kewa Pueblo, and we'll walk to the river. I remember a spot Mr. Montoya liked over there."

"You'll get my gear?"

Carlos opened his car door. "I will."

"Do we need a license?"

"Only if we get caught," Carlos laughed.

He drove back to his apartment thinking about what he'd do with fish if he caught them. He'd only cooked fish a couple of times. He'd cleaned dozens of them, but his mother had cooked them. Would he take them to her? Ask her to make him supper?

He could taste the crisp, salty crust on her delicious tender filets. His mom made the best fish on the pueblo, of that he was sure. But, being at his parents' meant fighting off his mother's emotional pleas, and that was simply too painful.

He couldn't handle seeing her misery, knowing he was to blame. Knowing that, until he figured out his life, he had to stay right where he was, no matter how much it hurt her.

*

A group of Alonzo's co-workers were gathered in the break room on Monday morning. One of the other analysts, Kate Cunningham, was doing her best to convince them to attend the Navajo Nation Fair the following weekend. He couldn't understand why anyone would hesitate.

She was a stunning beauty, with eyes the blue of lake water in spring, and blond curls as wild as the winter wind. He'd heard many of his colleagues talk about asking her out, but didn't know anyone who had.

"What about you, Alonzo? Any chance you'd like to go?" she asked.

"To Navajo Nation Fair?"

"Yes," she said.

"I'm not Navajo."

When she laughed, every man in the room smiled. "And I'm not Irish, but I still celebrate St. Patrick's Day. Come on, be a sport. I'll even drive."

That wouldn't happen. "I'll think about it."

Without a doubt, a different direction from the pueblo.

*

By Thursday, the idea had begun to appeal to him. It was something different to do on the weekend. He went by Kate's desk in the late afternoon, glad nobody else was anywhere around. "Still interested in going to Navajo Nation?"

"Absolutely."

"Okay."

"Really? That's super. Do you want me to drive?"

Absolutely not. "That's okay. I'll pick you up. Sunday morning. Seven or so. It'll take two or three hours to get there. You should eat breakfast." He cringed inside when he heard his own words. He sounded as pushy as Paolo.

"Shall I pack a picnic?"

"No. There'll be plenty of food for sale."

"Thanks, Alonzo. Nobody else was game. I know we're going to have a great time."

"See you then," he said, and walked back to his desk.

A date with a White woman. It couldn't get much different from that.

CHAPTER 4

Early Saturday morning, a reluctant sun sat on the distant rim of the Sandia Mountains, wrapped in a bright golden-orange *manta*. Alonzo parked off the road near the entrance to the Kewa Pueblo. It wasn't far from home, but far enough that Paolo was unlikely to go fishing there.

He sat drinking coffee and watching the sunrise evolve from brilliant orange to shimmery tangerine to gilded lemon. He could take a picture, but then who would he show it to?

Luz?

Yes, Luz.

He got out of the car, pulled out his phone, and began taking pictures. The sunrise diminished in the camera's lens. He looked back and forth from the mountains to the screen. He took several shots, each one a disappointment. Was this what Luz had been trying to explain weeks before?

Carlos drove up, parked behind him, and got out. "Taking up photography?"

Alonzo didn't answer.

"I've got your stuff. At least your mom thought it was yours. I guess it might be Paolo's."

His hands itched as he walked toward his cousin's car.

Paolo was very particular about his gear. He wouldn't appreciate Alonzo using it. And, Alonzo wouldn't want to.

The grip of the beaten up pole was as familiar as the warm hand of an old friend. He picked up his tackle box. "They're mine."

"Your mom packed some prune pie for us."

"Great."

They walked to the river, silent as they passed three old men comfortably ensconced in their private reverie. Nodding in greeting and respect, the two continued to walk an acceptable distance downstream.

Carlos found Mr. Montoya's spot, far out of sight and sound of the old men. They sat on a large, flat rock under a huge cottonwood tree, and began to prep their gear.

"My dad thinks prune pie is the perfect bait," Carlos said, unwrapping the fragrant treat.

"Not a chance. Give me that."

He took a bite of his mother's signature pie, and fought the unbidden emotion that collected in his throat. He swallowed two lumps: only one of them was pie.

Warmth slowly crept up and over Alonzo and he unzipped his sweatshirt. "It's going to be hot today."

"I'm glad we're not dancing."

Alonzo didn't answer.

"I said I'm glad we're not dancing."

"Yeah."

"Aren't you glad, too?" Carlos grinned at his cousin.

"*Ma'aku.*"

"Why should I be quiet? Am I bothering the fish? Or you?" His pole jerked. "This could be a big one." Carlos finessed the line, letting it out a little, pulling it back, giving the fish the chance to escape if he was clever. Or lucky.

Alonzo was so busy watching his cousin that he missed the initial jolt on his own line. A wildly spinning reel chattered and commanded his attention. The drag on the pole was considerable. There was no need to finesse. He reeled and pulled, reeled and pulled.

Carlos drew his fish from the water. He extracted the hook, mumbled a prayer of thanks, and put it into the water in the ice chest he'd brought. He looked over at Alonzo, who was struggling. "I think maybe you've caught Grandfather."

Alonzo pulled up again on the bending pole. The fish was either young and strong or old and shrewd.

"Probably a catfish. Want some help?"

"I've got it."

The fish fought like a warrior. When Alonzo finally pulled it out of the river, both men gasped.

"It's huge," Carlos said. "It must be fifteen pounds!"

Alonzo held the thrashing fighter as best he could and extracted the hook. Sadness settled on his shoulders. Mr. Montoya wasn't there to share in his victory.

Nor was Paolo.

He tipped his head toward the ice chest. "Will it fit?"

"I think so."

Carlos took the struggling fish from his cousin and crammed it into the ice chest, where it continued to battle. "I bet those old men have been after this beauty forever."

Alonzo baited his hook and threw it back into the water. He unwrapped the towel around the prune pie and took another piece.

The sun had crawled up the sky, brightening the day and warming the soft breeze that ruffled the leaves in the cottonwood tree above. Birds chattered, scolding Alonzo for moving away from the pueblo.

Carlos pulled off a piece of the sweet treat in the towel. "I was thinking, we should go ahead and make that planter box you were working on for my mom."

Alonzo kept his eyes on the river, letting his gaze float slowly downstream with the current.

"Erin says the rose is doing really good at her house. Wasn't that the intention, so Mom could have roses?"

Erin's intention. Not his.

"Lon?"

"Yeah."

"What do you think?"

"About what?"

"The planter box."

"You do it."

"I don't know anything about it."

"Get Paolo to help you."

"You're kidding."

"No."

"Paolo hated the idea. He'd never help. Come on. It'd make my mom happy."

Alonzo couldn't spend that much time on the pueblo. He'd be trapped if he did. He felt like the fish he'd caught— thrashing and fighting for his freedom.

Panic pounded in his chest.

Without any warning, he reached over, picked up the ice chest, and turned it upside down over the water. The two fish hit the surface with a loud splash.

Grandfather, stunned at first, slapped his tail, then darted beneath a boulder and disappeared.

Carlos jumped up. "What the heck?"

"Let one of the old men catch him."

"Geez, you're nuts, Lon. Absolutely nuts. Did you have to throw mine back, too?"

"You'll catch him again." Alonzo reeled in his line, laid his rod aside, and leaned back. He had no need for fish.

"Are you ready to go?" his cousin asked.

"No."

"You sure?"

"Yeah."

Sharing silence with Carlos was familiar and easy. His cousin caught six fish before the day had warmed, and Brother fish had gone home to sleep.

The two packed their gear and started back to the cars.

Carlos opened his trunk and put the equipment and the

ice chest inside. "What are you doing tomorrow?"

"Going to Navajo Nation Fair."

He cousin's dark eyes held a dozen unspoken questions.

"One of the other analysts in my office wanted to go."

"Why?"

"She thought it sounded like fun."

"She?"

"Yeah."

Anyone else would have asked for details. Not Carlos.

"Are you coming back for dinner?"

"Not today."

"Let's do this again."

"Yeah, we will."

"Will you think about the planter?"

"I did. It's a bad idea."

"Was it a bad idea last spring?"

Alonzo thought a moment and then said, "Probably."

Of course, it hadn't been a bad idea. If his trial with tomatoes and beans was successful, it might have huge implications for increased crop production on the pueblo.

He knew that two plants in two pots would only be a start. He would have to devise a way to water several rows of crops. And, he'd need more room to do that.

His patio was far too small.

*

When Kate opened her front door on Sunday morning, Alonzo felt his breath yanked out of him as fiercely as if he'd jumped off a cliff at the ancient pueblo.

She looked beautiful. Her golden curls were still damp; her face was bright and fresh, as if she'd just finished scrubbing it. Her tawny skin contrasted against a white dress like sun against sand.

"Good morning," she said.

"Hi."

"Would you like a cup of coffee? I made a pot."

"No, thanks. I had a cup earlier. Are you ready?"

"Yes." She put a key into a small pouch and stuck it into a pocket. "All set."

"It might be cold by the time we come home."

She pulled a pristine white sweater from the hall rack. "I'm good to go."

When he opened the car door for her, he wished he'd thought to have it washed. Dirt he hadn't noticed only minutes before, accused him of neglect.

"I've been reading about the Navajo Nation," she said as they pulled out of the parking lot. "Why are their lands so big and the pueblo lands so small?"

He glanced over at her, wondering if she was actually interested or merely making conversation. "The Navajo were nomadic and the pueblo people were agrarian. We only needed enough land to grow crops."

"Do you grow crops?"

The simple question brought uneasiness to his chest. "My family does."

"On the pueblo?"

"Yes."

"But you don't live there."

"No."

"Why did you leave?"

"I was tired of watering crops."

Her laughter eased his deep confusion. Perhaps the day held more fun than he had imagined.

*

The line of cars outside the parking lot at the fair stretched farther than they could see.

"Good thing we came early," Kate said.

"If we'd come late, there wouldn't be a line."

"You're just saying that."

By the time they parked and walked into the fairgrounds, Alonzo's empty stomach was growling a loud complaint. "I wonder if anyone is making sopapillas."

"Is that a traditional Navajo dish?"

"No, but it sure would taste good."

He settled for an apple from one of the many farm stands. "I'll save my appetite for Navajo tacos at lunch."

Kate threaded her arm through his. "What's first?"

He fought the instinct to jerk away, shocked by her familiarity. A pueblo girl would never be so forward. Such a public display of an intimate nature made him feel conspicuous and uncomfortable.

He did his best to hide his discomfort. "The rodeo and the powwow aren't until later. I guess we should start with the arts and crafts."

"Perfect. Just what I was thinking."

The minute they entered Gorman Hall, Alonzo knew that he was in for a long day.

"Oh, wow," Kate exclaimed, taking it all in. "This is fantastic. There must be a hundred booths. I want to check out every one."

The building was crowded with artists offering all the traditional Navajo art forms: jewelry, rugs, blankets, baskets, paintings, and pottery. Kate stopped at each booth, looking at the artist's wares with interest.

Alonzo watched her easy interactions with the vendors. It wasn't only that she was beautiful, which everyone certainly noticed, but that she had a way of connecting that was captivating. She was as clever as Coyote.

By the time they'd seen every booth, Alonzo was starving. The tantalizing aroma of fresh cooked food filled the air outside the hall, and heightened his hunger.

Kate took in a deep breath. "What is that I smell?"

"Fry bread."

"I wasn't hungry until I smelled that. Can we get some?"

"Sure."

They bought Navajo tacos at the first stand they came to.

"This is huge," she said. "How can anyone possibly finish a whole one? I may need your help." She struggled through her first bite, chewed slowly, and swallowed. "Never mind. I'll manage."

Her body may have been slight, but her appetite was substantial. She ate the entire taco, then licked her fingers. "Yum. Let's get another one of those for dinner."

After they'd eaten, they found seats in the arena to watch the rodeo, the steer wrestling, the tie-down roping, and the ladies barrel race.

Kate began taking pictures with her phone, so Alonzo pulled his out as well. It wasn't something that he would normally do, but practically everyone in the crowd was taking photographs.

Every shot he took was blurred. He had no idea how to stop the action when a rider streaked by them, but he knew there must be a way.

Alonzo was amused at how Kate cheered and clapped for people she'd never seen before in her life. He was tempted to take a picture of her, but decided against it. It felt too intimate. Too invasive. Too intrusive.

"Can we go watch the dancing now?" she asked after the barrel race.

"No bull riding?"

She coughed. "It's getting too dusty here."

They walked to the dance circle, where she chose a spot in the shade. "It isn't as crowded as I expected."

"Guess people would rather see a bunch of guys get thrown off a bull."

Performers did a traditional harvest dance, a squaw dance, and an eagle dance. Alonzo noticed that many of the Navajo costumes were more colorful than those at his pueblo and wondered why. Would a nomadic people come into contact with other groups who might influence their dress? It certainly made for interesting photos.

While Kate was engrossed in the performance, Alonzo took pictures. He thought of Luz walking around the plaza at PICC, and tried to see things as she might.

After several bad shots, he managed to get one good photo of a young Navajo girl in a bright fuchsia blouse, who stood waiting on the sidelines. Her long dark hair blew across her face, and he snapped the shot as she was pushing it aside. He stared at the resulting shot with satisfaction.

Finally.

"Are the dancers good?" Kate asked him.

He nodded. "Pretty good."

"Do you ever dance?"

He hesitated. "Only on feast days."

He didn't mention PICC. He didn't want her showing up there unexpectedly.

The final dance was the hoop dance, one of Alonzo's favorites. The story told of the circle of life—of harmony and continuity. He'd wanted to learn it when he was small, but no one in his village was expert enough to teach him.

The lone dancer was good, his movements quick and sure. Alonzo was impressed, if not a little jealous. He knew it took talent along with lots of patience and practice.

"Look," Kate said, pointing toward the dancer, "the hoops are just like wings. How does he do that?"

"I wish I knew," he admitted.

*

The sun was setting as they pulled out of the parking lot.

"When you were getting our drinks, I heard someone mention code talkers. Is that some sort of sign language?"

"No. During World War Two, about four hundred Navajo were recruited by the Marines to serve in their communications division. Their language is only spoken among themselves, and it turns out it was undecipherable by the enemy. The code talkers served in the Pacific. I read we wouldn't have won the battle of Iwo Jima without them."

"No kidding?"

"You have to wonder about a government that spends years punishing children for speaking their native tongue, then depending on them to do exactly that to fight a war."

"That's crazy."

He nodded. Like so much of how the government dealt with Native Americans, he thought.

"Oh, look!" she said, pointing to a sign. "There's a memorial right here, honoring the Code Talkers."

"For all the good it does. They were treated like trash when they got home. Couldn't get jobs, couldn't get loans, and couldn't get respect. They went from being heroes to being hobos." Alonzo stopped when he realized he sounded exactly like Paolo. "Sorry. Sure. Let's check it out. I heard that it's an impressive monument."

They followed the circular path below Window Rock, pausing when they reached the 16 stark, dramatic bayonet sculptures. The dark, sharp forms stood in striking contrast to the famous, round window of sandstone beyond. Several other visitors stood nearby, many speaking in native tongue.

Kate moved along the circle toward Window Rock. "I don't suppose we can go up there."

"Not anymore. Folks used to climb up to have their pictures taken in the window, but the sandstone was wearing away, so now it's off limits."

Kate took pictures with her cell phone before they continued back to the car.

"If it weren't so late, we could go up to Four Corners."

"Is that where the states all touch?"

"Yes. Arizona, Utah, Colorado, and New Mexico."

"Who do you suppose determined it was that spot?"

"Someone who wanted to make some easy money."

She laughed. "You're a cynic."

He started the engine. "No, I'm a realist."

Paolo was the cynic.

*

When he got home that night, he pored over the pictures he'd taken. The shots of the sunset were terrible, though he couldn't say why. The rodeo pictures were equally unsatisfying. He knew exactly what he'd been after, but it did not translate to the screen.

He opened Luz's book and studied her photographs. Why were they so special? So dramatic? So effective? After the second time paging through the book, he realized that each photograph had a single subject, but the angle or lighting turned the shot from simple to spectacular.

He considered his own pictures again, trying to see how he might have used a similar approach. Back and forth, from his to hers, convinced him that she had a genuine talent.

Had she been born with it or learned it?

He switched to his browser and searched for a community class in photography.

An hour later, he ordered a textbook for his new class. If it was learned, he could do it as well as anyone else.

Carlos called him the next day. "How was your date?"

"It wasn't a date."

"Sounded like a date."

"It wasn't."

"Did she ask a bunch of stupid questions?"

"Like what?"

"Like, what does it feel like to be an Indian?"

"No."

"Did you ask her out again?"

"No."

"Why not?"

He thought a moment. "I don't know."

But, of course, he did know.

He was not sure if this was the right direction, either.

CHAPTER 5

Kate stopped by Alonzo's office on Tuesday morning, her bright smile the perfect start for his day. "Thanks again for going with me to Navajo Nation. It was so much fun."

"Anytime."

"Really?"

He wasn't sure what that meant.

"A bunch of us are going to the State Fair this weekend. You should come with us."

He had no plans, especially now that he and Carlos wouldn't be dancing at PICC.

Why not? What would it hurt?

"Yeah? Sounds good."

"I'll let you know when we decide about timing. I want to go to the parade on Saturday morning, but a couple of the guys say that's too early for them."

"What time does it start?"

"Eight-thirty."

"That's not so bad."

"We'd have to get there earlier to park and get a good place to sit."

"Whatever you decide is fine with me. I don't mind

getting up early." No big deal. He did it every day.

"Thanks, Alonzo. I'll let you know."

When he saw her again on Friday, she'd had no luck convincing any of the others to join them for the parade. "We'll meet them at the Ferris wheel at ten-thirty."

"Works for me," Alonzo said. "Nobody will be able to say they couldn't find it."

Her grin was killer. "So, what do you think for time? I imagine if we're there by seven-thirty, we can find a good place. I'd like to be right on the street if we can."

"That's fine. I'll pick you up at seven."

"Perfect. See you then."

*

They walked along the crowded sidewalk Saturday morning, searching for a place to sit.

"I had no idea there would be so many people here," Alonzo said. "There must be a thousand little kids."

"Everybody loves a parade," Kate said, stopping short as a toddler stumbled in front of her and nearly fell. "I read somewhere that this is the biggest parade in New Mexico."

The parkway was strewn with beach chairs and blankets and backpacks. Sheriff's deputies were already patrolling the route, warning parents to keep their children out of the street.

"What about there?" Kate asked, pointing to a small space between two already rowdy groups. The lack of shade from a tree or building left a narrow spot completely vacant.

"Sure. You can sit. I'll stand. I want to take some pictures anyway."

"We can take turns."

Alonzo thought it was a perfect opportunity to try some of the techniques he'd been reading about. He had his cell phone fully charged and was ready when the lead-off unit and the Governor's car passed by, kicking off the festivities.

Floats, drill teams, bands, clowns, cheerleaders, and

wheeled vehicles of every variety paraded by. Alonzo took pictures standing up, sitting down, and even kneeling by the curb. He dismissed the notion that lying on the ground was a good idea. Better safe than squashed.

He started deleting the disappointing shots, but after some consideration, decided to keep them to look at more closely when he got home. He might learn from them.

"Show me," Kate said.

"No."

"Why not?"

"They're no good."

"Come on."

"I'll show you later," he said, but doubted he would.

The horses, wisely placed at the end of the parade, pleased the crowd more than any of the other entrants. Alonzo saw youngsters all around them, jumping and yelling and trying to reach out to touch the animals.

He watched several horses shy away from outstretched arms. He imagined he could have ridden Maasr'a in the parade, but K'akana would have been nearly impossible to control. Some horses were far too temperamental to endure that much agitation.

The blast of an air horn down the street startled everyone, and freaked a young rider. She yanked on her reins, and spooked her horse. The animal bucked and threw her, screaming, to the pavement.

Alonzo could sense what was coming. He shoved the phone in his pocket.

Bystanders rushed to help the girl; the horse panicked and took off running toward where Kate and he stood watching.

With no time for a second thought, Alonzo leapt past Kate, jumped into the street, and began running in the same direction as the horse, looking over his shoulder, keeping the animal in sight.

He could do this. He and Paolo had done it dozens of times when they were boys. He could still do it.

Heavy hooves shook the pavement as the horse reached his side. Alonzo said a quick prayer to Mother Earth, stretched out, grabbed the horse's mane, and jumped, swinging awkwardly but soundly onto its back.

He leaned over, clutching the horse's broad neck, and spoke the gentle native words Mr. Montoya had taught him years before. "You are safe. We are one. Mother Earth guards us and protects us."

Gradually, the horse quieted and slowed. Alonzo kept talking calmly, until the horse finally came to a stop.

The crowd roared, the horse reared, and Alonzo struggled to quiet him again.

After a time, a couple rushed up, the tall man grabbing the reins. "Easy, Galaxy. Easy, boy." The horse responded, snorting loudly and throwing his head.

Alonzo patted the animal, and thanked Mother Earth.

"That was quite a stunt," the man said. "You must be one of the rodeo riders."

"No."

"Well in that case, thank you for your courage."

The woman beside him said, "I told my husband our daughter wasn't strong enough to handle him in a parade."

A girl about Felicia's age came limping up. "Thank you," she said to Alonzo. "The horn scared him."

"I saw," Alonzo said, dismounting. He patted the horse.

The man spoke to his daughter. "I'd better take him."

The girl agreed, obviously not happy.

Alonzo nodded to them, patted the horse once more, and walked back down the street toward Kate. The crowd on both curbs applauded wildly.

"That was amazing!" Kate said when he reached her side. "How in the world did you do that?"

"We did it all the time when we were kids," he said, keeping his voice low. "Unless you owned a horse, the only way to ride was to catch someone else's. My brother and I used to spend every summer riding."

"I'm impressed."

"Don't be. It was more good luck than anything else."

"It didn't look like luck."

One of the mounted sheriff's posse reined up in front of them. "I'm not sure if I should thank you or arrest you," he said. "That was very dangerous. On the other hand, you averted a complete disaster."

"He's a hero," a fellow sitting nearby said. "He deserves a medal."

The deputy cast a dubious eye on the fellow, and then looked back at Alonzo. "Take care of yourself."

"Yeah, I will," Alonzo said.

As the deputy rode away, Alonzo leaned down and spoke quietly to Kate. "Let's get out of here."

They pushed through the crowd and made their way toward the fairgrounds, where the silhouette of the giant Ferris wheel was stark against the bright blue morning sky.

Kate threaded her arm through his and said, "You were terrific, the way you caught that horse."

"I didn't catch him, he caught me. It wasn't a big deal. Let's not mention it."

"Are you kidding? It was huge. You were incredibly brave."

The fawning tone made him cringe. Worse yet was the look on her face, as if he truly had done something special instead of reacting instinctively. He was sure an act wasn't brave if it didn't involve a decision.

"Wait till I tell everyone. They'll be as impressed as I am. You'll see."

"No."

"No, what?"

"No, I don't want you to tell them."

She stopped and gazed up at him with confusion. "What do you mean? Of course we'll tell them."

Even if his upbringing didn't demand modesty, Alonzo was not one to brag. "I'm asking you not to. What I did was reflexive, not brave. Let's keep it between us."

She started to argue but stopped when he shook his head.

"Please, Kate. Please, just forget it."

He could tell by the way her shoulders stiffened that she didn't only disagree, she didn't understand.

But, she honored his request, and he spent the rest of the day in blissful anonymity.

*

The next morning, Alonzo took his time scrolling through all the pictures he'd taken at the parade. The subjects were colorful and interesting, but not a single shot captured what he was after. In some, the movement blurred the focus; in others, the background detracted and spoiled the shot.

His favorite was of a young Indian boy, dancing with an older child, perhaps his brother. The boy looked uncertain, maybe frightened. The older boy was touching the younger one's shoulder, encouraging him.

It was badly out of focus, but it pulled at Alonzo's heart the same way Luz's pictures did.

Late in the afternoon, he remembered that he'd turned his phone off before the parade. He switched it back on, and it immediately began buzzing with messages, fourteen of which were from Felicia.

Instead of reading them, he called his sister, sure that something horrible must have happened.

"Lon, finally!"

"What's wrong?"

"Nothing. You're famous, Lon. Have you seen?"

"Seen what?"

"The video. It's gone viral."

"What are you talking about?"

"The parade yesterday. Somebody recorded you on their cell phone. Look it up. Hashtag horsemanhero. It was even on local news last night. They want to know your name."

"Oh, geez."

"You were amazing, Lon. You saved a little kid's life."

"What kid?"

"He was in the street. Right in front of you. Didn't you see him?"

"No."

"Look it up."

"Okay. Listen, don't tell anyone my name."

"But…"

"K'ayama! I don't want this. Please."

"Okay. Okay. Whatever."

"Have Mom and Dad seen it?"

"Yes."

"Don't show anybody else. If anyone mentions it, say it isn't me."

"They know it's you, Lon. It's obviously you."

"No, it isn't. I wasn't there."

"You're so weird."

"Yeah, I know."

"When can I come visit?"

"Soon."

When he hung up, he deleted all the messages without listening to them and turned the phone off. He grabbed his keys off the table, drove downtown, and went to a movie, where it was dark, and cool, and nobody could recognize him.

*

He turned his phone on the next morning and found two dozen more messages. He deleted them all with the exception of one from Carlos which said, "Fishing next Saturday? Same place, same time."

Alonzo replied, "Yes," and turned the phone off again.

The teasing began the moment he reached his office. By nine-thirty, it was unbearable.

"I told you we should tell them," Kate said after she'd found him barricaded in a darkened meeting room. "If we had, it would be old news by now."

"With any luck, there'll be a tsunami or a nine point five earthquake somewhere, that will take over the news. This is ridiculous. It was no big deal."

"It was a pretty big deal to that kid's parents. The horse would have trampled him to death."

"They should have been holding on to him. Besides, I didn't even see him. I was focused on the stupid horse."

"It's not the horse's fault."

"I know. But, I don't want it to be news."

"You do know that the local station wants to interview you, right?"

"Why do you think I'm hiding out?"

"You should do it and get it over with."

He didn't know how to explain it to her. "I'll think about it." The lie slid out much easier than he would have imagined, and far easier than he would have liked.

Sad.

A pueblo woman would have understood.

*

He drove to the university that evening, excited to start his photography class. Walking from the parking lot to the arts building, he noticed students checking him out with unusual interest.

His clothes were clean and unremarkable; his hair was trim; he looked much as he had when he'd taken his degree there years before.

Groups of students stood talking outside the classroom; many stopped when he reached the door.

"You're the guy, aren't you?" one girl said. "From the parade?"

"He is," a fellow standing next to her agreed. "He's the

horseman hero. We have a celebrity in our class!"

Alonzo felt a cold force slowly squeeze his insides; he felt sick, trapped, and desperate to escape. His brain did a rapid search for an out. "Is this Physics 101?" he asked, pointing at the door.

"No," the girl said. "This is Elements of Cell Phone Photography."

Alonzo pulled out his phone and pretended to look at something. "Wrong place," he said, turning. "Thanks."

He heard the girl call out as he walked away, "That's the guy. The one who saved the kid. The one they want to interview."

He ducked into the stairwell and raced up to the floor above. If anyone chased him, surely they'd head down. He found a dark, empty room and sat researching cell phone photography until well past the hour.

Turned out there were plenty of online courses.

CHAPTER 6

By the end of the week, most of the reporters who had been hanging around or calling Alonzo's office had given up and moved on to other news. He hadn't heard from anyone in his family, so he knew Felicia had told them he didn't intend to talk about the incident.

Carlos said nothing about the video gone viral when he left a message confirming their fishing trip. But, Alonzo knew that his cousin would not be able to resist the urge to tease him about it. Teasing was Carlos's favorite form of entertainment.

Alonzo arrived at Kewa Pueblo early on Saturday morning. He texted Carlos, "Meet you at our spot." Then, he walked along the bank, searching for a perfect picture.

He passed the three old men they'd seen before, huddled silently together, as if they had frozen in place. Their faded, rumpled clothes looked as ancient as the pueblo itself and could have emerged from an old photo of their ancestors.

They would have been perfect subjects for Luz's book on Kewa, but it was a picture she'd never take. Alonzo wondered how many untaken pictures she'd left behind.

His simple nod of respect did not prompt any reaction.

A pool not far from their fishing spot reflected the tall cottonwoods on the bank as clearly as a well-polished mirror. He began taking shots from various angles and heights.

Once again, the pictures on his phone screen were a disappointing contrast to what his eyes saw. Back and forth, scene to screen, he was so engrossed in his effort, that he didn't hear his cousin walk up beside him.

"Hey, Starman," Carlos said, "perfecting your selfie?"

If it had been anyone else, Alonzo would have recoiled. Instead he said, "I'm detailing the scene of your defeat."

"What defeat is that?"

"The great fall fish-off. I'm confident after our last trip that you don't have a chance of winning."

"This from the guy who threw Grandfather back in the river."

"I caught him, didn't I?"

Carlos opened his tackle box. "I don't know, did you?"

After they'd prepared their poles and dropped lines in the water, Carlos offered Alonzo a slice of prune pie.

"Your mom's or mine?" Alonzo asked.

"Can't you tell the difference?"

Alonzo took a bite and savored the sweet treat. "Mine."

"Yep."

Silence circled around, wrapping them in a familiar comfort perfected over years of fishing together. A sharp tug on Alonzo's line focused his attention on the unseen warrior beneath the glassy surface.

"Nice one," Carlos said when Alonzo pulled the foot-long trout from the water. "Are you keeping him or throwing him back?"

"Will you take him to my mom?"

"Sure." Carlos chuckled under his breath. "Of course, I'll tell her I caught it." He opened the ice chest so Alonzo could deposit the thrashing fish. "You could take it yourself."

"Next time."

"Not ready to talk about the video?"

"No."

"You put on quite a show."

Alonzo rebaited his hook and threw the line back in the water.

"Mr. Montoya would have been pleased."

"Mr. Montoya would have kicked my butt for being so stupid. That horse could have killed me."

"Not likely. But, he sure could have killed that kid."

"I never saw the kid."

"You knew a kid was possible. That's why you acted."

Was that why?

"You never talked to any reporters."

"No."

"The kid's parents wanted to thank you. They said you were a hero."

"I told you, I never saw him."

"That doesn't make what you did less courageous."

Alonzo shook his head. "Courage means a thought process. You have to recognize the risk and decide to act anyway. I acted without thinking. That's not heroic." After a pause he added, "Some would call it crazy."

"But not those parents."

Alonzo was tired of arguing and disappointed that Carlos didn't agree. His tenuous connection to the pueblo felt frayed and fragile. If Carlos didn't understand, who would?

He took another piece of his mother's prune pie, a pueblo boy's sweet security blanket.

"What were you doing there, anyway?"

"Kate asked me to go to the fair."

"You're dating?"

"We went to the fair."

"Two fairs."

"It's no big deal."

"Have you seen Luz?"

Alonzo turned to look at his cousin. It wasn't like him to

ask so many questions. "No."

"She likes you."

"Yeah? Why so interested in Luz?"

"No reason. I just thought you should know."

Carlos pulled in the next three fish, adding them to the ice chest treasure. "Have you thought any more about building the planter box for Mom?"

"No."

"I'd help you. Dad, too, I think."

"I doubt that. He was totally against the idea."

"I heard Mom talking about it again. She was trying to convince him to build it."

Alonzo poured his attention onto the fishing line, willing it to bob with another bite.

"What do you think, Lon?"

"No."

"Why not?"

"I told you, it's a bad idea."

"Actually, it's a terrific idea."

"Then you build it."

"What are you afraid of, Lon?"

His jaw clenched on words that threatened to spill out and fill the air with poison.

"It could be good for the pueblo, especially now that it's so dry every year."

Alonzo wondered if someone had put him up to this; his mother, or his father, or Julia. Carlos wasn't the build-a-planter-box type.

"Will you at least think about it?" his cousin pressed.

He would keep asking, Alonzo knew. There was only one way to make him stop. "Yeah. Don't ask me again. I'll tell you when I've decided."

For Carlos, there was only one acceptable answer.

Was it one Alonzo could live with?

*

Sundays were hard.

Mondays were easy because there was work.

Sundays never seemed to go fast enough, especially now. Alonzo had to admit he missed the dancing. Even harder to accept was that he missed seeing Luz.

She'd said that she sometimes worked in the gift shop at PICC on the weekends. He could call and ask if she were there, but that felt awkward. Instead, he dressed, ate two tomatoes, and drove to the center.

She stood behind the counter, helping the first in a long line of customers. He realized he'd arrived just after the first performance. Stupid. He should have planned it better if he wanted to talk to her.

And, he'd forgotten the book for her to sign.

Loser. Capital L.

He should leave; he could come back during the two o'clock performance, when she'd more likely be alone.

"Hey, Alonzo," she said, waving to him.

"Hi, Luz."

"Were you looking for something?"

"No. I came to have lunch."

He started toward the café, then noticed a stack of flyers on the counter that said: Jemez Harvest Festival. He took one, folded it, and stuck it in his jeans. Then, he went into the café and ordered green chili and fry bread.

The waitress had barely put down his meal when Luz peeked into the café. "Hi, Luz," she said. "Need a menu?"

"No. I only have fifteen minutes."

"What about a drink?"

"Sure, thanks. An orange soda."

"I'll be right back."

"Is there room for me?" Luz asked Alonzo.

"Absolutely."

"I was supposed to be off this afternoon, but two people called in sick."

"Have you had lunch?"

"Not yet."

He pushed the basket of blue corn tortilla chips toward her. "Help yourself."

She took several and ate one. "Thanks. I'm starving."

"When are you off?"

"At four."

Without thinking he said, "How about dinner? Do you have plans?"

"No."

"Would you like to go somewhere?"

"Sure," she said, with no hesitation.

Maybe Carlos was right.

"Did you have someplace in mind?" she asked.

"No. What sounds good to you?"

She considered it. "How about Saint Clair Bistro?" she said. "I think they have live jazz on the weekends."

"Okay." He now regretted having ordered such a big lunch. "Should I pick you up here?"

"Why don't I meet you?" She took another handful of chips, and gave him a smile in exchange. "Thanks. This'll hold me over." She stood as the waitress returned with her soda. "What time?" she asked Alonzo.

"Whenever you want."

"Six?"

"Six works," Alonzo said.

"I'll make a reservation. We probably don't need one on a Sunday night, but you never know."

He watched her walk out of the café, pleased she hadn't said a word about the video. He was sure she must have seen it. Everyone in the southern states had seen it. The video had been viewed by nearly three million people.

Alonzo was not one of them.

*

The bistro was crowded and noisy, but not with jazz. Bands only played on Friday and Saturday nights. Luz had requested a table on the patio, and they were seated as soon as they arrived. The menu was what Alonzo's father would call "a little too uptown".

"Everything sounds delicious," Luz said. "I love the way meals are described so artfully that you can taste them."

Another talent she had that Alonzo did not.

She ordered pecan crusted trout and white wine; he ordered a burger and a beer.

"You didn't bring your books." She grinned, and Alonzo's heart lost a beat.

"No." He hadn't even bought the first one yet.

"I could write my name on a napkin, and you could tape it inside the cover."

"Would that help with resale value after you're famous?"

"Only if you have the full set of nineteen."

"Have you been working on Laguna?"

"I've started. I went there a couple of weeks ago, walked around, and figured out where the shadows fall during the morning and late afternoon. Laguna is closed to photographers, but last month, I sent my books and a request to the tribal council."

"And?"

"And, they granted me limited access."

"Good job."

"Day after tomorrow is Laguna Village Feast, the second biggest celebration of the year. I'm spending the day there."

"Hoping for a bunch of unexpected surprises?"

Her smile was slow and intimate, acknowledging without words, that he remembered what she'd said. "I wish I understood Keres. I learn so much when I can talk to the elders; some of them don't speak English."

She had to know where he was from; she had to know his pueblo was one of seven that spoke Keresan.

"Do you want an interpreter?"

"Do you want to spend a hot day in the sun?"

"No different than feast day at home."

"Can you take a day off work?"

"It's strange, but I haven't felt very well this weekend. I'm thinking I'll be pretty sick by Tuesday."

"That's too bad. For work, anyway. If you're sure, it'd be great to have your help. The thing is, the best times to take pictures are the two hours after sunrise and the two hours before sunset."

"What do you do the rest of the day?"

"Scout. Frame shots. Talk to the locals."

"What time is sunrise these days?"

"Six-fifty."

"It'll take an hour to get there," he said.

"And another forty-five minutes to park and set up."

"That means we leave at five?"

"White time, not Indian time."

"Got it."

"I can pick you up, or meet you at the center."

He bristled. "I can drive."

"I've got tons of equipment in my car. It would be better if I drove."

She would know how uncomfortable that would be for him. She would know because, like him, she'd been raised on a pueblo, where, if a man were in a car, he'd likely be driving.

And, they were going to a pueblo.

She waited, silent, while he decided.

"Okay," he said at last. "I'll meet you at the center." No way would his neighbors see him being driven by a woman.

"Tuesday morning at five, at PICC. Shall I bring coffee?"

"I'm closer," he said. "I'll get it." Something else many pueblo men wouldn't offer to do. What else would be upside down before Tuesday was over?

*

59

At his office the next day, Alonzo spent a lot of time coughing loudly and clearing his throat with exaggerated drama. By four o'clock, his throat was genuinely sore. There was probably some cosmic justice involved.

"If you're sick," Kate told him, "you should stay home tomorrow. Nobody else wants a summer cold. They last forever."

"I'll think about it," he said, trying not to sound too eager.

"Get well fast, though. A bunch of us are doing an escape room on Saturday. I was hoping you'd come with us."

"Escape room?"

"Haven't you heard of them?"

"No." The familiar feeling of being the outsider tugged at his Indian gut.

"It's such fun. We all get locked in a room and have to figure out how to escape."

"You mean like a jail?"

The blue in her eyes deepened when she laughed. "No. Like a challenge. There are clues and tips. Things left around for us to find. We'll have an hour to figure it out. If we're desperate, we can get help from the staff."

"They lock you in?"

"Yes. I suppose you could get out if there was an emergency. Why? Are you claustrophobic?"

"No."

"Okay then. You want to go?"

Why not? "Sure."

"Our reservation is at two."

When he considered it again late that night, he wondered who in the world would have dreamed up an "escape room".

CHAPTER 7

Indian time.

It could be an issue.

It was for Paolo and Erin. Paolo was invariably late. Erin hated it. Felicia, by contrast, was always early, perhaps unconsciously making up for her older brother's tendency.

Alonzo was somewhere in the middle. Mostly it didn't matter. But, sunrise was unambiguous; if you missed the moment, it mattered. It wouldn't rise again for latecomers.

He set his alarm.

Then, he slept through it.

He was racing down the street toward PICC when he saw Luz pulling out of the parking lot.

Sunrise waited for no one, and neither did she.

"Sorry," he said, handing her a cup of coffee and setting the bag of tomatoes he'd brought her behind the seat.

He expected a lecture.

"Good thing you brought coffee," was all she said.

Laguna Pueblo lay 45 miles west of Albuquerque, between Interstate 40 and Route 66. The pueblo lands covered nearly half a million acres and had been inhabited since around 3000 B.C. Alonzo knew that Neyse's husband had a cousin who lived there, but he had never visited Laguna himself.

"Have you already decided where you want to start?"

"Yes. The mission church is the most recognized building on the pueblo. I want to capture it as close to the moment of sunrise as I can."

Which was why she would have left without him.

"I'm going to set up two tripods."

"One for sunlight and one for shadow?"

Her dark eyes left the highway long enough to caress his face. "Exactly."

"When will Mass begin?"

"I think around nine."

"Are you going to take photographs inside the church?"

"If they'll let me. Nothing sacred, of course. Just the pews, walls, floor, and windows. The last thing I want is to offend anyone."

He was sure that *someone* was going to be offended, especially if she used the telephoto lens she'd used at PICC.

*

The first thing Alonzo noticed when they got out of the car was the aroma of bread baking. It hung in the air as tangible as a map of home. He took a deep, nostalgic breath.

"Wonderful, isn't it?" Luz asked. "Maybe we can get some at the fair later."

He helped her unpack, and then set up one tripod as she set up the other.

"I don't imagine many people will be out this early," she said, "but I'd like you to stay with one camera when I'm working with the other one."

"Sure. Can I take some pictures?"

"As long as you make sure they're good."

"I'll try to surprise you," he said, and was rewarded with the smile he sought in reply.

The eastern sky brightened in subtle degrees, melting from pale grey, to pearl pink, to piercing orange.

The shadow of the mission, which lay sleeping on the cold, hard-packed earth, was roused by slender fingers of sunlight, and began slowly crawling toward its hiding place under the church.

Alonzo didn't see it move as much as he felt it move; felt the inexorable light give birth to another day.

He took a few pictures with his cell phone, but none of them captured the magical moment of creation. Seeing the results, he promised himself he'd enroll in one of the online photography courses he'd recently researched.

Luz came around the outer wall, camera in hand, glancing back and forth from the view finder to the screen. She took no notice of him; not a look, not a word.

The morning had brightened in ten minutes; the light on the mission walls had changed from pearl to oyster. By nine o'clock, Alonzo knew it would be the unyielding white of desert-bleached bones.

"Please?" Luz asked, holding out her camera to him.

He took it, surprised at how warm it felt in the cool air.

She took several pictures with the camera on the tripod, then unfastened it, collapsed it, and put the equipment in the car.

The door to the chapel was latched. "Guess that's all for here," she said.

They walked slowly down through the village, stopping periodically for her to take more pictures. Luz was silent, as if she walked in a world where Alonzo didn't exist.

She took pictures of things he didn't even notice: a cracked pot sitting on an adobe wall; an ear of corn bursting through its husk; a dog sleeping in an old wagon, whose missing wheel left it suitable for little else.

She took pictures of the ordinary and the unexpected, the beauty and the blight.

After an hour, she asked, "Shall we take a break?"

"Sure."

"Did you bring breakfast? You had a bag."

"I brought tomatoes."

"I brought bread."

"Perfect."

"Let's go down by the river," Luz suggested.

They found a spot near a small curve in the bank and sat.

Alonzo ripped apart the paper bag and offered Luz a tomato. "I have a knife if you want it sliced."

She picked up the smaller of the two fruits and took a bite as she would from an apple. A line of juice trickled down her chin and she quickly wiped it with the back of her hand. "A perfect breakfast," she said, unwrapping slices of bread.

Alonzo took a piece and tore it in half. His first bite tasted of tradition. "Did you bake this?"

"No." She sounded defensive. "Why? Did you grow the tomatoes?"

"Actually, I did."

"Seriously?"

"Yeah."

"At your apartment?"

"Yeah."

"How?"

He hadn't expected the question. It lodged in his brain like an invading enemy seeking out a weakness—a vulnerability he wasn't sure he was prepared to share. "It's a long story."

"We've got hours. The sun doesn't set until seven."

Where to start?

How much to tell?

"You don't have to tell me if you don't want to," she said, after the silence had lingered like a lazy dog.

"My sister-in-law and I worked on a self-watering system for plants last spring. There are specially designed pots available online. I got one to see if I could grow vegetables."

"Why? What did you and your sister-in-law plant?"

"Roses."

He got the pueblo girl look.

"Our Aunt Julia wants to grow roses in the yard by their house. In the summer, it's too hard to carry enough water from the river every day to keep roses alive."

"She wants to grow roses?"

"Julia's White."

That was all the explanation she needed.

"So, did she get her roses?"

"Not yet."

"Why?"

"The pot we used for our experiment is still at my sister-in-law's."

"But it worked? You grew roses?"

"Yes."

"So, your aunt could get one of the pots."

"She could. But it would only be good for one bush."

"She could get a dozen."

"She could."

"But she doesn't want to?"

"I think there's a better solution. A large planter box with a special net could collect dew at night to water the plants during the day."

"Can you get that online, too?"

"No."

"You're going to build it?"

"Probably." He surprised himself. Was he going to say yes to Carlos?

"Probably?"

"It's hard now, since I live in town."

The excuse was as flimsy as a child's cheap toy.

When she didn't reply, he knew she didn't believe him.

Had she backed him into that corner, or had he done it to himself?

"It's not exactly a popular idea. Our family has been in turmoil since we started working on it."

"But you believe it's a good idea?"

"Yes."

She was getting way too close.

He dug a small hole and buried the two tomato stems. "What's next?"

She gave him a sideways look, then took the hint. "We take a walk and talk to some villagers. I made a few connections when I was here before. I'd like to speak to those folks again and get some agreements about using their images."

"Agreements?"

"Yes. I never take pictures of anyone without their permission. If I'm going to publish a photo of anyone, I always get written permission. I never take pictures of anyone's full face. Profiles, sometimes, but never full on."

"Why not?"

Her look said he should know why.

The rebuke, however subtle, stung.

He stood. "Ready?"

She folded the cloth she'd used for the bread and stuck it in one of the many pockets in her cargo pants. When she started to get up, Alonzo offered her his hand.

Electricity shot up his arm when she touched him; a shock so powerful and unexpected that his breath caught in his chest like a rabbit in a hidden trap.

Her eyes said she'd felt it, too.

He turned away, giving her no chance to comment.

This could not be what he needed.

*

The pueblo was fully awake now. Many villagers were at Mass; some were setting up booths for selling their crafts; still others were busy preparing for the feast to be served to family and friends later in the day.

Luz was humble, even deferential, acknowledging people

they passed, and saying a few simple words of greeting. At the edge of the village, they approached a sun-kissed old man, who sat on a wooden bench in front of an ancient adobe home.

"This is Joseph," she said to Alonzo. "His grandson said he was willing to talk to me. The thing is, he doesn't speak English."

Alonzo greeted the man, whose eyes misted over when he heard the traditional, respectful words. For a long moment, the man merely stared.

"What's wrong?" Luz asked softly.

"I don't know."

When he finally spoke, his voice crackled with age and emotion.

Alonzo listened to the wandering story, which went on for more than three minutes. When he finally stopped, Alonzo turned to Luz to translate. "He says his mother came from my pueblo many years ago. Apparently he hasn't heard our dialect since she died."

"But he can understand you?"

"He says he'll try."

"I wish I knew how old he is."

"He'll tell us eventually. I'm sure it'll be part of his story."

"Ask him if his grandson showed him my book."

It was clear by the face he made that Joseph didn't think much of Luz's work.

"He saw it," Alonzo said.

"And was obviously impressed. If that's the case, why would he want to talk to me?"

"Should I ask him?"

"No." She thought a moment. "Ask him if he's going to the dance."

When Alonzo asked, Joseph looked at Luz with eyes that had seen much and missed little. The scope of his disapproval encompassed Alonzo as well as Luz. "Her camera doesn't belong here."

"Well," Luz said when Alonzo had translated, "that's unequivocal."

Alonzo saw tension tighten her stance.

"Does he want us to leave?"

The old man's eyes softened when he answered no. He considered Luz as if she were one of his grandchildren, and spoke gently.

When he'd finished, Alonzo translated again. "He welcomes you to sit down and he will explain why what you are doing is wrong."

"Oh, good. A lecture on why my life's work is a waste."

"Maybe you can convince him otherwise."

"Seriously?"

Alonzo gave her an encouraging grin. "Probably not."

The old man nodded toward a single chair, indicating that Luz should sit. Alonzo squatted near her, having been offered nowhere else to sit. His knees protested at the awkward angle that had once been so comfortable.

He'd been gone too long from tradition.

Without waiting for a question from Luz, Joseph began talking. He paused periodically for Alonzo to translate. His story began like so many of the elders on Alonzo's pueblo: he wasn't sure what year he was born, but he figured he was about ten when Pearl Harbor was bombed.

"That would make him close to ninety," Luz said

Joseph gave her a look which said she should be quiet.

When he was around six, his father had caught the "white man's sickness," and died.

"What's the white man's sickness?" Luz asked.

"Alcohol," Joseph said with disdain.

After his father died, his mother gave up living. She was a ghost before she was dead. When Joseph was eight, she was taken to a hospital in Albuquerque and never returned.

He had no siblings, so Joseph inherited his grandparents' attention.

That was all he inherited.

They were the poorest of the poor and often did without. He'd been hidden by his grandfather to avoid being taken away to boarding school. Consequently, he'd never learned English.

"He said that last with pride," Alonzo told Luz.

He told them how the old ways began changing when the railroad was built across their lands, continued when uranium was discovered and hundreds of his people went to work at the mine, then fell to practically nothing when the casino opened.

Joseph stopped while Alonzo translated, then leveled an accusatory glare at Luz. His next words were sharp as arrowheads. "White man's ways," he said in Alonzo's dialect, "and white man's machines, have killed our people. In my great-grandson's lifetime, we will disappear. She takes pictures of a dying people."

When Alonzo repeated the old man's words, he watched Luz's face twist with sadness.

"Harsh," she mumbled.

A young boy, dressed in traditional garb, approached the old man, who opened his arms to embrace him.

"My great-great-grandson," Joseph said. "Joey."

Joey squatted next to Alonzo. "Are you here for feast?"

"Yes."

A man joined the group, greeted Joseph and said hello to Luz. "I'm Joey's father, Antonio," he said to Alonzo.

"Alonzo Herrera," Lon said, offering his hand. "Your grandfather has been telling us his story."

Antonio smiled. "He'll tell anyone who'll listen."

"He's not enthusiastic about Luz taking pictures."

"No." Antonio spoke briefly to the old man. "I told him we are going to walk to the plaza."

Joseph looked hard at Luz. "No camera," he said in surprisingly clear English.

She put the black cap over the lens, pulled a cloth bag

from her pocket and wrapped it up. "No camera."

*

They didn't leave the pueblo until long after sunset. Luz had taken a second set of shots at the same locations as the ones she'd taken that morning.

Driving back toward Albuquerque, Alonzo asked, "Did you get what you wanted?"

"I hope so. I'm sure I got a few that are good. I won't know until I see them on my computer. This pueblo is hard because it's so big, but also because a well-known photographer, Lee Marmon, has spent his lifetime photographing Laguna Pueblo."

"He's from Laguna?"

"Yes."

"Tough competition."

"Yes."

"I wonder what Joseph thinks of him."

"Not much, I imagine. But, Antonio told me that Lee has given the younger generation a gift. Because of him, the villagers can see exactly how the pueblo used to look, the way their ancestors used to dress, and how the feast days were celebrated."

"He approves of your books?"

"He does."

"One out of two isn't bad."

"More like one out of a hundred."

"Nobody else gave you a bad time."

"No."

"Are you discouraged?"

"Not discouraged." After a few moments she said, "Unsure."

"You can't let one man's opinion stop you."

"It won't stop me, but it makes me think."

She was quiet for a long while, and Alonzo wondered if

that was all she would say.

He waited.

"I'm going against my parents' wishes; I'm going against many of the elders' wishes; I'm going against tradition. At times, it feels like I'm fighting the world."

He couldn't help but think they were both battling the world.

"You do great work, Luz. You can't stop."

"You like my pictures?"

"Yes."

"And yet, no autographs."

"I'm waiting until I have the full set."

"That may be a while."

"But you're going to continue, right?"

She turned toward him long enough for him to see her dark, perceptive eyes. "Are you?"

"Am I what?"

"Going to continue. With the planter box?"

She hit a soft, vulnerable spot Alonzo had done his best to hide. "I don't know," he said. "Maybe not every good idea should come to fruition."

"Maybe not. But yours should." Her look was a challenge.

"So should yours," he told her.

CHAPTER 8

Alonzo felt a cold chill the moment they entered the escape room, known as The Shack. Kate's group had been told it was a serial killer's hideout, and its grim, evil atmosphere heightened their collective anxiety.

Seconds later, the others were already searching for clues to find the way out.

"Remember," a voice from outside said, "the killer will be back in an hour. You have fifty-nine minutes to escape. Otherwise…" The laughter, though forced, sounded truly sinister.

"Isn't this great?" Kate asked, clasping his arm.

"Yeah, terrific."

His fellow "prisoners" pulled items from drawers, looked under and behind furniture, and even used a black light searching for hidden messages.

"Forty-five minutes left," Kate said.

Alonzo paid more attention to her than to the challenge of escaping. She was alive with excitement, offering solutions, shouting answers to clues, and reminding them constantly of the elapsing time.

Alonzo felt the tension in the room grow as the minutes

shrank. He knew it wasn't real, knew no one was coming back to kill them. And yet, the feeling in the shack was so menacing that his heart rate ramped up each time Kate called out the remaining time.

His coworker, Mike, glanced at a group of alphabet blocks. "It says *dear*," he insisted.

Alonzo peered over his shoulder, wondering how he seemed so sure so quickly. There were other possibilities.

"Yes. But it could say *read*," Kate cried. "Look—now it makes sense!" She rearranged the letters, and they pounced on their next move.

Yelling with excitement, they made it out with only seconds to spare.

Kate was elated; Alonzo was exhausted.

"We're all going to Maxine's diner for supper," Kate said. "Are you interested?"

"Not this time," Alonzo told her quietly. "I'm beat. I was up half the night. One of my neighbors had a party," he said, hoping she couldn't read the lie in his eyes.

She looked disappointed, but didn't argue. "Then I guess I'll see you Monday."

"Yeah. Thanks for including me."

He drove home trying his best not to compare the day at Laguna with his afternoon in The Shack. In the end, he couldn't escape the thought that white folks had a strange way of entertaining themselves.

*

He met Carlos on Sunday morning for what was becoming their regular fishing trip.

"Escape room?" Carlos repeated when Alonzo told him about his adventure the day before. "Since you're here, I assume you broke out."

"Yeah."

They were walking back to their cars after each one

having caught his day's limit.

"Will you take my catch to my mom?" Alonzo asked, sure his cousin would oblige.

"No."

Alonzo wasn't certain he'd heard him right. "Did you say no?"

"I did."

""Why? Is it too far to carry such a heavy load?"

"Your mom told me not to bring any more fish. She said to tell you to bring them yourself."

"If you'd told me that earlier, I wouldn't have bothered to come."

"Which is exactly why I didn't."

Alonzo had no use for six fish, even if he did feel like cooking, which he didn't. He supposed he could give them to some of his neighbors at his apartment.

"Take her the fish, Lon. She misses you."

"I know."

"Well?"

"You should have told me."

"She asked me not to."

Of course she did. He couldn't blame Carlos. "How about this…you take them to her and tell her I'll come for dinner tonight."

"You'll really come back?"

"Yeah."

"I'll have hell to pay if you don't show."

"It'd serve you right."

Carlos put the ice chest and gear in his trunk. "You'd better come, Lon."

"Yeah, I will."

"I'll see you later."

"Why? Are you having dinner there, too?"

"I'll wangle an invitation. Nobody does fish like your mom."

*

He spent the day trying to come up with an excuse. Total waste of time.

There were none.

Felicia saw him pull up in front of the house and was on her way out to greet him before he'd opened the car door.

"I'm glad you're early," she said. "I want to talk to you."

He knew it was coming, he just didn't know what her angle would be.

"Balloon Fiesta starts on Friday. It'd be the perfect time for me to spend the weekend."

"No."

"Why not?"

"Because traffic next weekend will be nuts. I'm not going to leave my apartment."

"You promised."

"No, I didn't."

"Yes you did. At Paolo's wedding. You said I could visit."

"I said sometime before Christmas."

"It is before Christmas."

"It's two months till Christmas."

She pulled on his arm, stopping him before he stepped into the house. "I did what you asked me. About the video. You asked and I did it. Now, I'm asking."

He put his arm around her waist. "Did you talk to Mom about visiting?"

"Heck no. You'll have to convince her."

"She's not gonna like it."

She grinned up at him, and kissed his cheek. "You'll figure a way. Like you always say, you're her favorite."

Victoria was in the kitchen, preparing Alonzo's most loved dishes, and singing along with the radio. "You're here," she cried, rushing to hug him. "Felicia, get your brother something to drink."

"I'm fine, Mom."

"Are you hungry?"

"Yeah. But I don't want to eat before dinner."

"I have green chili."

"That's fine. I'll wait."

Felicia gestured wildly behind her mother's back and then said, "I'm going to finish my homework," and went to her room.

"How are you, Dyaami?"

"Fine."

"You're too thin."

"I'm fine."

She returned to the stove, where she stirred the contents of two pots. The aroma could have flattened him. He wished he could bottle it and take it back to his apartment.

"Mom, Felicia wants to come to my place for a visit. How about next weekend? It's Balloon Fiesta."

"Are you sure you're not hungry?"

"No. Mom, what about next weekend?"

"What about it?"

"Felicia wants to come. It's okay with me." He paused. "Mom?"

Victoria stirred with renewed energy.

"Mom."

His mother put the worn wooden spoon down beside the stove, and turned slowly, her eyes as weary as Alonzo had ever seen them. "Your brother married a White woman. He's gone. You moved to Albuquerque. You're gone. Can't you leave me my daughter?"

"She wants to come for the weekend, Mom. She wants me to take her to the Balloon Fiesta."

"That's how it starts. One weekend."

"Mom, you can't tie her up here."

Victoria glared at him with the eagle eyes of his childhood. "It's her home. It's your home. I don't want her at your apartment. If she wants to go see the balloons so badly, your father can take her."

"Mom…"

"*Ma'a,* Dyaami."

When his mother said stop, the discussion was over. Felicia would not be spending the weekend in Albuquerque unless, for some reason, she had to be hospitalized.

*

Alonzo was not surprised when Paolo and Erin arrived. His mother hadn't said she'd invited them, but he knew she would. Victoria would fight to reunite her two sons until she'd accomplished the task or she'd gone on to the next world.

Paolo greeted him with a clumsy embrace. "Good to see you, Lon."

"You, too," Alonzo said, aiming for sincerity but probably missing.

Erin's hug was closely supervised by his brother. "How are you?" she asked.

"Good." He wondered where the comfortable closeness they'd shared in spring had gone. Killed, he imagined, by the truce he'd made with Paolo.

Erin walked into the kitchen. "Can I help?" she asked Victoria.

Her mother-in-law smiled, but shook her head no. "I've got it."

"Carlos says you've had good luck fishing at Kewa," Paolo said.

"Yeah."

"He told me you caught Grandfather and then threw him back."

"It didn't seem right. He belonged to the old men."

"We have good fishing here, you know," Paolo said. "We could go together some time. Or, we could go riding. You obviously haven't lost your touch."

Alonzo shot him a don't-start-with-me look.

"Pretty impressive, Dyaami."

"More like pretty stupid."

"You saved a kid's life."

"I never even saw him."

"Horseman hero is…" Paolo started, but Alonzo interrupted him.

"Ridiculous. Completely ridiculous. And, I don't want to talk about it."

Alonzo could have hugged Carlos for choosing that exact moment to walk in the front door. "It's about time. We've been waiting for you to have a beer."

"That's hard to believe," Carlos said.

Alonzo went into the kitchen and got three beers. When he handed one to Paolo, he added a cautionary stare. He was not going to discuss the parade.

*

Felicia pouted all through dinner, despite efforts by the entire family to drag the dour look from her normally happy face.

"Paolo and I can take you to Balloon Fiesta," Erin offered. "His friend, Greg, will be flying. We could go early, if you want, and watch them get the balloon ready."

Felicia shrugged, her slim shoulders speaking louder than words. It wasn't about the Balloon Fiesta.

"Who wants more fish?" Victoria asked.

Alonzo knew she wanted nothing more than to get past the subject of Felicia and Albuquerque.

When no one else spoke, Carlos said, "I'll take another piece. I wouldn't want Lon's hard work to go to waste."

"May I be excused?" Felicia asked.

"Yes," Victoria said, sounding relieved.

The girl disappeared down the hall, and they heard her bedroom door close.

"I don't see why she can't go to Albuquerque," Luis said.

Victoria stood with the abrupt force of an earthquake. "It's none of your business," she said to her youngest son, and she walked like a warrior into her kitchen.

Her husband looked hard at his son. "Best to stay out of it."

Luis mumbled something under his breath, which his father ignored.

Alonzo marveled at how much more Luis could get away with than he or Paolo ever had.

Erin began clearing the table, and the men went into the living room. Before long, Erin brought in a tray with plates of pineapple upside down cake. There might be a melding of male/female roles in Albuquerque, but it hadn't reached their corner of the pueblo.

*

Driving back to his apartment, Alonzo wondered why he hadn't told Erin about the success he'd had with his tomato plant. He'd taken four of the bright red fruits to his mother, who had sliced them and served them with dinner.

But, she hadn't mentioned that Alonzo had grown them, and neither had he.

The turmoil he and Erin had created was alive and well, albeit silent.

CHAPTER 9

During his years at University, Alonzo had attended Balloon Fiesta several times. The nine-day event had started nearly fifty years before and was one of the major tourist attractions in Albuquerque. He'd paid little attention to it in recent years, other than complaining about the traffic jams it produced.

But of course, Kate was not just paying attention, she was trying to organize a group to attend on opening weekend.

"Come on, guys," she was saying to their co-workers when Alonzo arrived at work the next morning.

One of the other analysts snickered. "You're nuts, Kate. Nobody wants to get up that early on a weekend."

"Alonzo doesn't mind getting up early." Kate's Miss-America-smile could move a man, Mohammed, or a mountain. "You'll go, won't you Alonzo?"

No came so naturally to him those days, reacting with instinctive protection against months of people pushing at him: go fishing; go out with Luz; go to the fair; move back home. Make someone else happy.

But then there was that smile.

"What time?" he asked.

"Morning Glow is at six-thirty on Saturday. Mass Ascension is at seven. Of course, we'd need to get there earlier if we want to watch them get the balloons ready."

A recently hired admin frowned. "What is Morning Glow? Sounds like people have been drinking all night."

Kate laughed. "No. It's a pre-dawn tradition, when the pilots fire all the burners at the exact same time, and the balloons shine like giant lightbulbs. From everything I've read, it's breathtaking."

"So then, what's the adjusted time?" Alonzo asked.

"Five?"

Seven other employees groaned.

Alonzo said, "What the heck? Sure." He had the sense she would have hugged him if he hadn't turned quickly toward his desk. "You should probably give me a wake-up call."

"No problem," she said.

No problem as long as they didn't run into Paolo and Erin. The last thing he needed was a game of twenty questions.

*

It was inevitable.

How could it not be?

Greg's balloon was in the third row Alonzo and Kate walked down at the fiesta grounds on Saturday morning. Paolo was working with the crew; Erin stood to the side, camera in hand, watching more than taking photos.

If Alonzo had been alone, he would have turned away and avoided them.

"Lon!" Erin called. "I didn't know you were coming."

Paolo turned at the sound of Lon's name. "Hey, Dyaami." He glanced at Kate, and realizing Alonzo was not alone, smiled broadly. "Hold on a sec," he said to another crew member. He made some adjustments on the ropes that held the balloon, and told Greg, "I'll only be a minute."

Greg gave Alonzo a quick wave and continued working.

"This is my brother, Paolo," Alonzo told Kate, "and his wife, Erin."

After the brief introduction, Paolo said, "I can't stop now. How about lunch later?"

Kate looked at him with the innocent expectation of one who had no idea the invitation involved entering a minefield. "I'd like that," she said, setting off the first explosion.

"I would, too," Erin agreed. Blast number two.

"Country Line? One o'clock?" Paolo suggested. "Order me a beer in case we're late." He nodded at Kate and hustled back to the burgeoning balloon.

"I'll call and make a reservation," Erin told them.

And, without Alonzo saying a word, the plan was made. A double date with disaster, he thought. He'd spent scant time with Paolo and Erin since the wedding. What would they talk about?

They moved along, Kate engrossed in the drama of the balloons, knowing nothing of the drama in his family.

"It's almost time for Morning Glow," Kate said, switching her phone to camera mode. "Don't you want to take some pictures?"

"Yeah, I do."

"I read that this is the most photographed event on earth," Kate said, snapping a picture of a pilot adjusting the flame of his balloon's burner.

"That's probably more advertising than actuality."

She turned and grinned at him, the glow from a balloon nearby softening her features. "Cynic."

"Realist," he said, snapping a shot of her smile.

As crews around them fired their burners, the balloons burst into radiant colors—intense yellows, riotous reds, brilliant blues, and glorious greens. Alonzo took several quick shots, knowing that if he didn't move fast he'd lose the moment.

But, none of the pictures pleased him. He began searching for something different; something he hadn't seen in a dozen posters or magazines.

He noticed a child, a boy about five or six, watching a balloon flare with a blast from a burner, his silhouette turned black from the brilliance behind. Alonzo crouched and waited. The second firing of the burner brought the boy into stark relief against the balloon, and Alonzo took the shot.

Satisfaction coursed through him when he looked at the result on the screen. It was exactly what he'd been after. Every element was in place; every part of the photo mattered, counted, added to the overall effect.

He started to show it to Kate, then stopped. For some reason, it was private.

Instead, he followed her as she walked past balloon after balloon, taking a video of the radiant airships.

"This is so much more beautiful than I imagined," she said, her voice barely reaching over the roar of the blasting burners. "It's like a fairyland."

"Fairyland wouldn't be this noisy."

But, it was a bit like a fairyland, like being suspended in a bouquet of balloons, where everywhere Alonzo looked, his view was filled with dazzling brilliance.

"It's like Alice in Wonderland meets The Wizard of Oz," Kate said. "I want to jump into one of these baskets just to see where it will go."

"It'll go in a big circle," he told her.

"What do you mean?"

"There's a weather phenomenon here called the Albuquerque Box. The air near the ground is cooler and blows south. When the pilot is ready to come back, he takes the balloon to higher air, which is much warmer, and blows north. Lots of the balloons land exactly where they started."

"That's amazing." She peered at him. "Don't you think it's amazing?"

"I guess."

"What do *you* think is amazing?"

"I think it's amazing that dozens of balloons don't crash into each other during Mass Ascension."

"That's because of all those guys in the striped shirts, right? The ones they call Zebras?"

"No. Those guys are actually a team of white collar prisoners doing community service."

"I thought," she began, but his laughter stopped her. She shoved him and he nearly fell. "Careful," she said, threading her arm through his. "I wouldn't want you to get hurt."

He stiffened. What would Paolo think if he saw her hanging on him like a Christmas ornament?

"Oh, Alonzo! One is going up. Mass Ascension is starting!"

Alonzo had never been so grateful to see a cell phone. Taking pictures required both of her hands.

"Where do you think we can get the best view?" she asked, taking another picture.

"I have no idea. Let's walk around and see what looks promising."

Two, three, four balloons at a time lifted off the ground, and rose gently and gracefully into the sky. Gradually, the bright colors faded into indistinguishable dots.

The two moved as fast as they could, stepping between balloons, and chase crews, and other sightseers, intent on doing exactly the same thing as all the other onlookers.

Alonzo took shot after shot. Some were okay, but the thought of the photo of the boy's silhouette gave him a sense of triumph.

"It sure is different in the sunlight," Kate said. "I didn't realize how many balloons were here earlier."

"The website said they expected nearly six hundred entrants."

"And not two of them are alike." She shaded her eyes, looking into the bright sky. "It must be fun to create the designs."

They stood and watched as two crews packed up balloons which never launched.

"That must be a huge disappointment," Kate said. "There has to be so much preparation and anticipation."

"Not to mention expense. Entrance fees, travel costs, fuel, taking the thing to the balloon wash…"

"How do they wash a balloon?"

He laughed. "You are so gullible."

"Don't you think it's cruel to make fun of people?"

"I'm not making fun. I'm teasing." He must be spending too much time with Carlos. "Do you want to go watch the chainsaw carving?"

"Do you?"

"This is your party. It's up to you."

"I'll pass. What else can we do? We aren't meeting your brother for another three hours."

"Have you ever been to the Balloon Museum?"

"No."

"I haven't either. But, I heard it's interesting."

"Let's check it out."

"It's not far. We can walk."

They were not the only ones with the same idea. Families with children crowded around exhibits highlighting the history and exploration of balloon flight.

"What an awesome place," Kate said. "It's perfect for kids."

Groups squeezed together around each display; many were interactive and required patience to engage.

"Listen to this," Kate said, reading from her phone. "The first hot air balloon was launched in seventeen-eighty-three. Its passengers were a duck, a sheep, and a rooster. It stayed in the air for fifteen minutes before crashing."

"Guess they weren't given landing instructions."

"Like that poor dog they shot up in a rocket about a hundred years ago."

"People can be cruel to animals."

"It's better now, don't you think?"

"Yeah," Alonzo said. "These days they're considerate of animals and cruel to other people."

Her sad eyes hurt his heart. "Do you actually believe that?"

A sorrow born of years of oppression welled up inside him. "I do." And then, to avoid being called a cynic, he added, "But, it's getting better."

It was after twelve by the time they were finished seeing all the exhibits at the museum.

"Unless there's something else you want to do, we can head over to the restaurant," Alonzo said. The sooner they got there, the sooner they could leave. "Traffic is bound to be heavy no matter which way we go."

Paolo's car was in the parking lot when they arrived; he and Erin were already seated at a table, looking at menus.

"I ordered you a beer," Paolo said when the couple joined them. "Sorry, Kate. I wasn't sure what you'd want."

"No problem," she said. "Water is fine."

"What did you think of Fiesta?" Erin asked.

"It was fantastic. I loved every minute. Now I'm dying to go up in a balloon. I haven't been before."

"It's something you'll never forget," Erin said. "But, I think the Santa Fe area is more interesting, more beautiful, more striking even. That's where I'd go."

Paolo glanced at his wife with amusement. "Is Greg paying you to advertise?"

"No. But that's not a bad idea," she said. "I wouldn't mind a side job."

"What do you do?" Kate asked.

"I teach high school English. Paolo teaches History. We both work at Bernalillo High School. What about you, Kate?"

Alonzo relaxed. The focus was on them and not him. Maybe this wouldn't be so bad.

Later, his brother insisted on paying the bill. "You can

get it next time," he told Alonzo when he objected.

There wouldn't be a next time if Alonzo could avoid it.

"I'm going to the ladies room before we leave," Kate said.

Erin pushed her chair back. "I'll go with you."

Paolo smiled at his brother as the two women walked off. "They could be sisters. Now I understand why you don't want to move back home. You found your own Erin."

Alonzo's eyes narrowed, and his hands balled into fists. He unclenched his jaw and said, "She isn't Erin, and she isn't mine." He was on his feet before he realized it.

"Alonzo, wait..."

But Alonzo was afraid that if his brother said another word, he might slug him. "Thanks for lunch," was all he could manage before walking out.

*

"What's the deal with you and your brother?" Kate asked him as they drove back to her apartment.

"What do you mean?"

"The tension during lunch was heavier than my workload."

"I'm not sure what you're talking about."

"I may be blond, Alonzo, but I'm not stupid. If you don't want to talk about it, say so."

"I don't want to talk about it."

"Fine," she said, in a voice which assured him it was anything but.

He walked her to her apartment door, dragging along with them the silence that had not been broken on the ride.

"Thanks," she said simply.

"Yeah. Any time."

She glared at him with eyes that said, *not anytime soon.* "See you Monday."

"Yeah."

He drove home in the silent company of irony.

*

Late that night he pored over the pictures he'd taken at Fiesta. He began by dumping all those that were out of focus or had no particular subject. Then, he trashed the ones that looked like a dozen posters or postcards he'd seen.

The remaining seven shots all pleased him, but one he returned to again and again: the silhouette of the small boy against the luminous balloon. Something about it tugged at his insides and made him smile.

He pulled Luz's phone number up and with barely a second thought, texted her the picture. No message, just the picture.

In less than a minute, his phone pinged.

On the screen was a photo of three balloons silhouetted against a blazing red-orange sky, floating into the dazzling sunrise.

It grabbed his breath and yanked it out of his body. He stared at it for a full minute.

He switched back to his camera and scrutinized his own pictures. Not one was worth sending her. He knew it wasn't a contest. It was a conversation, wordless and intimate. Still, he wanted to hold up his side.

As he considered his response, his phone pinged again. The screen lit with a huge question mark.

She was waiting.

He searched through the emojis and stopped at a fried egg in a skillet. He sent it.

Seconds later, she sent back a clock.

He returned the number nine.

She sent back a photo of herself standing in front of PICC.

A thumbs up from him settled it.

They had a date.

CHAPTER 10

Alonzo was surprised when he pulled up in front of PICC the next morning. The parking lot was nearly full, and more than a dozen people were carrying large boxes into the center. He stopped at the curb where Luz stood waiting.

"Good morning," she said, getting into the car.

He handed her a cup of coffee. "Good morning."

She took the cup and wrapped her hands around it. "Thanks. It's chilly this morning."

"I thought we could go up to The Range in Bernalillo. Everything around here is crowded because of Balloon Fiesta."

"The Range is good. I like their blue corn pancakes."

"What's going on at the center?"

"The Invitational Art Festival." She took a tentative sip of coffee. "Fifty Native American artists from New Mexico are invited to participate every year. Unfortunately, I wasn't one."

"Their loss."

"It's quite an honor. I hope I'll be included one day, but I'm not optimistic. They're looking for more traditional art, like pottery, jewelry, and blankets. I don't think photography is very high on the list."

"That's too bad."

"Jemez has an open air market next weekend. I'll have a booth there."

Was that an invitation, he wondered?

The Range was crowded. They waited nearly half an hour before they were seated.

"Thanks again for the coffee," Luz said after they'd ordered.

"No problem."

"I liked your picture."

"Thanks."

"Was it a surprise?" she asked.

"Not really. I'd taken another one right before that. When I saw what was wrong, I was ready for it."

"The learning curve."

"I liked yours, too. I don't think it would be as dramatic in sepia," he said.

"No, I don't either."

"Yours might work in black and white."

"You think?"

"I do. Let's look."

"How?" he asked.

"Show me the picture."

Alonzo found the photo on his phone and handed it to her.

"See here at the bottom? You can make all sorts of adjustments in color, hue, and intensity. Of course you can crop. You can change the tilt. You can even post online or send the picture to someone right from here. These camera phones are amazing." She changed his photo from color to black and white and handed it back to him.

He had no idea there were so many options. He'd barely taken a dozen pictures before he met Luz.

"It's interesting, but it makes the picture feel cold. I don't like it."

"I don't either. But sometimes, it surprises you."

"Your favorite thing, surprises."

She smiled. "Yes."

"Have you taken a lot of photography classes?"

"I have. I love learning what the equipment can do. The digital age has changed photography dramatically. The thing it hasn't changed is sensitivity. Artistic eye. People can learn everything there is to know about a camera and still take lousy pictures."

"If you have an artistic eye, you know they're lousy."

She grinned at him. "And if you have an artistic eye, you learn to expect more mediocre pictures than masterpieces."

"You're too hard on yourself."

"Not at all. I'm asking people to pay for my work. I owe it to them, if not to myself, to offer my very best."

"Have you decided on the pictures you'll use from Laguna?"

"I've narrowed it down."

"I'm curious to see what you choose."

"I found a few pictures on one camera that I don't remember taking."

"Surprises?"

"The one of the two crosses is interesting."

"Thanks."

"You had to do some work to frame that one."

His face warmed with her praise. "Which pueblo is next?"

"Kewa, I think."

"They're conservative. Have you talked to anyone about photographing there?"

"Yes. They gave me limited access, exactly like Laguna. They want me to have an escort when I'm there."

"As if you don't know the traditions."

"They're a little different in each village. I'm happy to follow their rules."

When they finished their breakfast, Alonzo said, "Carlos

and I go fishing on the river at Kewa. I can show you the spot if you'd like."

"I would."

The freeway was crowded with Fiesta traffic, so Alonzo took the back roads, roads he preferred anyway. Half an hour later, he parked in the spot where he and Carlos always met.

"I don't suppose you have your camera," Alonzo said.

"I never leave home without one." She opened her bag and took out a compact digital camera. "It's small, but it's powerful. It even has a decent zoom lens." She slipped it into a pocket in her jacket. "I don't want to advertise. They didn't expect me today."

"We probably won't see anyone. It's too late for fishing."

They walked along the bank, climbing over rocks and skirting around trees and brush. As Alonzo suspected, they met no one along the way.

As if compelled by an invisible force, Luz stopped at the exact spot where Alonzo and Carlos fished. She sat on the flat rock, pulled out the camera, and began framing.

More than anything, Alonzo wanted to take pictures of her. The braid hanging down her back was thicker than a rope and glistened like black onyx. She was beautiful, especially now, engrossed in what she loved.

An obliging fish swam near the surface, perhaps sensing that Luz posed no danger.

Alonzo heard the soft whir of the telephoto lens extending toward the water. He stood perfectly still, not wanting to spoil her concentration. She was in that alternative world he'd observed at Laguna, where there was no place for him.

"Brother fish says he knows you," she said, her voice a stiletto slicing the silence.

He shivered, but not from cold.

She stood, said something to the fish in her native tongue, and the fish darted under the rock.

"This is our spot."

"Yes," she said simply.

She knew.

They continued walking down river, stopping whenever Luz spotted something that intrigued her.

After nearly an hour, Alonzo said, "If we're going to walk to Albuquerque, we should have packed a lunch."

"Are you ready to head back?"

"I was thinking we could check out the exhibit at PICC."

"I'd like that, too. But, let's walk on the other bank."

They found a spot where the river narrowed, took off their shoes, and made their way across.

Alonzo took out his phone and began taking pictures. He tried not to aim for the same things Luz was shooting, but found her focus irresistible. He ended up taking pictures of her taking pictures.

She didn't comment on it; he wasn't sure if she realized what he was doing. But, he had a feeling she knew. She didn't miss much. She had at least six senses.

And, she could talk to fish.

*

They had to park several blocks from the center, which was more crowded than Alonzo had ever seen it.

"I wouldn't have thought so many people would be here," Alonzo said as they made their way out to the plaza.

"I think they come over from Balloon Fiesta. Maybe they figure they're already out, they may as well make the most of the day."

Luz paused at every artist's booth, introduced herself, and commented on the art. She never mentioned her own work, although some of the artists recognized her.

"Hey, Alonzo."

He turned. "Hi, Natoma. What brings you here?"

She laughed. "You mean besides a great art show?"

Someone else might have said the same words and made

him feel foolish. But, Paolo's former girlfriend was well-known as a kind woman, and her smile made all who received it feel washed with warmth.

"My boyfriend is dancing."

Luz turned from the artist she'd been speaking to. "Hello."

"Natoma, this is Luz Fragua. She's a photographer from Jemez."

"I've seen your books," Natoma said. "They're beautiful."

"Thank you."

"Natoma is from my pueblo," Alonzo said. "Her boyfriend is dancing today."

"Maybe you know him," Natoma said. "Lorenzo Espinosa? He's from Laguna."

"I do know him. I've taken several pictures of him. He's a wonderful dancer."

Natoma's quick smile was tinged with pride. "I think so, too."

The drums began a steady beat, and Natoma turned.

"Nice meeting you," Luz said, and Natoma nodded in agreement.

"Do you want to watch the dancing?" Alonzo asked her.

"Not especially. Do you?"

"No."

"I'd like to load the pictures I took on my computer and see what I've got."

"Send me one," he said.

"Only if you'll send one back."

"Okay."

He walked her to her car.

"Thanks for breakfast. And the river walk."

"Anytime," he said. Unlike Kate, Luz did not suggest another outing.

He wasn't discouraged. He'd already decided to go to the Open Air Market at Jemez the following weekend, where she'd told him she would have a booth.

*

Alonzo did not look forward to seeing Kate again, sure that their recent disagreement would make things strained or awkward at work. He avoided the break room for two days.

On Wednesday morning, her bright smile and cheerful greeting showed no sign of lingering discord.

"Good morning," she said, passing by his desk.

"Hi."

She didn't stop. And, she didn't encourage him to attend the Brewfest that weekend, which many of their colleagues planned to do. Something had changed when he refused to talk about his issues with Paolo.

He wouldn't have talked about it even if he understood it, which he didn't. Things with his brother had changed, too, at the same time that Alonzo's feelings for Erin had. Those connections needed to be reestablished, and Alonzo wasn't sure when, or if, that could happen.

*

On Saturday morning, the sky was the color of cold ashes dragged out of an horno. Rain was in the forecast. Alonzo knew that would be a factor in attendance at the Jemez market. It was also the final weekend of Balloon Fiesta, and he wondered if the airships would be allowed to fly.

His phone pinged as he was walking out to his car. On the screen was a photo of the famous red rock mesa at Jemez. Striations of rich earth, stacked like sliced crayons, vibrated against a bright blue sky.

He knew Luz had not taken the picture that morning.

He scrolled through the photos he'd taken during their walk along the river and decided on one of the bank, a similar stack of color where wet earth and rock met dry.

Her response was a set of clapping hands.

He sent a picture of a cup of coffee with a question mark.

His phone pinged almost instantly. A selfie of her smile.

He stood staring at it. God, she was gorgeous.

He drove to Bernalillo, where he bought two coffees and a sandwich at Starbucks. He wrapped her coffee in his jacket. Jemez was only half an hour away, but he wanted it to be steaming when he handed it to her.

Alonzo arrived after nine o'clock and found the parking area empty; not a good omen. He walked around the booths looking for her. He greeted artists who were sitting quietly with their work, waiting for patrons who may have found more agreeable activities on a miserable morning.

He finally saw her photographs, carefully hung from the framework of a canopy at the farthest end of the field, creating an intimate space which would also serve as shade should the sun appear. She nodded and smiled at him with slow eyes when he handed her the coffee. "Good morning."

"Not so much," he said.

"Oh? Why?"

"It's cold."

"It'll be hot by eleven." She took a tentative sip of coffee. "Like this. Thanks."

"Anytime."

He walked around the entire booth, considering each picture. A copy of the horse nuzzling a hand hit him with the same intensity as it had at PICC. "This one is my favorite."

"Why is that?"

"It reminds me of when I was a kid. My brother and I took care of our neighbor's horses. He taught us to ride."

"He taught you well."

He knew she was referring to the incident at the parade. Tension tightened his chest. He would be so disappointed if she mentioned it. He'd counted on her understanding.

Apparently she did, since she said nothing more.

He relaxed and the tension drained.

A young man approached the booth, the same man who Luz had left PICC with a few weeks before. He nodded to Alonzo and spoke briefly to Luz, who shook her head no.

The man frowned, argued with her, and then huffed off.

"Sorry," she said. "Have you two met?"

"No."

"I should have introduced you."

"Probably not the best time. He didn't seem very happy."

"No. He's dancing today and wanted me to dance with him. I told him I can't leave the booth. He doesn't get it."

"Do you dance with him often?"

"Occasionally."

"Which dances?"

"The hoop dance."

"You do the hoop dance?" he asked, surprised.

"Yes."

He didn't know any woman who did the complicated dance. Few on his pueblo knew it. When Alonzo had tried to learn it, he'd tripped and fallen so many times he was sure he'd break his neck.

"When did you learn?"

"When I was about two."

"Seriously?"

"Yes. Have you ever heard of Tony Whitecloud?"

"No."

"He was pretty famous way back. He brought the hoop dance to Jemez years ago. Before World War Two. In fact, he toured all over the U.S. with Gene Autry, selling war bonds in the forties."

"He taught you?"

"Not exactly. He was my great-grandfather. Most of our family has learned hoop dancing. Some say it originated with the Plains Indians, but in our family, Tony Whitecloud was the creator."

"That's some legacy. Your whole family dances with hoops?"

"Some of my cousins have competed at Nationals. One even got into the finals. But, it's hard to beat somebody like Nakotah LaRance."

"Who is he?"

"He danced professionally with Cirque du Soleil; even traveled all around the world with their show."

"Is he Jemez?"

"No, he's Hopi."

"Have you seen him in person?"

Her smile was as soft as a spring sunrise. "He's one of my cousin's best friends. We all went to Las Vegas to see *Totem*. It was great. Out of context, the dances aren't the same, but I loved the show. It's as close as I've ever been to knowing someone famous."

"Did it take you long to learn?"

"I don't remember. They start little kids with one hoop and work up from there. I've been asked to help teach, but I don't have time. As you know, it's not only the dance, it's the significance of the circle of life; the healing element of the ceremony."

Alonzo felt her connection to her pueblo as solidly as if she were holding it in her arms. It tugged at his own roots growing deep within, urging them to life.

"When will you dance again?" he asked.

"My cousin and I are dancing at the Winter Indian Market in Santa Fe next month."

"When is that?"

"The weekend after Thanksgiving."

"Nothing sooner?"

"We might dance at Jemez on San Diego Feast Day."

"Maybe I'll come."

"Our dances are closed."

He pulled his best Paolo grin from his pocket. "I think I can pass."

"Oh? Do you speak Towa?"

"Why? Do they give everyone a quiz?"

Her laughter was wind chimes and roses, light and sweet and brushed by the air. "No. Only insolent outsiders."

With just four words she chastened and charmed and challenged.

She was definitely Coyote in disguise.

*

Luz called him early in the week. His heart took a stammering beat when he saw her name flash on his phone. "Hi. What's up?"

"I want to ask a favor."

"Big or little?"

"Big. For me, anyway."

"Tell me."

"After you introduced me to Natoma, I remembered some pictures I took of her about a year ago. She was in the crowd during the dancing at PICC."

"Probably watching Lorenzo."

"Yes. You're right. He was in the same group of shots. Anyway, I studied the pictures of her, and even though they were not especially well framed, it was clear that the camera loves her."

He could see why.

"I'd like to do an entire series on her. Casual. Formal. Street clothes. Traditional dress. If it works out, I'm going to start a book called *Women of the Pueblo*."

"Seriously?"

"Yes. Do you think she'd agree?"

"I have no idea. I don't really know her all that well. She didn't go out with my brother for very long."

"Do you have her phone number?"

"No."

"Could you get it from your brother?"

"I can get it." Not from Paolo.

"I'd appreciate it."

"Would you take pictures at the pueblo?"

"Some. A few at Tent Rocks. Maybe some at the lake. And, I'd love to get her dancing."

"The Christmas dances are next. But, they're closed."

"I think I can pass."

"Not with your camera."

"True enough." She paused and then said, "Call me when you get the number, okay?"

"It's going to cost you."

"I'm prepared to pay."

But it wasn't money he wanted, it was time.

Time with her.

"I'll get it."

He'd call Carlos. That guy could get a phone number from a rock.

CHAPTER 11

Alonzo wasn't surprised when Natoma called. Carlos had delivered on her number, which Alonzo had given to Luz. She'd lost no time.

"Alonzo?"

"Yeah?"

"It's Natoma."

"Hi. What's up?"

"I just talked to your friend, Luz. I was hoping you could tell me about her."

"Tell you what?"

"Anything. How long have you known her? Is she seriously doing a book on pueblo women? Is she weird?"

"Weird?"

"Well, nobody has ever called me and asked to take a bunch of pictures of me before. It seems weird."

"I don't know her very well. She is a photographer. She's published two photo-essay books. She wants to do one on each of the pueblos. She does those old-fashioned looking pictures, in sepia tones."

"If I agree, would you come too?"

"If you want."

"She said she wants to get together this weekend. Are you busy?"

"No. Did she say where?"

"She didn't. I told her I'd call her back. I'll let you know."

"Okay."

There were worse things in life than hanging out with two beautiful women.

*

On Thursday night, Luz called. "Natoma said she asked you to be there when we get together on Saturday."

"Is that a problem?"

"Actually, it is."

He wasn't sure how to respond.

"The thing is, Natoma won't be as natural with someone there watching, as she would be if she were alone."

"I don't think she'll agree if someone she knows isn't there."

"Yes, she told me that. So, I wanted to establish some guidelines with you."

"Like what?"

"Probably the most important thing is, don't talk. If I'm giving Natoma directions or a suggestion, and she's talking to you, I'm not going to get the shot I want. If she's paying attention to you, or looking at you for approval, she won't be looking at the camera."

"Don't talk."

"Yes. To her or to me. I don't want to be interrupted while I'm working."

"Okay."

"Can you do that?"

"Sure. I'll bring duct tape."

"No hand gestures either."

"I get it."

"Thank you."

"So, where are we meeting?"

"At PICC on Saturday at eight o'clock."

"I thought they didn't open until ten."

"They don't. I've got a key. I want the morning sun in their plaza. It's a public space, it's neutral, and she says she's been there many times, so it's familiar."

"Okay."

"Would you do one more thing?"

"What's that?"

"Bring something to do or to read, so neither one of you is tempted to look at, or talk to the other."

"Are you giving her all these rules, too?"

"No."

"Why not?"

"Because I don't know her. This is between you and me."

"Fair enough. Is that it?" he asked.

"It is."

"Okay, then, I'll see you Saturday."

*

Late that night, he switched on the TV and ran through the few channels provided by his landlord. A PBS program on water harvesting immediately caught his attention, and he watched with renewed interest.

When it ended, he realized that growing beans on his patio would not prove his case. Perhaps that was why he'd never actually planted them. The methods he saw in the program were already working elsewhere.

Alonzo was sure that increased production would be advantageous for pueblo households; greater production might give rise to new vegetable varieties. And, additional sales in the surrounding communities would help the families who relied on crops for income.

Inspired, he pulled out the sketches he'd made months

before and began a list of the supplies he'd need. The soil by Julia's house was not conducive to growing much other than weeds. A free-standing planter was a must. Supplies wouldn't cost much, and he knew Carlos would help.

His uncle was another matter. Tony had been against the idea when Erin proposed it initially. Alonzo wasn't at all sure he and Carlos could convince him differently now.

He texted his cousin. "Fishing Sunday?"

Moments later a reply flashed on his screen. "Time?"

He sent back: "Kewa 7:00."

His phone pinged immediately with a thumbs up emoji.

In no time, they had a plan.

*

Alonzo expected Natoma to be dressed in pueblo attire on Saturday morning. Instead, she was bundled up in a white parka, a multicolored ski hat, and bright red mittens. She greeted Alonzo with a sweet smile. "*Kuwe tzi.*"

He grinned. "Sorry, but I'm not allowed to talk to you."

Luz glanced over at him from where she was setting up a tripod. "Good morning. Thank you for coming."

He and Natoma watched Luz attach a camera to the tripod, and a cable to the camera. "I'm going to have you sit on the bench by the horno," she told Natoma. "We're going to talk for a while, get to know each other a bit. I imagine this is a little uncomfortable for you. It would be for me."

The two women smiled at each other as if they shared a secret.

"What about me?" Alonzo asked, aware he was already intruding.

"Over there," Luz said, pointing toward two chairs by the door to the center. "I brought a couple of books for you."

He grinned at her. "Didn't trust me?" He pulled out his cell phone and waved it at her.

"Good." She turned to Natoma. "Are you comfortable?"

"I'm a little cold."

"I should have started a fire in the horno. Sorry."

"I'll be fine," Natoma said, rubbing her arms.

Luz sat on the bench next to Natoma and lowered her voice. Alonzo couldn't hear what she was saying, but he could see Natoma smile, and then laugh, and then gradually, relax. All the while, Luz had the cable in her hand and he had to assume she was taking pictures.

An hour and a half later, other employees began arriving at the center, and Luz began breaking down her equipment. Alonzo hadn't said a word to either of them from the moment he sat down. He had taken two quick pictures with his phone, but was sure Luz had noticed, so he'd put it away.

Natoma walked over to him. "Are you bored?"

"No. Were you?"

"Not at all. She's nice. And, she's interesting."

"Not weird?"

Natoma flushed. "No."

"Are you going to do it again? You know, take more pictures?"

"Yes. She wants to take some at Tent Rocks." She lowered her voice and asked, "Would you come, too? I'd feel more comfortable if you were there again."

"Sure. If you want. But, I think you're safe."

"It's not about safe. It's about," she paused, then finally said, "familiar. I don't know her. If you're there, it'll be familiar."

"No problem. When?"

"Next Saturday."

Luz approached, carrying a camera bag heavy with equipment. "So, next Saturday?"

Natoma nodded.

"Closer to sunset would give us the best light, I think. Can we say three-thirty? I'll meet you there. I'll need to walk around beforehand and figure the best places to shoot."

"Okay, I'll see you then," Natoma said, and she

disappeared into the center.

"So," Alonzo said, "was it good?"

"Yes. She's a brilliant subject. Like I told you, the camera loves her."

"Why not? She's beautiful."

"It's more than that. She has a quality that comes through the lens and transcends her appearance. It's a sort of magic that's hard to define and impossible to fake. But, the camera always recognizes it."

"Would any camera recognize it, or only yours?"

Her almond eyes narrowed. "What a good question. Let's check out those pictures you took."

"What pictures?"

"The ones on your phone."

"You noticed."

"I see everything."

"That's scary," he said, pulling out his phone. He tapped on the camera and enlarged the first picture he'd taken.

"Well, it's not the best composition I've ever seen, but look at her face. Even in profile, the combination of strength and softness comes through. It's like the camera sees inside her, to who she really is. What about the others?"

"The others?"

"You took more than one."

He swiped the screen and a picture of Luz appeared. Her head was tilted toward Natoma, listening to what the other woman was saying. Luz had a simple smile of contentment on her face.

"Not bad. You could have tightened the shot a bit. The background isn't very interesting."

He thought she might be embarrassed. Or annoyed. She didn't appear to be either.

"I'm glad you can make it next weekend. I imagine she'll be okay on her own after that."

"We can drive out together, if you want."

"I need to be there earlier. About two o'clock."

"That's fine. Shall we meet here?"

"Sure."

He carried her equipment out to her car and watched her pack it carefully into the back seat. "I bet you're going home to load them on your computer."

"I bet you're right."

"Send me one."

"Only if you'll send me one back."

"Tomorrow."

"Deal."

He watched her drive off, trying to imagine a photo he could take before tomorrow that would be worth sending.

*

Clouds crowded the sky early that evening, piling one on top of another, pushing the smaller ones together. Alonzo wondered if they would squeeze out any rain. He took the tram to the top of Sandia Peak, hoping the sunset would prove worthwhile.

He was not disappointed.

He took shot after shot as the sky exploded with color. Clouds that had been grey turned a dazzling orange, as if his mother's pumpkin pie filling had spewed into the heavens. The last photo he took was of a blackened distant mountain, crowned with the sun's brilliance and topped with orange foam.

He stared at it on the tram all the way down the mountain, trying to decide how he could have made it better. He tried to see it through Luz's eyes instead of his own.

His phone pinged with a text.

Luz.

He put it in his pocket. He would wait until he was at home to look at it; wait until he was alone; wait until he could savor it like the final Christmas gift.

Once home, he poured himself a beer, tuned to a local

station on the radio, kicked off his shoes, and sprawled out on the couch. He was almost afraid to open the text—not that he'd be disappointed, but that it might have disappeared.

There was no message, only a photo.

Natoma was sitting on a low wall, her head tipped, her eyes uncertain, as if she were trying to solve a problem. The sun had caught in her hair and the light caressed her face. The picture was in color, which he hadn't expected.

The photo showed more than her beauty, it showed her nature. Her soul. It laid her bare and revealed her core. It took his breath away.

He wondered how Natoma would react; wondered how he would feel if he were that exposed.

It occurred to him that in the wrong hands, a camera could be a weapon.

*

Carlos was already at their meeting spot on Sunday morning when Alonzo arrived. He was sitting in his car with the door open, eating prune pie and drinking coffee. "You're late. Too bad. I ate your pie."

"I've killed for less."

"So I've heard." Carlos reached into the back seat and handed Alonzo a large, heavy bag. "It's from your mom."

"How did she know I was coming?"

"How do you suppose? My mom told her."

Alonzo peered into the bag, found a pie, and took out a piece. He wrapped the bag in a blanket in his trunk, making sure the car would be in the shade when they returned.

Fish weren't biting that day, which didn't bother Alonzo in the least. After forty-five minutes without a nibble, he said, "I was wondering…would you still like to build a planter box for your mom?"

Carlos looked over at him. "Sure. Why? You getting bored in Albuquerque?"

"Sort of. I've been thinking about it. We could plant vegetables instead of roses. If it works like it should, it would be possible to increase food production in the fields. People could even grow crops right by their houses."

"That wasn't the plan. The plan was for Mom to have roses."

"Yeah. I know. But, this is a better plan."

Carlos shook his head. "Not for my mom."

"I got another one of those pots like Erin's. I'll bring it to your mom. Then we can build a big planter with a dew catching net. We'll grow roses *and* vegetables."

"I guess that works."

"Do you think your dad will agree?"

"It may take some convincing. Mom'll manage, I think."

"Would it be better if I asked him about it?"

"Maybe." Carlos was quiet for a while. "There's nothing happening here," he said, nodding at the river. "We could go talk to him now."

Alonzo hadn't expected for it to happen quite that quickly.

"Well?"

"Yeah, I guess. If we're going to do it, I suppose the sooner we start, the better."

They packed up, walked back to the cars, and drove to Tony and Julia's. Alonzo knew that he'd have to go and visit his mother before he left, but first he had to convince his uncle that a self-watering planter box would be a good thing for everyone.

Julia welcomed him with a warm embrace. "Where's my dinner?"

"Brother fish is on vacation," Carlos said. "Where's Dad?"

"I think he just got out of the shower. Why?"

"We want to talk to him about building a planter box."

Julia looked from her son to her nephew. "Really?"

"Yes. You still want that, don't you?"

"I do. As long as it doesn't start a tribal war."

Tony came into the kitchen, his hair still wet from the shower. "Fishing bad?"

"Worse than bad," Carlos said.

Tony poured himself a cup of coffee. "So, you came back for breakfast?"

"Not really," Carlos said. "We wanted to talk to you about something."

"I hope it isn't that rose business again."

Alonzo glanced at Carlos, certain they'd chosen the wrong moment. They needed to give this more thought.

Julia turned to her husband and in a voice Alonzo had never heard before, said, "Tony, I don't ask for much. I'm asking for this. It won't hurt anyone or diminish anyone or inconvenience anyone. If Alonzo and Carlos believe they can make it work, I'd like to help them. Please."

Alonzo watched his uncle working through his silent resistance, his face masked, yet readable.

"Some people aren't going to like it," he said.

"And I don't like what some people do, either. But, I don't try to stop them, do I?"

"If it works the way we think," Carlos said, "a self-watering system could be used in the fields and increase food production for everyone. It could be an advantage to the entire pueblo."

"Only if they're willing to accept it," Tony said. "Which many will not."

"That would be their loss," Carlos said.

Tony looked at Julia for a long time. Alonzo wasn't sure what passed between them, but Tony sighed and said, "Okay. Let's give it a try."

"You mean you'll help?" Carlos asked.

"I don't think your mom will let me live here if I don't."

"*Da'waae*," Julia said, kissing Tony's cheek.

"Where do we start?" Tony asked. "Do you have a plan?"

"Not with me," Alonzo said. "It's at my apartment. I

didn't think this would happen so fast."

Julia coughed. "Fast? I've wanted this for twenty years."

"I bought a second pot like the one Erin has. I'll bring it, and we'll plant a rose for you right away."

"It's not going to bloom in winter."

"It has to survive winter," Alonzo said. "If it does, we'll build a bigger planter for more roses in the spring. Meanwhile, I'd like to see if we can get beans to grow this winter. The ideal would be growing food year round."

"That's pretty optimistic," Tony said.

"We won't know if we don't try."

Tony gave him an I-can't-argue-with-that nod; a nod that said true enough, rather than I give up.

"I'll make a shopping list, and order the drip net online. I'll bring the pot next Sunday, and if Aunt Julia will choose a rose, we can plant it. I could buy the lumber, but I don't have a way to get it here."

"You won't buy it," Tony said. "I will."

Alonzo had hurt his pride.

"We can go to Santa Fe and get the lumber on Saturday," Tony said.

"Uh, I have plans on Saturday," Alonzo said.

Julia's eyes didn't question him, but Carlos's did.

"Email me the list," Julia told him. "Tony and I can get as much as possible on Saturday, and you can start work on Sunday. I think we're all available on Sunday."

Alonzo's chest filled first with relief and then with anticipation. His uncle had agreed. Soon, they'd start building the project he'd dreamed about for months. Sweet satisfaction wrapped around him like familiar warm arms.

"How about some breakfast?" Julia asked. "Scrambled eggs and prune pie?"

It was all Alonzo could do not to say, *just like home*. He was not prepared to give voice to the notion that this was where he belonged.

CHAPTER 12

When Alonzo arrived at his office Monday morning, his head was focused on work, but his heart was focused on the planter box. More and more, he felt divided from his life—a strange sense that he had divorced himself from himself.

"Have you heard Kate's news?" Pete asked, stopping briefly at his desk.

"What's that?"

"She's moving back to Phoenix. A teaching position she's wanted came through. She's leaving in two weeks."

She hadn't mentioned it to him. The truth was, they'd barely spoken during the past couple of weeks.

"I'm glad for her," Alonzo said. "Especially if that's what she wants."

"I'm surprised she didn't tell you," Pete said. "I thought you two were dating."

"Dating?"

"Yes. We all thought so."

Dating? They all thought he and Kate were dating?

"Not dating. Just friends."

Pete walked to his own desk, and Alonzo wondered what he'd missed.

Late that afternoon, Kate caught him when he was walking out to his car. "I suppose you've heard."

"Yeah. Pete told me. Congratulations. Sounds like that's what you've wanted."

"Not exactly. But, I couldn't seem to get what I wanted here."

"What did you want here?"

He was shocked when she leaned over and kissed his cheek. "You're sweet, Alonzo. But, you're clueless. How could I have made it any more obvious?"

"Oh, geez."

She smiled, her face tinged with regret. "It obviously wasn't mutual or you would have figured it out by now. I did want the teaching job. I still do. But, I would have stayed if things had been different with us."

"I'm sorry, Kate. I didn't understand."

"That's one of your qualities I find so attractive, I think."

"That I'm clueless?"

"That you're sweet. You're kind. And, you're genuine. You're one of the good guys."

"I wish I'd realized."

"There's obviously something missing or you would have. It's okay. I'm good. I am planning a party before I leave. I hope you'll come."

"Of course."

"Great. I'll give you the details when I work them out." She gave him a rueful smile and turned toward her car. "See you mañana."

"Yeah," he said, still shaken by her admission. How did he miss it?

Loser.

Capitol L.

Or, maybe L stood for something else.

*

Saturday morning was cold and overcast, and Alonzo wondered if Luz would cancel the shoot. But, by noon, the October sun had broken through, and the day sparkled with a light only seen in autumn.

Alonzo drove to PICC, where Luz's car, but no Luz, was in the parking lot. He found her in the plaza, taking pictures of the same fellow she'd left the center with weeks before. He was dressed in full costume, and Alonzo assumed he must have danced at the noon performance.

"Hey, Alonzo," Luz said. "Is it that time already?"

"Whenever you're done."

"I'm sure Michael is done," she said, smiling at him. "Have you two met?"

"No."

She made the introduction and then said something to Michael in their language.

His response was a quick, broad smile.

"I'm ready," she told Alonzo.

They walked out to her car, which he knew she'd insist on driving. He prayed they wouldn't run into anyone he knew at Tent Rocks.

"Are you planning a book on pueblo men?" he asked as Michael came out of the center.

"No. I've applied to do a one-woman show in the spring, and I wanted more diversity in my portfolio. Michael is an ideal subject."

"Does the camera love him?"

"It certainly does."

He couldn't help wondering if she did, too.

*

An hour later, when they pulled into the parking lot at Tent Rocks, Luz said, "I'm going to walk around to see where the shadows fall and where the light works best." She took one camera out of her bag and covered the others.

Alonzo followed silently as Luz slipped seamlessly into a space that was hers alone, framing shots crouching low, perched from above, and occasionally, straight on.

Her intensity fascinated him. She was absorbed in another dimension, silent and serene. A small smile never left her lips, as if the experience was so satisfying she was wrapped in a cocoon of pleasure. Alonzo had the feeling that if he spoke, his words would shatter her world.

By the time Natoma arrived, Luz had set up two tripods and laid out baskets, blankets, pots, and jewelry, to use as props.

Natoma was every bit the woman the camera loved, especially in her traditional dress. Her thick black hair hung half-way down her back, glistening like deep rich velvet. This Natoma was the woman warrior of pueblo legend.

"Are you ready?" Luz asked her.

"I'm nervous."

"You'll be fine. If I ask you to do something or pose in a way that's uncomfortable or awkward, tell me."

"Okay."

Luz turned to Alonzo. "You know the rules, right?"

"Be invisible."

The two women smiled at him, and a peace he hadn't known in months settled in his chest.

The sun slid slowly toward the horizon; shadows moved in tandem, growing longer as day turned to twilight. Luz and Natoma developed a verbal shorthand, understanding each other with a minimum of words and gestures. Alike, yet different, they shared a world he could never enter.

Alonzo wondered if it was because they were both women, or both naturally artistic, or both under the spell of the moment.

He couldn't decide which woman was more beautiful, Natoma, in front of the camera, or Luz, behind it. He wondered again if anyone had ever photographed Luz. He wanted to take pictures of the two of them with his phone, but knew doing so would not only disappoint Luz, it would very likely make her angry.

When the light no longer supported the day, Luz said, "I'm afraid that we're going to have to quit."

"That's a relief," Natoma said. "This is way more work than I could have imagined."

"You should have told me if you were tired."

Alonzo watched Natoma search for words to say she'd never quit. Instead, she said, "I'm fine."

"Is that it?" he asked

"For today," Luz said. She looked at Natoma. "I'd like to get some pictures of you dancing. If you're willing, I could arrange a time at PICC. Also, I wanted to talk to you about a designer in Santa Fe, Patricia Michaels. Have you ever heard of her?"

Natoma shook her head. "No."

"She's a Native American artist from Taos. She does some wonderful things...very organic. I'd love to get some shots of you in two or three of her outfits."

"Do you know her?"

"Yes. She's a friend. I'll talk to her and see if she'd be willing to let us use some of her samples. I'll let you know."

Natoma smiled, and Alonzo saw how the camera could love her. Her beauty lived at several levels of her being.

"I'll call Patricia and find out if she's agreeable. If the pictures I take are good enough, she might even want to use them for ads. You never know."

Advertisements? Alonzo's chest tightened. Tendrils of anxiety wrapped around his lungs and slowly squeezed. He was sure that if Paolo heard that, there would be trouble.

Luz continued. "Thanks, Natoma. I appreciate your doing this. I'd like to show you what I've got. Could we get together, maybe at PICC?"

"Sure."

"Can I come, too?" Alonzo asked. "I could be invisible."

"That's up to Natoma," Luz said.

"It's fine with me. He's endured all this," she said, sweeping her arm toward the darkening hills.

"I'll put together a set of the best shots. There's a meeting room at the center we can use. I'll talk to them about when it's available."

"Thank you. Then I'll see you," Natoma said.

They followed Natoma down the road toward the pueblo and then took the cut-off to the highway south.

"You're happy with the photos?" Alonzo asked.

"Yes. I have a feeling at least a couple of them are brilliant. I won't know for sure until I get them on my computer, but I think she may be the best subject I've ever photographed. Oh, and Alonzo, thanks for not getting in the way."

"Yeah. I do invisible really well."

The headlights of oncoming traffic glared at them, and lit her face in profile. Once again, he thought about photographing her. He felt sure that his camera would love her as much as hers loved Natoma.

When they pulled into the nearly empty parking lot at PICC, he asked, "Do you want to go get dinner somewhere?"

"Sure."

"What sounds good?"

"Just about anything. I didn't have any lunch."

He thought a moment. "Have you ever been to Farm and Table?"

"No."

"It's supposed to be pretty good. I read that they use locally grown produce, meat, cheese, and wine. Are you game?"

"Absolutely. Would you mind driving? I'd feel more comfortable leaving my equipment in the lot here than having my car out on the street."

"No problem," he said, happy to be out of the passenger seat and into the driver's.

*

The restaurant was cozy and crowded, but their timing could not have been better. They were seated on the patio minutes after they arrived, reading the menu and anticipating a relaxing evening after the long afternoon.

"They don't offer a very big selection," Luz said, "but all the plates around us look delicious."

"It says right at the top that they honor the New Mexico growing season. There are probably fewer choices in fall than in the spring."

"Maybe they should find more growers. Farmers who are willing to experiment, to try new things, or new ways." She looked at him with such piercing intimacy that he nearly turned away. She waited then, demanding a response without saying another thing.

"My uncle agreed to help me build a planter. He and my cousin. In fact, I sent him a list of supplies we need last week, and he and my aunt were going to shop for them today. We'll start work on it tomorrow."

Her eyes held his with pleasure. "Tomorrow?"

"Yes."

"I'm glad. It's a good idea."

"I hope it works."

"It will."

She smiled, and he let himself be convinced.

"Send me a picture. I want to see it."

"I doubt if we'll finish it in one day."

"Send me one of the tomato plant."

"Okay."

Paolo would never bother sending pictures; Paolo would take Luz to the apartment and show her in person. But, Alonzo wasn't Paolo, and inviting a woman to his place was so outside his realm that even imagining it was a stretch.

"Will you send me one from today?" he asked.

"Give me time to go through them first."

"I'd like to see one from late in the afternoon, when the sun was behind the rocks."

"You liked that light?"

"Yes."

"It's the best. It's soft and mellow, it's flattering, and it's romantic. Good lighting for a woman."

"Morning light is good, too."

"I think it's sharper. Evening light lulls you."

"Have you thought of other women you want to put in this book?"

"Only one, so far. She's from Jemez. She's my cousin, actually. She isn't beautiful, but she's strong, with distinctive features that tell about pride and determination."

"Have you asked her?"

"Yes." Luz grinned. "She said no. It isn't easy, I know. A camera can feel invasive."

He wasn't sure if she was referring to her camera or the #horsemanhero video. They still had never spoken about it, even though he was sure she must have seen it.

"I asked one girl at Acoma, and she agreed, but her parents talked her out of it. It may be easier now that I have shots of Natoma that will show my work, and my intention."

"The books show your work."

"Not of people. I told you I've been careful about that. This book will be different, much more personal. It's hard to let a camera get that close...to let everyone see into you."

"I know."

She was quiet, waiting, he supposed, for him to say more. When he didn't, she looked back at the menu.

What could he say? He wasn't a hero.

*

"Thanks for treating, Alonzo," Luz said as they left the restaurant. "I wasn't expecting that."

"I invited you."

"Still, we could have split the bill."

"Maybe next time," he said.

"I really enjoyed it. Everything was so good. Delicious, and so fresh."

"Even though they were out of a couple of items."

"They need another supplier. Someone who can keep up production year round."

"Maybe," he said, opening the car door for her.

They talked about photography on the way back to the center. He thought again about asking her to his apartment, but it didn't feel right. He wasn't a virgin, but his familiarity with such things would be considered experimental rather than experiential.

He was a novice. He imagined that at her age, Luz was far more knowledgeable.

"So, you'll send me a picture?" she asked when she got into her car.

"Yeah."

"And I'll send you one from today."

"Right."

"Thanks again for dinner," she said, and closed her door.

He watched her drive down the street.

Again.

He'd made no move, and neither had she.

Was Michael competition, or was Alonzo missing something, as he had with Kate.

For the first time in months, he wished he could talk to Paolo.

*

Alonzo could smell Julia's cooking the minute he stepped out of his car the next morning. She was frying bacon, he was sure. He knocked and heard Carlos yell, "Come on in."

Tony and Carlos sat at the table eating, while his aunt

was busy in the kitchen.

"Are you ready to work?" Carlos asked.

"Not before he eats," Julia said. She put a warm arm around Alonzo. "French toast and bacon sound good?"

"Sounds great!"

She poured him a cup of coffee and nodded toward the table. "Melon?"

"Sure." He hadn't bothered to stop at Starbucks, since he knew his aunt would insist that he eat the minute he got to their house. If you arrived at a pueblo home at mealtime, you'd be served a meal; if you arrived at any other time, you'd be served a meal anyway. Food was the reception committee of the pueblo.

"We got most of the supplies in Santa Fe yesterday," Tony said. He speared a slice of melon and dipped it into a pool of syrup on his plate. "They didn't have a couple of things on your list, but Julia will run into Albuquerque today and get them."

"I ordered two screens. They should come sometime next week," Alonzo told him.

Julia handed him a plate stacked with thick slices of French toast and a pile of crisp bacon. "Juice?"

"No thanks, Auntie."

Tony ate another dripping piece of melon. "We won't be ready for screens for a while. Even if we finish the planter, we'll need the soil first."

"I brought the pot like Erin's," Alonzo said. "It's in my car. I thought maybe Auntie should plant a rose here, to see how it does this winter."

As Alonzo ate, they discussed the plan for the day's work, the items Julia would pick up in town, and when they could plan to finish the project.

"Your mom is expecting us for dinner," Julia told him. "No excuses. You're here and you have to eat."

He'd expected it. "That'd be great. I miss her cooking."

"You're only a move away from enjoying it every night."

Tony's look was a silent warning against his wife pursuing the issue.

"Anyway," Julia said, "she's making all your favorite dishes."

"The rest of us will just have to suffer," Carlos said.

Alonzo kicked his cousin's foot. "You could stay home."

"Like that's going to happen."

Tony stood. "Let's get at it. The day is only going to get hotter."

Julia reached for Alonzo's plate. "Did you get enough?"

"Plenty, thanks."

"I'll make lunch when I get back from town. There's sun tea on the back porch, and there's plenty of water."

Tony gave her a brief hug. "Don't worry. We'll be fine. Go to town. Choose your rose bush."

"There may not be much of a selection this late," she said.

"Actually," Alonzo said, "bare root roses are usually available beginning the first of November."

The others all looked at him in surprise.

"I did a lot of research last spring."

No one spoke.

"I'll get the planter box," he said, and hustled out, hoping the entire day wouldn't be filled with verbal sink holes.

*

They stopped only long enough to eat lunch, laboring the entire day, and by dinnertime, they stood back and admired their efforts.

"It's bigger than I imagined," Julia said.

"It will be a good test for its adaptability," Alonzo said. "If we want to use the system in the fields, we have to find out how self-watering works large scale, not just in a pot."

"Speaking of pots," Tony said, "we should get the rose bush planted."

"I'll do it," Julia said. "The instructions couldn't be more clear. Besides, I like to get my hands dirty."

"Speaking of dirty," Alonzo said, "if you don't mind, I'd like to clean up before I go to my folks."

"Of course," Julia said. "There are fresh towels in the bathroom."

He'd brought clean clothes, knowing he'd end up at his parents' for dinner. He stood under the pounding spray, treasuring the relief it gave his aching muscles, which had lifted and pulled and nailed all day long.

"I'll see you at my folks," he told his aunt and uncle, and walked the short distance to his parents' home. His mother greeted him like a returning warrior. Alonzo gave her a warm embrace, and kissed her cheek.

"Are you hungry?" she asked.

"Smelling your cooking always makes me hungry."

"Lon!" Felicia cried, joining them. "I didn't know you were coming."

"I didn't either," he said, even though he did.

"Are Paolo and Erin coming, too?" the girl asked her mother.

"They are." Victoria looked at Alonzo, her eyes defiant.

"That's great," he said. There was a time it would have bothered him. No more. He barely remembered the yearning, a hangover from his youth that had lingered far too long.

His mother's smile was a gentle caress of relief. "Good."

The peace lasted less than five minutes.

"*Kuwe tzi?*" Paolo asked Alonzo when he and Erin arrived.

"Good," he said. He gave Erin a brief, brotherly embrace. "How's school going?"

"Really well. I have a terrific class this year. What about you, Lon? What have you been up to?"

"Not much."

"He and Carlos are building a planter box for Aunt Julia," Felicia said.

Alonzo watched Paolo's face squeeze tight with disapproval.

"Why?" Paolo asked, his voice as tight as his face.

"She wants a rose garden."

Paolo started to say something else, but Erin took his hand. "Would you get me a soda, please?" A subtle message between husband and wife. The subject was closed.

However, Alonzo knew that Paolo had not said all he intended to about the planter box.

*

Much later, after Victoria had packed him a week's worth of food, and Felicia had pestered him about a visit, Alonzo said good night to his family. He was not surprised when Paolo followed him out to his car.

"So, what's the real deal with the planter box?"

Alonzo wanted nothing more than to avoid an argument. He measured his words as carefully as he would ingredients for his mother's posole, "Julia wants a rose garden."

"That's it?"

"We're going to try growing beans."

"Why?"

"If the system works, we might be able to increase production of produce in the fields."

Paolo's face hardened, his eyes as cold as petrified wood. "Why are you so hell bent on changing things?"

"Life changes, Paolo. It's inevitable."

"Not here."

"Yes, here. We didn't always have running water, indoor bathrooms, or TV. You even have a cell phone. What makes this so distasteful? Three months ago you said you were sorry you hadn't helped Erin."

"That was about her, not the planter. And, it was about roses. You want to change our ways, our traditions. It's the wrong path, Lon. The wrong direction for the pueblo. And, it's wrong for our people."

Alonzo opened the door to his car and put the bag he carried on the passenger seat. "You have your opinion, Paolo. I don't agree. And, I don't want to argue. I didn't ask for your help, and you can be sure I won't. Let's leave it at that."

Paolo's sharp eyes strafed Alonzo's face as he turned away, and Alonzo felt the cutting pain of his brother's fierce disapproval.

He drove away, smarting from something worse than an argument.

CHAPTER 13

Luz's familiar car was the only one in the parking lot when Alonzo pulled in at PICC early Saturday evening. Moments later, Natoma pulled in beside him and gave him a slow, shy smile.

"Are you ready for this?" he asked as they walked toward the entrance.

"Not really."

"Kinda surreal, yeah?"

Alonzo texted Luz that they were at the front door, and she soon appeared with a ring of keys.

"Are you excited?" Luz asked Natoma.

Natoma gazed down at her scuffed moccasins. "I wouldn't say that exactly."

"The photos are wonderful, which I knew they would be. You don't need to be nervous." She led them to a room in the back where she'd set up her computer and a large screen. "Sit anywhere."

"That's a big screen," Natoma said, her face a grimace.

"I like it because it shows me all the details."

Natoma sat. "Wonderful."

Alonzo was glad it wasn't going to be pictures of him

on display. He flashed on the video that had dominated Facebook the month before; the video he had still never watched; the video more invasive than a hunter's knife.

Yes, he was very glad.

Luz dimmed the lights and flashed the first photo on the screen—a shot of Natoma's hands holding a large woven basket filled with corn.

Alonzo could feel Natoma slowly relax, her sigh like a light wind brushing his cheek on a soft summer evening. Luz knew her subject. Smart woman.

Luz moved from tight shots of Natoma's hands to long profile images, and finally, full figure photos that were strikingly beautiful. The sequence was like a story unfolding on the screen.

No one spoke.

When she finished, Luz turned the lights up slowly, allowing them to return to the room gradually. "What do you think?" she asked Natoma.

"It's strange. It's almost as if it isn't me."

Luz glanced at Alonzo, her eyebrows raised like living question marks.

He groped for a word that would capture his reaction, but not a single one appeared.

Luz's questioning eyes turned to worry. "No?"

"*Not* no," he said quickly. "They're wonderful. Every one of them. Better than wonderful. How will you choose which ones to use for your book?"

"I haven't thought that far ahead. We still have one more shoot. I spoke to my friend, Patricia, and then sent her a couple of these shots. She's delighted to have Natoma model some of her clothes. As I suspected, she mentioned using her for advertisements."

Alonzo squirmed inside his skin.

Natoma stared into her hands. "I'm not sure…"

"You don't have to decide tonight," Luz said quickly "Patricia said to figure a few dates that would work for us and let her know. We'd do the shoot in Taos."

There was a long pause before Natoma said, "Weekends would be best." She looked at Alonzo. "Will you go?"

"If you want me to."

"Okay," Luz said.

Alonzo noticed she kept her voice low and calm, as if she were gentling a jittery colt.

"I'll call Patricia and tell her we're good any weekend." She turned off her computer and began packing up.

Natoma stepped toward the door. "Thanks, Luz."

"You can't leave," Luz said.

Natoma's dark eyes clouded. "Why?"

Luz laughed. "The front door is locked. Hold on a sec, and we'll all go out together."

Natoma drove out of the parking lot, leaving Luz and Alonzo standing next to Luz's car.

"The photos are amazing," Alonzo said.

"She's the perfect subject. She's got it all. She seriously could be a model."

Alonzo smiled. "So could you."

"Hardly."

"I bet I could take pictures of you that are every bit as flattering as the ones you took of Natoma." He had no idea what possessed him to say something so bold; to assert that he might approach her level of expertise. He braced himself for an attack.

"You think so?" Her voice was amused. "And where would this photo exposé take place?"

Was she teasing or was it a challenge?

He thought for a bit, trying to imagine a setting that would be a suitable backdrop. "Bernalillo."

"Bernalillo?" She sounded like he'd suggested the South Pole.

"Don't look at me like that. I know a perfect spot."

A smile licked her lips.

"Well?"

"Well what?"

"Are you game to be on the other side of the lens?"

She squinted, as if narrowing her gaze would make his motive more clear. "On one condition."

"What's that?"

"That you let me photograph you as well."

"You've taken dozens of pictures of me."

"Only here. And only dancing."

"Why would you want anything else?"

"Curiosity."

Anxiety grabbed his gut. What would she see? How deep could the lens go? Which of his secrets would be exposed?

When he didn't respond she said, "Scared?"

"No," he answered without hesitation.

"Well then?"

"Okay." There seemed to be no other answer if he intended to take pictures of her.

"When?"

"Early morning," he said.

Her laugh was the wind; light, sweet, buoyant. "When?"

"Tomorrow."

"What time?"

"Six o'clock. Here. I'll drive."

"Do you have a camera?"

"I have a cell phone."

"You're a real pro."

"It's good enough to make my point."

"Okay, then I'll see you at six. Are you bringing coffee?"

"Are you bringing breakfast?"

She laughed again, and he felt a strange sensation. He was falling. Much as the feeling alarmed him, he didn't know how to stop it.

"I'll figure something," she said, opening her car door.

He should say something else. He should stop her.

His arms ached to hold her. He wanted nothing more than to bury his face in her hair and breathe her in like pure oxygen.

Paolo would have done it.

Alonzo watched her start the car and, with a wave, drive out of the parking lot.

Loser?

Maybe.

Scared?

Damn straight he was!

*

He woke the next morning before his alarm. He showered, dressed, and walked through the silent complex to his car. It wasn't until he was sitting at the drive-thru window at Starbucks that he thought about the clothes he'd put on.

Luz had been specific about Natoma's clothes. Surely if she'd wanted him in native dress, she would have said so. He wondered what she'd wear; wondered if it mattered. He hoped he could get the shot of her he imagined; the one that would please them both and prove him right.

The parking lot at PICC was empty. He was early. He sat sipping coffee, glad that he and Tony had finished the planter the day before, including filling it with rich, dark soil. The screens had been delayed, and they couldn't complete the project until they arrived.

"Good morning," Luz said when she finally showed up. "Sorry I'm late."

He handed her a cup of coffee. "You okay?"

"I stayed up until almost three this morning. I start working on my photographs and lose all sense of time."

"We can postpone if you want."

"After I made the effort to get here? No way."

He tuned the radio to a local station and headed north

toward Bernalillo. "Say, weren't you supposed to bring breakfast?"

"Yeah. I was hoping you wouldn't notice."

"There's a Starbucks in Bernalillo. We can get another cup of coffee and a sweet roll or some banana bread."

"Sounds perfect. Especially if they warm it." She shivered. "I always forget how cold it gets in the fall."

He turned up the heat. "There's a blanket in the back if you want it."

"No. This is good." She took the sleeve off her coffee cup and held her hands around it. "Where are we going?"

"You'll see."

*

He led her through a stand of cottonwoods to the bank of a slow moving stream, where he spread a blanket on the cold, damp ground. A profusion of shimmering golden-leaved branches hung over them, a copious canopy of color.

Luz tore open the bag of banana bread they bought at Starbucks and offered Alonzo a slice.

"Not right now, thanks. This light won't last." He pulled out his phone, confident that it was fully charged. He'd studied several online videos on portrait photography the night before and was alive with ideas.

Luz broke off a piece of bread and put it into her mouth.

Alonzo focused the camera and took his first shot.

"Now wait a minute," she said, resting her hand on his arm. "Unflattering pictures are not allowed."

He grinned. "Fair enough. Same applies to you."

"Of course."

He dropped to his knees and leaned down low, shooting her in profile, her obsidian hair in stark contrast against the vivid foliage.

She nodded, realizing what he was after. "Good idea."

She'd left her hair loose, and it hung down her back like

a curtain of black silk.

Alonzo felt a nearly irresistible urge to run his fingers through it, to see if it was as soft as it looked. Instead, he took several more shots from the low vantage point before standing.

"Let me know if you want me to move."

"Do you think you could get up in that tree?" He pointed to a golden globe of brilliance, its dark trunk and branches nearly as black as her hair in the morning glare.

"I suppose. Can I finish eating first?"

"Sure." He sat down on the blanket and picked up the other piece of bread. The sun was in no hurry, but sent forth blazing yellow rays to herald its rising.

"I was wondering," Luz said, "if you finished building that planter box. The one for your aunt?"

"We did."

"Really?"

"Yes. In fact, we filled it with soil yesterday morning. I'm still waiting for the screens."

"How will those work in winter? You'll have water from rain and snow, won't you?"

"That's one of the unknowns. We'll have to figure it out as we go along."

"We?"

"My aunt and uncle. Carlos, too."

"I thought your family opposed the idea."

"Some still do. But, my aunt convinced my uncle it was worth trying."

When they finished eating, he pulled her to her feet.

"I'd like to see the planter."

"Oh? Why?"

"I'm curious."

"Why?"

She looked into his eyes. "Because it sounded important to you." Her words were simple, her voice, an intimate caress.

Alonzo couldn't answer. He felt as though she'd seen into his very being. As if she, like her telephoto lens, had extraordinary powers. She'd come as close to his core as anyone ever had. All he could manage was a quick nod.

Half an hour later, the sun sat on it haunches above the Sandia Mountains, surveying its kingdom. Sunlight jumped from branch to branch, illuminating the leaves with fire.

"Your turn is done," Luz said. "I'm taking over."

He smiled at her bold declaration, so unlike a traditional pueblo girl. He wondered if she'd learned it because of, or in spite of her upbringing.

As she took her camera out of a bag, she asked, "Did you get what you were after?"

"I think so. If not, we'll have to try again."

"Hold on. That wasn't part of the deal."

"No?" He folded his arms and turned his back to her. "Then I'm going on strike."

He heard the click of the camera, followed by a soft laugh. "Oh, yeah. That's you."

He turned to a smile that rivaled the sun. He wanted more than anything to reach out, pull her in, and feel her warmth; to surround her with his being.

But, he couldn't get himself to reach past the invisible, yet tangible impediment that stood between them: Erin's rejection.

Alonzo had done everything he could think of to banish the painful memory, but it stood, an implacable ghost before him. He was not ready to risk that possibility again.

"Can you get up in that tree?" Luz asked.

"I can. If you don't make me look like a monkey."

"Is that how I looked?"

"You may never know."

"Aren't you going to show me the pictures?"

"Only the good ones."

"Well, I'm going to show you all the ones I take," she said sounding confident.

"I don't want to see them," he said, walking toward the tree.

"But what if I want to use them?"

"Help yourself. I don't care."

He swung into the tree as easily as he swung onto a horse.

"Move over," she said, and she climbed up across from him.

He marveled at her instinct. "You're a show-off."

"I'm a veteran. 'Not my first rodeo', as they say."

It reminded him that he wanted to go riding with her. But she was already giving him instructions.

He'd ask her later.

*

They walked downstream to get the shots Luz wanted, climbing over rocks and through bushes, warming as the sun made its inexorable climb up the sky.

"We'll have to call Uber to get a ride back to the car," Alonzo teased.

"They'd never find us."

"Pueblo Uber would."

"There's a pueblo Uber?"

He laughed. "If there's not, there should be."

"There is. It's called search and rescue."

"You must have taken every possible shot by now. Aren't you about done?" he asked.

"That's an interesting question, and one I ask myself on every shoot. Am I done? Have I missed anything? Would the next shot, the one I don't take, be the best shot?"

"If you didn't stop, you'd still be on your first shoot."

She lifted the camera and said, "Smile."

He grinned, self-conscious at the proximity of the lens.

"Okay," she said, looking at the picture on the screen. "I'm done."

"Did you get what you were after?"

"Not really. But I'm not giving up. The right shot will happen, though maybe not this morning."

He wondered how she knew.

Something about the first rodeo, he guessed.

*

"Listen," Luz said as they drove away from the river, "I brought a few prints of the pictures I took of Natoma—the ones she seemed to like the best last night. I thought maybe we could take them to her, since we're so close to your pueblo."

His brain spun, not expecting the request. That would mean facing other people there; it would mean running into his family; it would mean explaining Luz.

"Did you already have plans? If you do, it's no problem. I'll call her and arrange…"

"No. It's fine. Maybe just a little early."

"We won't be there till ten."

"Crack of dawn for some."

But, not for Natoma.

She answered the door when they knocked, her smile warm and welcoming. "Good morning."

"Who is it?" came a woman's harsh voice.

"Some friends," Natoma said. She stepped outside and closed the door behind her.

"I hope we're not intruding," Luz said.

"Not at all. What's up?"

Luz handed her a manila envelope. "I printed a few of the shots that I thought you'd like to have."

"Thank you." Natoma took the envelope and dropped her hand to her side.

"Aren't you going to look at them?" Alonzo asked.

Natoma glanced behind her at the closed door. "Not right now. I was helping my mom with some things. I'll look at them when I'm finished."

"We should have called," Luz said.

Natoma touched her arm. "No. It's fine. I'm glad you came. But, I'd rather take my time looking at them."

"I get it," Luz said. "One other thing and then we'll go. I spoke to Patricia. She said this coming weekend or the one after would work for her. Could you do either one?"

"For the photo shoot in Taos?"

"Yes."

"Either one is fine. What's best for you?" Natoma asked.

"Sunday is San Diego Feast Day at Jemez," Luz said. "The following weekend would be better for me."

"That's fine. Either day. Just let me know."

The voice from inside the house was strident. "Natoma! I need you in here."

"I'm coming," Natoma said. "Call me about the details. Maybe we could all drive together."

"Sure," Luz agreed. She and Alonzo stepped off the porch. "We'll see you."

"Thanks again for these," Natoma said, holding up the envelope.

"That obviously wasn't the best timing," Luz said as they backed out of the driveway.

"Yeah. Sorta strange."

"Let's go by your aunt and uncle's. You can show me the planter."

More strangeness.

"Would they mind?" she asked.

"No. I think it would be fine."

Julia welcomed them with hugs, hot coffee, and fresh muffins. "What brings you here?" she asked.

"I wanted to see the new planter," Luz said.

"What do you think of it?"

"It's big."

Julia nodded. "It is. And speaking of big, Carlos said

you have the biggest camera he's ever seen."

Luz grinned. "It's the lens that's big, not the camera. It can be intimidating if you're on the other side of it."

Carlos wandered out from his room, yawning and rubbing his eyes. "I thought I heard your voice, Dyaami." He tipped his head toward Luz in greeting. "What brings you here so early?"

"It's nearly eleven," Julia said.

"Where's Dad?"

"He drove into town for mulch and amendments for the soil." She poured her son a cup of coffee.

Carlos sat next to Alonzo. "What's happening?"

"We took some pictures to Natoma, and as long as we were here, Luz wanted to see the new planter."

"Pictures?" Julia repeated.

"Yes," Luz said. "I've done a couple of photo-shoots with her. She's a brilliant model. We're doing another one with a designer friend in Taos next weekend."

"You didn't tell me," Carlos said.

Alonzo shrugged. "You didn't ask."

"Who is the designer?" Julia asked.

"Patricia Michaels. Have you heard of her? She was on Project Runway a few years ago. She has a fabulous line of high-end indigenous clothing."

"Yes, I've seen her things. I understand she's designing interiors now, too."

"I'm not surprised. She's so talented."

Just like you, Alonzo thought, but wouldn't say in front of his family. Bad enough they'd shown up together. How long before everyone in the village knew?

What had he been thinking?

He should have said no. Found an excuse.

Carlos gulped his coffee and pushed back his chair. "I'd like to hang out, but I'm dancing this afternoon, and I need to feed Mr. Montoya's horses before I leave."

"You're going to be late," Julia said.

"I'll feed them," Alonzo offered. "We're in no hurry."

"Seriously?" Carlos asked.

"Sure."

"You know where everything is?"

"Yeah."

"Great! Thanks, Lon. I owe you. You guys can ride if you want. Maasr'a would love that."

"She's not dressed for riding," Alonzo said. This was getting out of hand. They'd feed the horses and they'd leave.

"Maybe another time," Luz said. "I love riding."

Alonzo tucked away the idea. Another time they'd go riding. Another time and another place. Someplace where people didn't know him; didn't know what a fool he'd been. Didn't wonder if he was doing it again.

When Alonzo led Luz toward the car Julia said, "You're going to drive?" She shook her head. "You've lived in town too long. Leave the car. Your uncle will be back shortly. He'll want to meet Luz, and show off the planter. Come back after you finish with the horses. We'll have lunch."

Alonzo knew what that meant.

The entire family would be there.

*

Maasr'a whinnied when Alonzo patted him, whispering familiar words that Mr. Montoya had taught him. K'akana stamped with impatience, pushing at Alonzo with his head as if to say, hurry up.

Luz stood outside the fence, taking one picture after another as Alonzo greeted and then fed the two animals. "You've known them for a long time."

"Yeah."

Maasr'a paid more attention to Alonzo than to the grain in the basket.

"It seems like maybe he's missed you," Luz said.

"It's been a while."

"We should go riding one day."

He didn't respond.

"Or not," she said after a bit.

"K'akana is hard to handle," he said, nodding toward his brother's horse.

"My uncle has horses," Luz said. "We could ride at Jemez."

Alonzo felt strangely guilty talking about riding another horse in front of Maasr'a. "Yeah. I'd like that," he said, keeping his voice low.

Luz laughed softly. "Don't want any hurt feelings?"

He looked at her with gratitude, her insight pleasing him. Would she please others? "I have a funny feeling you're going to be meeting my family," he said.

She turned, as if expecting someone to be behind her.

"My aunt will call my mom and tell her I'm here. Everyone will show up for lunch."

"Okay." She watched him grimace. "Is that a problem?"

"Not a problem, exactly. But, you know how pueblo families can be."

"I certainly do."

"Are you ready?"

"I'll be fine. It's not my family. Are *you* ready?"

"No."

"Let's go for a walk. To the river or the fields. Show me where you'll try your watering system when the planter is a success."

He finished up with the horses, told them he'd be back to visit them soon, and then took Luz to the fields. Many had large pumpkins, gourds, and squash growing. A few lay fallow, Mr. Montoya's among them.

"I'll use Mr. Montoya's field if the planter works the way I hope. There will be some who disapprove, but with my uncle's support, it should be fine."

They walked along the river, the water low in

anticipation of the autumn storms.

"I suppose we should get back," Alonzo said at last.

Luz smiled up at him. "Don't be so glum. Your family is no different than anyone else's."

Maybe not to her.

Maybe not yet.

CHAPTER 14

Julia's dining table was crowded with family and food. They were all there, of course. All except Paolo.

"He'll be so disappointed he missed you," Alonzo's mother told him. "I wish you'd called."

"I didn't know," Alonzo said. "It was last minute. Luz wanted to bring some photographs to Natoma."

Victoria's never-miss-a-thing eyes narrowed. "Natoma?"

When Alonzo faltered for further details, Luz said, "Yes. I'm working on a photo essay of pueblo women. Natoma agreed to model for me."

An awkward silence fell over the room; a deathly silence that said more than any words.

"Have you been working on it for long?" Erin asked.

Alonzo felt his heart squeeze, and he silently thanked her for bringing the conversation back to life.

"Not this particular project. I've been working on a series about the pueblos, combining the history, traditions, and inhabitants of each of the nineteen villages."

"They're called *Sunlight and Shadow*," Alonzo said, having found his voice. "The pictures are all in sepia tones. They're really incredible."

Luz flashed a brilliant smile at him. "Thank you."

"I'd like to see them," Erin said.

Julia nodded, her mouth full. "I would, too," she finally said.

"Don't leave me out," Felicia said. She looked at Luz. "Do you have any of them with you?"

Luz's sweet smile caressed the girl. "No. But you can see them at PICC."

"Can we get them online?" Erin asked.

"I'm afraid not. The books are difficult for me to upload."

Luis took a second helping of Julia's green chili, and said, "Do you have a website?"

"I do. But it's very elementary. I don't know enough to make it look professional, and hiring someone to do it for me is pretty expensive."

Alonzo watched his parents as they digested what Luz said. He could see them evaluating, contemplating, judging. It was clear that Luz was not the traditional pueblo girl his mother envisioned for him.

"Have you always liked photography?" Tony asked, his tone one of interest rather than interrogation.

"Yes. Since I was a kid, cameras have fascinated me."

"Have you taken many classes?" Victoria asked.

"Oh, yes. I have a B.A. in Fine Arts from the University of Arizona. They're one of a handful of places where you can major in photography."

Alonzo's mother's face was unreadable.

"But everything has changed so much since I graduated. Digital cameras improve every year. Much of what I learned is already obsolete."

"When did you graduate?" Victoria asked, masking her obvious interest by serving herself more salad.

It sounded innocent enough, but Alonzo knew better. Luz was stepping into a time trap, and he was helpless to stop it.

"Almost fifteen years ago. It doesn't seem possible."

Everyone did the math. Alonzo could see it on their faces.

She was in her mid-thirties, close to ten years older than he. Alonzo wanted to jump in and protect her from their disapproval, but what could he say?

She was an outsider, a foreigner, and even worse, an old woman by his mother's reckoning.

Erin rode in on a pristine horse, rescuing Luz from the oppressive stillness. "I feel the same way about my teaching credential. It seems like concepts change on a daily basis; new theories, new ideas, new studies. I'm never sure I'm going about things the best way."

Alonzo loved her at that moment as he'd never loved her before. She'd saved the day a second time.

"Self-doubt can be constructive if it leads to progress," Julia said.

Ramon nodded. "Too often it leads to inertia. Or apathy."

Felicia squirmed with impatience. "When can we go into town to see Luz's books?"

"I'm busy this coming weekend, but I could go the following Saturday," Erin said.

"That works for me," Julia said. She stood. "Meanwhile, who wants pie? Victoria brought apple and peach."

"Can we go that weekend, Mom?" Felicia asked.

Her mother smiled, but Alonzo could see the exact place where it stopped before reaching her eyes. "I don't see why not."

"Then it's set," Erin said. "I'll drive if you'd like."

Julia placed two pies on the table, along with a stack of dessert plates. "Pie, Luz?"

"Yes, please. Peach, if there's enough. It's my favorite."

Julia dished up the first slice and asked, "Whipped cream?"

"On, no, thank you. I think it dulls the sweetness of the fruit."

Now that was helpful. Alonzo could see reluctant approval wash across his mother's face. She would never put whipped cream on a fruit pie.

Luz took a first, delicate bite, and then a second. She looked at Victoria, her eyes surprised. "I think this may be better than my grandmother's."

"Best on the pueblo," Tony said. He patted Julia's arm. "Yours is second."

"Second place gets a medal, too," Felicia said. "Besides, Aunt Julia makes the best Navajo tacos."

"And turkey," Luis said. "Sorry, Mom, but she does."

"No problem," Victoria said. "I'm happy to do the pies for Thanksgiving."

Julia smiled at Luz. "You're welcome to join us if you'd like."

"Thank you," Luz said. She glanced at Alonzo, clearly unsure about an answer. When he looked as uncertain as she did, Luz said, "I'd have to check at home. My mom usually needs my help on holidays."

"Of course," Julia said.

Alonzo's legs began to itch.

Time to go.

Definitely, time to go.

*

Before they drove out of the yard, Julia had extracted a promise from Luz that she'd consider coming for Thanksgiving, Victoria had extracted a promise from Alonzo that he'd call her, and Felicia had extracted a promise from Victoria that she could spend the following weekend with her brother in Albuquerque.

"Your family is nice," Luz said, snugging her seat belt.

"Yeah."

"Tell me again why you moved?"

"I didn't like the commute." It sounded reasonable, but Alonzo sensed that Luz didn't believe him.

"I could never leave Jemez," she said. "I think I'd wither to nothing if I left the pueblo. It feeds me. It fuels my work."

"You went to school in Arizona."

"I did. And living away was awful. I felt a part of myself die each day I was gone. I promised myself I'd never do it again."

His heart ached thinking of how he'd once felt the same. It hurt too much to speak of it, so he changed the subject. "You said Sunday is Feast Day at Jemez?"

"Yes."

"Maybe I'll bring Felicia. Are you going to dance?"

She tipped her head to indicate she was.

He wished he could take pictures of her dancing. He knew better than to even say the words out loud.

"I'll also be dancing at Winter Market in Santa Fe."

It was as if she'd heard his thoughts. "When?"

"The weekend after Thanksgiving."

"Will you have a booth?"

"No."

He heard the disappointment she'd tried to conceal. "How many artists will have displays?"

"A hundred and fifty."

"How many photographers?"

"I don't know."

"Do you know any of the exhibitors?"

"Just Patricia." Her eyes rested on his cheek. "Will you come?"

"Sure." He couldn't bring himself to ask if she wanted him to.

They drove back to town listening to an oldies station on the radio. When they reached the center, Luz said, "It was a nice day. Thanks."

"Any time."

"Are you sure you don't want to see the pictures I took this morning?"

"Yeah, I'm sure."

"Let me know if you change your mind."

"I won't."

"Would you like to go riding sometime?"

"Yeah."

"After Feast."

"Okay."

She opened the car door. "Maybe I'll see you Sunday."

"Yeah. We'll be there."

He waited until she'd left the parking lot before he started back to his apartment. He could hardly wait to look at the photos he'd taken of her that morning.

He downloaded the pictures from his phone to his laptop, and then scrolled through them, quickly the first time, and then slowly the next.

Geez, she was gorgeous!

And, as he suspected, there wasn't a shot where she didn't shine. There were bad shots, poorly framed or badly focused. But, Luz was beautiful, regardless.

He wanted to send one to her; to show her how he saw her. He wanted to send her the best one.

He knew it would take time to decide which it was.

He popped open a beer.

It would absolutely take time.

*

Kate stopped at his desk the following morning. "If you're not busy on Friday night, a bunch of us are getting together at Howie's."

"I guess that's your last day?"

"It is."

"Are you excited about moving?"

"I am. So, will you come?"

"Sure."

"Great." Her smile was as wide as the world and seemed to take in everyone. "I'm glad. I wasn't sure if I put you off a couple of weeks ago."

"Not at all." He couldn't blame her for him being a loser.

"I'm glad. You're a special guy, Alonzo. And, I'll never forget that day at the parade. You'll always be my hero."

He felt his ears burn with embarrassment.

"I know, you don't want to hear that."

"No."

"Okay, Well, I'll see you later, Friday for sure."

She walked away from his desk, greeting others as she passed by. She reminded him of someone, but whom?

"Alonzo, could you take a look at this?" one of his co-workers asked, and Alonzo pulled his thoughts away from the beautiful blond woman.

*

That evening Alonzo went through all the photographs again. He deleted the ones he considered bad; bad framing, bad focus, bad form. He pondered the ones that remained, considering which was good enough to send to Luz.

Ultimately, he narrowed his choice to two. In one, she was sitting by the stream, her face reflected in the still water; in the other, she was sitting in the tree, golden leaves surrounding her jet black hair like a halo.

After ten minutes of indecision, he texted her the shot in the tree. It was her smile that convinced him. She looked like she was remembering a wonderful day in her childhood.

Then he waited.

It was a full five minutes before his phone rang. "Hi."

There was a silence, and then he heard a choked, "Hi."

"What's wrong?" he asked, alarmed.

"I…it's…" and then more silence.

"Luz? What happened? Are you hurt?"

"No. I'm…I'm just so touched. The picture…it's…"

Alonzo held his breath.

"…amazing."

"I told you that you're beautiful. Do you believe me now?"

147

"I believe you have the eye of a photographer."

"It's not the camera. It's you. You can't take a picture of what isn't there."

She laughed softly. "Now you even sound like a photographer."

He wanted to ask her out. But, he knew if she was dancing that weekend, she'd be going to practice every evening during the week. "I guess I'll see you at Feast."

"Right. And Alonzo, thank you."

His heart swelled. "Any time."

*

Howie's was crowded and noisy. Kate had reserved a table for twenty-six, and it took up nearly half of the room. Alonzo had arrived late, which meant he was at the far end of the table and unable to hear a lot of what Kate said.

He knew most of the people there, though none well enough to call them a friend. An older woman from the records department sat next to him and kept asking him questions about the reservation.

"A pueblo is different from a reservation," he told her, but she wasn't inclined to rethink her questions.

After half an hour, he got up, headed toward the men's room, and slipped quietly out the front door.

He was watching the news, and drinking his second beer when Kate called him late that night. "What happened? You disappeared."

"My sister called me. She was stuck and needed a ride." He'd settled on the story as he'd driven home, sure she would call.

"I wish you'd said goodbye."

"I didn't want to bother you."

"That could never happen, Alonzo. Far from it. I wish you'd bothered me a lot more."

The part of him that felt so awkward with women,

squirmed. She had wanted something from him that he didn't have to give. He'd given that to Erin, and, he realized, he'd never reclaimed it.

It wasn't love, it wasn't attention, it wasn't interest. It was something more ethereal—harder to define. It was more like possibility; the idea that a relationship might happen.

"You there?" she asked.

"Yeah."

"Well, if you want to visit Phoenix one day, give me a call."

"I will." He tried his best to sound sincere. There was no chance he would ever go to see her in Phoenix.

"Take care of yourself."

"Yeah. I will. You, too."

After he hung up, he thought of Erin again. Two beers on an empty stomach made him pensive. He thought about all the years he'd dreamed about her, fantasized about her.

He was over it.

But, he hadn't reclaimed the essence of himself. He'd left it with her, then somehow forgotten about it.

He wanted it back.

He needed it back.

There was someone else he wanted to offer it to.

*

His phone woke him the next morning.

Felicia.

"Hi."

"You're coming, right?" his sister asked.

"I'm on the way."

"Liar. I know I woke you up."

"I'll be there in half an hour."

"Liar."

"An hour, then."

"Don't go back to sleep."

"I won't."

He dressed, got coffee at Starbucks, and drove to the pueblo. His sister was standing at the front window when he pulled up in front of the house.

"Good thing you're here," Luis said when Alonzo opened the front door. "She's about to have a stroke."

Felicia hit him with her backpack. "I am not."

Victoria called from the kitchen. "Are you hungry, Dyaami?"

Felicia glared at him. "If you are, you can take me out to breakfast."

"Thanks, Mom. I'm fine. I think we'll take off."

Victoria walked in, drying her hands on a towel. "Not too late tomorrow night, please."

He gave her a forceful hug. "No."

"You can have dinner here if you want."

Felicia's eyes were as sharp as eagle claws.

"We might go out." He grinned at his sister. "Give her the full experience."

His mother's look was not happy. "Well, I'll have leftovers for you."

He kissed her cheek. "That'll be great."

They headed back toward Albuquerque, Felicia humming a half-familiar tune.

"Where are we going?" he asked her.

"I don't care. Wherever you want."

"Great. I want to go back to my apartment and go back to bed."

"Anywhere but there."

"The mall?"

She hesitated.

"A movie?"

"What's playing?"

"I have no idea."

"What else is there?"

"Everything. Why did you want to come if you don't

have an idea of what you want to do?"

"Are we going to Jemez tomorrow?"

"We can if you want."

"What would you do today if I wasn't with you?"

"Sleep."

"You would not."

"Do laundry."

"Seriously?"

"Probably not. I avoid doing laundry until I've worn everything at least twice."

She leaned toward him and sniffed loudly. "I hate to say it, but I think it's about time."

He laughed and tugged on her hair. "Make up your mind, or my autopilot will take us home."

"The mall. Then lunch. Then a movie. Then dinner. Then rent a movie to watch at your apartment."

"I'll need a nap somewhere in there."

She giggled. "You can sleep during the movie."

*

Alonzo offered to sleep on the couch that night, so Felicia could have the bed, but she refused.

"Sleeping in the bed would be the same as being at home," she said. "What's the fun in that?"

"That couch isn't very comfortable."

"It's perfect. I'm sure I'll sleep fine."

The buzzer sounded on the microwave, and Felicia jumped up to get the popcorn. "Good thing we went to the market. No wonder you take food when Mom offers. There's nothing here to eat."

"Don't tell her. She worries too much as it is."

"I won't."

Alonzo started the movie she'd chosen, and was soon asleep.

An hour later, Felicia nudged him. "You may as well go

to bed. I can turn the TV off by myself."

"You sure?"

"Yes."

"Okay, then. See you in the morning."

He was surprised how late she slept. An hour after he got up, he snuck out, closing the front door as quietly as he could, and drove to Starbucks for coffee. When he returned, she was up, dressed and ready to go to breakfast.

"Where do you usually eat in the morning?" she asked.

"In my car," he admitted, "on the way to work. But, if we're going to Jemez for Feast, we can stop for breakfast at a place I like in Bernalillo."

"Okay then, let's go!"

"Bring your stuff. We won't come back here before I take you home."

"Alright. But, I can come again, right?"

"I don't know. You weren't much help."

"I'd hate to have to tell Mom about your empty shelves."

He pushed her toward the door. "I think blackmail is against the law."

"So is child labor."

A considerable wait at the restaurant meant that by the time they'd eaten and were on the road again, it was nearing noon.

"I hope we don't miss the dancing," Felicia said.

"They'll dance all day, the same as we do."

"Do you think they'll have a carnival?"

"Probably. Their pueblo is three times the size of ours. I can't imagine they'd have a Feast Day without a carnival."

The red rock formation that distinguished Jemez Pueblo emerged from the red earth that stretched out on either side of the highway. They parked and walked to the plaza, where they stood along with several hundred other spectators, watching two young men executing a brilliant eagle dance.

The beat of the drum set up a rhythm in Alonzo's heart, and he had to make a conscious effort to keep his feet from moving in time to the cadence. Dancing was the pulse of his blood.

"They're good," Felicia whispered.

He nodded. "Yeah." But after a few minutes, he felt a familiar impatience growing. He wanted to see Luz.

It seemed like a small eternity before her clan was entering the plaza, moving as one toward the fulfillment of tradition. She was dressed like all the other women, her white-skirted dress pristine. They all looked alike save for Luz. She stood out in his heart and in his eyes.

Her beauty was serene and timeless, like the pueblo itself.

He made no move to announce his presence. Doing so would have violated every tenant of their tradition. But, he willed her to know he was there, to feel his being, his support. He willed her to feel the fullness in his heart, now, right now, now that he'd recognized that he was in love.

CHAPTER 15

"Are we going to Luz's house to eat?" Felicia asked when the dancers took their mid-day break.

"We weren't invited. Besides, I have no idea where she lives. We can get Navajo tacos at one of the booths."

They walked around the carnival, bought tacos from a vendor whose line was nearly twenty people long, and then returned to the plaza to watch the afternoon dances. The weather had cooled as it often did in mid-November, and Alonzo knew the men in heavy buffalo garb were grateful.

Luz danced two more times before the end of the day, and each time, Alonzo's heart filled with pride. He wouldn't tell her that, of course. Dancing was not to celebrate the self, it was to celebrate life: the earth, the people, and the world. Still, he was proud of her. Some feelings couldn't be denied even if tradition demanded it.

Before he and Felicia left, Alonzo took a picture of the sun setting on the brilliant red rock hills. He'd send it to Luz later, so she'd know he'd been there.

"I think we'll head for home," he said to Felicia. "I'll take you to dinner the next time you visit."

"I get to come again?"

"If you want."

She turned the radio on, tuned in a local station, and began singing along with the popular vocalist.

Alonzo was happy to drive in silence. He'd pulled a warm robe of content around himself, and talking would have torn it away.

Felicia was in her world, and he was in his.

All was well.

The moment he opened the door to his parents' house, the feeling fled. Nowhere was the familiar fragrance of his mother's cooking. The house seemed as cold as if it were sick.

"What's wrong?" Alonzo asked his mother, who sat on the couch watching television.

"Nothing."

"Don't you feel well?" he asked, sitting down beside her.

"I'm fine."

"But, you're not cooking."

"Oh, I forgot to tell you; we're all going to Paolo's for dinner." Her smile was like a clever child's.

Had she truly forgotten, or had she trapped him? He could hardly refuse at that point.

"How was Jemez Feast?" she asked cheerfully.

"Good," Felicia said. "Except that we didn't go to Luz's house."

Victoria looked at Alonzo, questioning without words.

"I've never met her folks. It didn't feel right."

His mother shrugged, and though he tried to read her eyes, Alonzo wasn't sure what she might be thinking.

"We'll go to your brother's as soon as your father gets home. He's helping Tony work on his truck."

"Can I have a Coke?" Alonzo asked.

"You have to ask?" His mother's voice sounded wounded.

He patted her leg reassuringly. "Do you want one?"

"No."

Time moved on slow feet on the pueblo. They didn't arrive at Paolo and Erin's until after seven. Alonzo was pleased to find Neyse and Juan there.

"Hey," he said, hugging Neyse. "I haven't seen you in ages."

"Whose fault is that?" his cousin asked.

Juan nudged her. "*Ma'a.*"

Paolo clapped Alonzo on the shoulder. "How about a beer?"

"No, thanks."

The dining table was crowded when they sat down to eat. Erin had prepared a savory meatloaf, with mashed potatoes, gravy, broccoli, and a huge green salad.

"Do you eat like this every night?" Ramon asked.

Paolo smiled, pride brimming in his eyes. "Just about. Erin is a great cook."

Erin turned to her husband. "*Nachra.*"

Alonzo could see the love between the two and he felt suddenly happy for them; happy in a way he could not have imagined six months before. Happy, and contented.

Later, back in his apartment, he sent Luz the picture he'd taken from the parking lot at Jemez. In it, the sunset burned brilliant orange, and melted into the red rock hills, as if its heat had created them.

Moments later, his phone pinged. She'd sent a picture of the night sky blazing with stars from the Milky Way. He stared at it for a long time, then walked outside to see if the sky over his head was the same as the one over hers.

It wasn't.

He felt sad. Clearly, they lived in different worlds.

*

Kate's absence was palpable at the office that week. A shining light had gone out, and what remained was unexpectedly dull and dreary. Alonzo assumed that their group would rally and fill in the giant hole she'd left, but that week, the entire staff was dismal.

Some of the regulars went out for drinks on Friday evening, but Alonzo begged off. "Next time," he told them, although he doubted there would be a next time for him.

He was weary of work. He was weary of Albuquerque.

The screens for the planter box had finally arrived, and he'd arranged to take them to the pueblo on Sunday. He'd spent every evening that week, reading about winter gardening. Despite his initial optimism, he was starting to face the fact that the inevitable snow on the pueblo would kill most plants.

One possible solution was a hoop house, but much as it sounded like a pueblo-friendly structure, Alonzo feared that the large, plastic "tunnel" would offend some, if not most, of the villagers.

Was there always a price for progress?

*

Saturday morning, he met Luz at PICC. She'd agreed to let him drive to the shoot, he imagined because they'd be picking up Natoma, and his car was roomier than hers.

He helped her transfer equipment from her car into his, feeling a familiar thrill at being close to her again.

"Is that everything?" he asked.

"I think so. There's so much stuff in my trunk, it's hard to be sure."

"Do you have a different camera for late afternoon shoots?" he asked as he closed his trunk.

"Different filters, sometimes, but not a different camera."

He opened the car door for her, and she smiled up at him when the fragrant aroma struck them. "Coffee."

"Yeah."

"Thanks."

"Anytime."

Although it was cold when they arrived, Natoma was standing in front of her house, drinking from a bright red travel mug, the color a stark contrast against her bulky fawn-colored sweater.

"*Kuwe tzi,*" she said when she got into the back seat. Then, she said, "Uh, good morning."

"Good morning," Luz said, turning to her. "I hope you haven't been waiting long. It's cold out there."

"No, not long."

"Are you ready for our adventure? I think it's going to be really fun."

Alonzo glanced in the rearview mirror. Natoma looked like she was anticipating abuse more than an adventure.

"I'm kind of nervous."

Luz reached back and touched Natoma gently. "You have no reason to be. I've yet to take a picture of you that wasn't remarkable. Patricia is going to be so happy with the results today. Trust me."

Natoma sat back, but Alonzo didn't see much of the dread drain from her face. "You don't have to do this if you don't want to," he said when her expression didn't change. He pulled to the side of the road and turned to her. "We can call it off. It's entirely up to you."

Natoma gazed down at her hands, as if she held the answer there. After a few moments, she looked up and said, "You know, the first time I rode a horse, I was so scared I nearly threw up. Now, I love riding. I only learned that because I tried it." She smiled. "Let's do it."

They met Patricia at her workshop, a wondrous space of bright, colorful fabrics and objects. It was large, with ample room for work, as well as the seminars she taught for prospective designers.

After the introductions, Patricia said, "Based on the measurements you sent, I've selected several outfits. I'll have Natoma try them on, decide which ones suit her best, and then we can drive to the shoot site."

Alonzo sat down and waited while the three women went into a back room. He played a few games on his phone, checked his email, read two blogs on water harvesting, and watched several videos on winter gardening.

When Natoma emerged from the other room, she was smiling. "The outfits are beautiful," she said, her tone reverent. "So unique." She sat down next to Alonzo. "They're packing them now."

"Good."

"Thank you, Alonzo."

"For what?"

"For saying we could call it off. That made it okay for me to come."

"Sure," he said, convinced he would never understand women.

*

By the time the sun set, Alonzo was exhausted. He'd done absolutely nothing, yet he felt like he'd been dragged for miles by a ghost horse.

In stark contrast, Natoma seemed as fresh as a new colt. She had not just endured the pushing and prodding and photographing, she'd blossomed.

Again and again, Alonzo had heard Luz give Natoma direction, and then exclaim, "Yes! That's it. That's perfect."

Patricia helped Natoma change from one outfit to another, making adjustments and fixing Natoma's hair in different ways to enhance each ensemble.

The three quickly adopted a verbal shorthand that simplified their interactions and fascinated Alonzo. They were from three different pueblos, spoke three different native languages, yet they fell into sync, pulled together by invisible cords he could never see.

Luz walked toward him, taking the camera strap from around her neck. "Looks like we're finished. Natoma is going to change. When she's done, we'll help Patricia pack up, and then we can take off."

Alonzo noticed that while she moved slowly, her eyes sparkled with satisfaction. "You're pleased?"

"I am. I won't know for sure until I transfer them to my computer, but I think I have literally dozens of good shots. I've never had such a photogenic subject. If I'm not mistaken, Patricia is thinking about hiring a new model."

A sharp pain gripped Alonzo's insides, a warning shot that told him trouble lay ahead. He pushed the unpleasant notion away and focused on Luz's pleasure. The day's work had been all she'd hoped for. He could not know the future, regardless of his gloomy gut.

Patricia spoke quietly to Natoma as Luz and Alonzo packed equipment into the car. Even in the fading twilight, Alonzo could see struggle settle in Natoma's beautiful eyes. Whatever Patricia wanted, Natoma, too, had doubts.

From the look on her face, they were serious doubts.

Natoma rode in silence in the back seat. Luz chattered happily about the successful shoot, but nothing brought much response from Natoma. As soon as Alonzo pulled up in front of her house, Natoma opened the car door.

Luz turned to her. "Thank you, Natoma. I appreciate all you went through today. Modeling isn't easy, regardless of what people think."

"I enjoyed it," Natoma said.

But Alonzo heard an undertow beneath her words, a struggle with an invisible temptation.

"I'll call you when I've got the proofs ready," Luz said. "Maybe we could meet for lunch somewhere."

"Sure." Natoma said. "Thanks for coming again, Alonzo. It must be pretty boring for you."

"It's fine."

"Well," she said, "I'll see you."

As he headed toward the highway, Alonzo said, "I thought maybe we could go out to dinner."

Luz glanced down at her jeans. "Like this?"

Was she saying no?

"It doesn't have to be anyplace fancy."

"In that case, sure."

"Great. What sounds good?"

Luz thought a bit and then said, "Something different. Someplace I've never gone. An adventure." She looked at him, her eyes challenging. "Surprise me."

He felt pleasure rather than pressure. Where could he take her for a surprise? His usual choices were the three fast food drive-thrus near his apartment. He rejected the diner in Bernalillo and the rib place by Sandia Peak. Too ordinary.

He thought about the places the office group had gone when Kate had organized after-work get-togethers. Too predictable. Then he remembered the fondue restaurant where he'd gone with Erin. The Melting Pot. Perfect.

They stopped at PICC long enough to transfer the camera equipment into the trunk of Luz's car.

The restaurant was crowded. It was Saturday night, after all. But, they were late enough that the early diners were soon leaving, and they scored a small table in a corner where they could hear each other talk.

"Have you been here before?" Luz asked.

"Yeah." He held his breath, anticipating her next question.

"What's good? There are so many choices."

"Well, if you're hungry, we can do the four course meal."

"I'm hungry."

"Which fondue sounds best to you?"

"How about the Hatch Green Chili Cheddar?"

"Just what I was thinking."

After they'd ordered, Luz said, "So, how many pictures did you take today?"

"Not as many as you."

"Show me."

"I have to edit them first."

"Seriously?"

He laughed. "Absolutely. After all, I have to protect my reputation."

She leaned toward him. "Give me your phone."

He tipped his head toward hers. "No."

"I can't believe this."

"Why? I learned from you."

"I've shown you all the pictures I've taken."

"Hardly. You've shown me a carefully selected few. What I want to see are the rejects."

"Why?"

"I'd learn more."

"About photography?"

"No. About you."

Her eyes, so accustomed to focusing on a subject, narrowed in on him. "What's so interesting about me?"

He opened his mouth to tell her, at the same time as a server approached their table. "Incoming," he said.

They both leaned back, and the server placed a silver pot brimming with fragrant fondue on the table's warming plate.

"That smells fantastic," Luz said. She speared a piece of bread and dipped it into the thick bubbling concoction.

Alonzo did the same, warning, "Be careful. It's hotter than you might expect."

She laid her tongue against the steaming bread. "Oh," she gasped, and grabbed her ice water. "You're right."

The moment to tell her how he felt had melted faster than cheese in a hot pot.

"This is delicious," she said. "But, it must take hours to eat dinner if you have to wait for every bite to cool."

Works for me, he thought.

The second course was salad, followed by the meat course. When their server cleared the third course plates, Luz said, "I don't think I can eat another bite. You're going to have to finish dessert by yourself."

But, when the pot of rich, creamy melted chocolate

arrived, Luz said, "Forget what I said a minute ago." She speared a plump piece of pineapple and dipped it into the chocolate. She blew on it, then took a delicate bite. "You were right. Dark was the way to go."

After they'd tried all the various combinations, Alonzo said, "Marshmallow is the best."

"Not even close. The banana tops everything. But, I bet fresh strawberries would beat all the others, hands down. We'll have to come back in the spring."

When she smiled, Alonzo's insides tumbled into unfamiliar territory. She was talking about the future. Could she possibly be interested in him, too?

"Winrock Cinema is across the street," he said. "Would you like to see what's playing?"

"Sure."

Of course, they could have checked it on their phones, but neither one suggested it. Instead, Alonzo paid the bill, and they walked out to the parking lot.

"We don't need to drive, do we?" Luz asked. "It's right across the way. Let's walk."

"Okay."

They headed down the street, which was deserted, even though it was only eight in the evening. They stopped at the corner, and stepped into the crosswalk.

As they neared the center of the street, squealing tires split the quiet night. Headlights splashed toward them. Alonzo grabbed Luz's hand and started running. They hit the curb just as a car full of young men sped by.

"Geez!" Alonzo gasped. He pulled Luz close to him. "Are you okay?"

She nodded, her head against shoulder.

"That was way too close!" His heart pounded, racing in his chest like a spooked horse.

"You saved my life," Luz whispered.

He chuckled. "I wouldn't go that far. It's not like you were sitting on the pavement."

"You kept me safe. Thank you."

"Anytime." He kept his arm snugly around her waist as they walked to the theater. Standing in front of the box office, reading the posters of the movies being shown, Alonzo wondered why his heart was still hammering.

"What do you think?" Luz asked.

"The new *Star Wars* movie?"

"How would you know? Aren't they all the same?"

He shrugged. "What looks good to you?"

"The foreign film. The cinematography is supposed to be fantastic."

"That's fine with me. It's starting now. Good timing."

They made their way in the dimly lit theater and found two seats in the back. As his eyes adjusted to the dark, Alonzo realized there were only a handful of others there, and he wondered if they'd made a bad choice.

Luz reached over and took his hand. "I'm so happy. I've wanted to see this, but nobody else was interested."

He squeezed her hand. "You didn't ask the right person."

She didn't pull her hand away, and he didn't let go. Alonzo felt contentment settle over him, a warm, gentle sense of being exactly where he was supposed to be; a place he'd longed for and had finally found.

They left the theater two hours later, their hands still enfolded.

"Well?" Luz asked.

"Amazing."

"I knew you'd like it!"

"You knew?"

"I was pretty sure you would. Judging by the pictures you've sent me, it's obvious you have an artistic eye."

He squeezed her hand. "Thanks."

Driving her back to her car at PICC, Alonzo wished she lived in town. He wanted to take her home.

And then what?

He wasn't Paolo. He wasn't experienced with women.

The parking lot at PICC was deserted except for Luz's car. She checked the trunk, reassuring herself that all her equipment was safe.

She closed the hatch, satisfied, then turned. "Thanks."

"For what?"

"For a wonderful day. It was perfect from beginning to end. I especially liked it when you saved my life."

Tentatively he wound his arms around her. "Anytime."

When she laid her head against his chest, his heartrate doubled. "When can I see you again?" he asked.

She grinned. "Anytime."

He laughed when he heard his own familiar word. "Next Saturday?"

"I can't Saturday. I'm dancing at Winter Market in Santa Fe, remember?"

"Hoop dance?"

"Yes."

"What time?"

"I don't know."

"Will you have a booth?"

"No."

He heard the disappointment in her voice. "Soon."

"I hope so."

"You're a great photographer, Luz." He wished his confidence could reach into her heart and erase the doubt dwelling there.

She looked up at him with rare, raw uncertainty. "Do you think so?"

"Absolutely." His arms tightened around her. "What's wrong? Did something happen?"

"Not really. Not yet, anyway. I submitted an application for a show at Albuquerque Museum."

"The one in Old Town?"

"Yes. You know it?"

"I've walked by it. Does that count?"

She grinned. "No."

"Did you get a response?"

"Not yet. They'll make their decision the first week of December."

"Well then, we'll celebrate that weekend."

"Are you so sure?"

"I am."

When her eyes locked onto his, Alonzo felt himself falling into dark inviting pools. "Luz," he whispered. He leaned down and touched his lips to hers, gently, until he felt her press up to him, yearning.

Her arms were around his neck, pulling him to her with a fierceness he could not have anticipated. A crescendo of kisses, one after another, like music, building and building and building.

He pulled away when he felt a nearly overwhelming desire. He leaned close to her ear and whispered, "I'm a simple pueblo boy. I don't..." His voice faltered.

"And I'm a simple pueblo girl."

"I don't want you to think..."

"No expectations." She leaned up and kissed him gently. "Other than, when will I see you again?"

"Friday? After Thanksgiving?"

"Okay. Would you like to go riding?"

"Sure."

"My uncle has horses. He'd be happy for us to take a couple of them out."

"What time?"

"Noon? I can pack us a lunch."

He kissed her and nuzzled her neck. "I hope you're as good a cook as you are a photographer."

"I can't be good at everything."

But, he thought that anything Luz put her mind to would be brilliant. Luz was the light he'd longed for.

CHAPTER 16

Alonzo spent Thanksgiving Day in his apartment, watching football games, alone. Alone, but not lonely. He and Luz had texted photographs back and forth from the time he woke up; no words, just pictures. He knew she had thousands to choose from; he, dozens. He ended up looking online for additional options.

He could have gone home. His father would be watching football with his brother. But, he didn't want to answer his mother's inevitable questions about Luz, or why he didn't move back to the pueblo.

Erin and Paolo had insisted on hosting Thanksgiving dinner. Alonzo could not imagine how that conversation had gone. His mother and Julia had traded hosting the holiday for years. Were they content to step aside, or did they resent the younger generation wanting to step in?

It would be an interesting evening.

Later, Alonzo parked in front of Erin's house...Erin and Paolo's house. He remembered being there in the summer and shuddered to think what an idiot he'd made of himself, mooning over Erin. How long would it take for the pueblo to forget—for him to walk around with his head high instead of skulking around like a fool?

The house blazed with light and noise. Alonzo purposely arrived late, determined to avoid any possibility of time alone with his brother and Erin. His amorous feelings for her had long since disappeared, but the shame of his agonized adoration persisted.

"Finally," Paolo said when he opened the door. "Mom was beginning to worry." His brother clapped him on the shoulder and led him into the living room. "The prodigal son has arrived."

Victoria came in from the kitchen and scrutinized her son's face. "Are you okay?"

"Of course." He kissed her forehead. "What's the big deal?"

"You're late."

"I didn't think anyone on the pueblo knew those words," he said, giving her a quick hug.

"That's not a nice way to speak to your mother," Ramon said.

"Sorry."

"How about a beer?" Paolo suggested.

Alonzo nodded. "Thanks."

The living room furniture had been pushed aside to make room for a second table. Football blared on the TV, but no one paid any attention. Instead, they were all talking, their voices pitched more for a stadium than a sitting room.

Felicia brought his beer. "Why didn't you bring Luz?"

Even over the din, his mother heard the question and turned to hear his answer. "She said she had to help out at home."

"I hope you'll bring her at Christmas," his sister said. "I like her."

The look that passed across Victoria's face told Alonzo that his mother did not.

Erin welcomed him with a hug that would have been torture six months before. "I'm glad you're here."

"Were you worried, too?"

"I didn't have time to breathe, much less worry."

"It doesn't look like the party suffered much from my absence."

"We couldn't eat till you got here."

He glanced toward the kitchen. "Is dinner ready?"

"Not quite." She leaned toward him. "I'm sliding down the slippery slope of pueblo life. I say dinner at six, and I'm still not ready at seven. Very sad."

"If you mean that, you'll probably have a happier marriage."

"Probably," she agreed.

The resignation in her eyes made him sad. He suspected that Erin would be the one in their marriage making the most concessions.

When it was ready, Paolo carried the turkey to the dining room table. "Uncle Tony, would you carve? I'd hate to mess it up when Erin worked so hard on it." He put his arm around his wife. "Well done, Henateetz."

Alonzo saw reluctant approval on his mother's face, as if Erin's success both pleased and annoyed her. He wondered how long it would take for Victoria to fully accept her eldest son's choice.

And what about his own choice? Would Luz ever be accepted?

Alonzo sat down next to Luis, sure that his younger brother would not ask him any awkward questions. But, when Carlos pushed in on his other side, his confidence evaporated.

"How did the photo shoot go?" Carlos asked.

"Fine." Alonzo took a bite of turkey, giving the meal before him careful attention, and willing Carlos to shut up.

"Was Natoma any more relaxed?"

Alonzo did not have to look up to know Paolo's eyes had fastened on him. "I think so."

"When are we going to get to see the pictures?"

Paolo's eyes tightened, and Alonzo felt himself squeezed in their strangling grip.

"I have no idea," Alonzo said. "When are you dancing at PICC again?" he asked, desperate to change the subject.

"Sometime in January," Carlos said.

The conversation moved on, but Alonzo knew Paolo hadn't. He'd heard Natoma's name and had seen Alonzo's reaction.

The subject had changed; it was not closed.

"Who wants more turkey?" Tony asked. He held the fork over the platter like Poseidon's trident.

"I do," Luis said.

Carlos lifted his plate toward his father. "Absolutely. This is great, Erin."

"Thank you," Erin said.

Alonzo thought her voice sounded strange, and then he noticed that she'd barely eaten anything. Perhaps she was tired after working so hard that day. She really had prepared a magnificent feast.

"Lon?" his uncle asked.

"No. I'm good. I have to save room for Mom's pie."

"How do you know they're mine?" Victoria asked.

Alonzo smiled at her. "Because I'm your son."

*

The women did the clean-up; the men watched football; the usual division of labor at their family gatherings.

"Paolo," Erin called from the kitchen, "would you take the trash out for me?"

Paolo stood. "Sure." He tapped Alonzo's foot. "Come give me a hand."

He knew he should have left. He should have stood up the minute he'd finished his pie and said he had to go.

Stupid.

Alonzo took one of the trash bags from Erin and followed

his brother out to the side yard.

"What's the deal with Natoma?" Paolo asked after stuffing the bags in the barrel.

His brother's words set a small fire in his gut. "What deal is that?" Even in the dim light of the moon, Alonzo could see Paolo's jaw tighten.

"The photography deal."

"I don't know about any deal."

"Was Luz taking pictures of Natoma?"

"Yes."

"Why?"

He considered not answering; walking away; ending the conversation before it got really nasty. Instead he said, "I'll give you her number. You can call and ask her." He turned and started back toward the house.

"Dyaami."

Paolo's voice stopped him the way only an older brother's can.

Alonzo turned.

Paolo took a step toward him. "What's the deal with Natoma?"

His voice had dropped, and the words slammed into Alonzo like a locomotive.

"Why are you so concerned about Natoma?"

"I'm concerned about the pueblo."

"How could pictures of Natoma hurt the pueblo?"

Paolo's glare put Alonzo back years, sending time skittering to his childhood, when his brother could control him with a look. Instead of backing up, Alonzo stepped forward. "Luz wants to publish a book featuring pueblo women. Natoma was her first subject."

"How does she know Natoma?"

"They met at PICC."

"They met, or you introduced them?"

"What difference does it make? What are you so worried about, Paolo? How does this possibly affect you?"

"Anything that affects the pueblo affects me. It affects you, too, whether you realize it or not. A book of photographs of pueblo women brings us attention, and ultimately, that brings more outsiders. Outsiders bring influence. Negative influence."

Alonzo's first response, ugly and hurtful, was to point out that his brother had *married* an outsider. Paolo was the ultimate hypocrite. Alonzo swallowed the nastiness. "Somehow I doubt that Luz's photographs have the power to bring down the pueblo."

"Your attitude is what will bring down the pueblo."

"I wouldn't lose any sleep over it."

"I know you wouldn't. That's the problem."

"Why, Paolo? Why, exactly, is that a problem?"

"Indifference is the enemy of the pueblo. People stop caring, our traditions weaken, and the pueblo begins to disintegrate."

Alonzo could see that Paolo wanted to say something else; something he was sure he didn't want to hear. He had taken three steps toward the door when the words hit him in the back.

"Stay in town, Dyaami. You don't *belong* on the pueblo."

Like sharpened obsidian, the words pierced, and Alonzo's heart nearly stopped with the pain. He paused only long enough to make a decision, and then let himself out the side gate.

Paolo could explain his disappearance.

*

Friday was a beautiful high-desert day; clear, sunny, and wind-less. Luz's uncle had been happy for Alonzo and Luz to exercise his horses, and apparently confident that Alonzo could handle himself on horseback. He didn't bother to meet them at the barn.

Alonzo wondered if Luz had shown him the video.

172

They rode out toward Red Rocks, taking their time as Alonzo gradually became acquainted with his horse. Like so many pueblo ponies, it was accustomed to being ridden by many different people and seemed content with Alonzo on its back.

Summer had seared the surrounding vegetation, which was now dry and brittle. They followed a well-worn trail, not unlike the paths Alonzo and Paolo rode along at home.

Home.

The word stung.

Where was home?

"You're quiet this morning," Luz said.

"Yeah."

"Everything okay?"

"Yeah."

"How was Thanksgiving?"

"Fine." He felt her eyes searching for more. The story was too long, too complicated, too revealing to tell, even for a man whose pueblo was famous for storytellers. "How was yours?"

"Good. Everybody was happy, no major arguments, plenty of food, and Mom made the teenagers do the dishes."

"We don't set the bar very high, do we?"

"Our family gatherings have a way of turning into a giant tug-of-war, where people line up on one side or the other of an issue, and get louder and nastier trying to make their point."

Paolo's words from the night before burned in his brain. His brother had definitely made his point.

They stopped for lunch by a stand of trees near the river. Now, the trees were nearly bare, their dark branches stark against the mid-day sun. Alonzo spread out the threadbare blanket he'd tied behind his saddle, and Luz opened a bag of sandwiches, chips, and fruit.

"Why does food always taste better on the trail?" Luz asked.

"It's probably got something to do with survival and not knowing when or where your next meal is coming from. The ancients were probably really appreciative when they finally found something to eat."

When they'd finished, Alonzo laid back, his arms cradled behind his head. "Siesta time."

"Seriously?"

"Yeah." He patted the blanket next to himself. "You should never ride right after you eat. It's the same as swimming."

Her ponytail swung back and forth when she shook her head. "You know that swimming thing is complete bull." She stretched out beside him. "But, it's true about riding."

Contentment filled his chest, pushed up and sent Paolo's words flying away. For that moment, he was exactly where he belonged.

*

When he woke he was alone. A cool breeze blew fat grey clouds from the west and splattered shadows across the red rock. He sat up, looking for Luz. He turned when he heard one of the horses whinny, and saw her, camera in hand, framing a shot.

She'd unsaddled her horse, leaving only the woven blanket on its back. He watched as she moved from one angle to another, speaking softly in her native tongue, a Pied Piper of ponies. She was completely engrossed and didn't acknowledge him until the horse stomped a foot when he approached.

"Straighten the blanket for me," she said softly.

It was the voice she'd used with Natoma.

Alonzo ran his hand across the horse's flank, and crooned Mr. Montoya's soothing words. He heard the camera's familiar click once, twice, over and over as he stroked the horse's shoulder and then its head.

Luz directed him quietly, easily, expertly. She was no stranger to the animal. Alonzo wondered if this were the horse in the photo at the center.

"Jump up on her back," Luz said. "She won't mind."

He wrapped his hand in the horse's mane and leapt onto her back. The blanket shifted, and he nearly slid off, but the horse stood steady.

Luz took shots of his hands, his legs, and his boots, moving slowly, confidently, all the time reassuring the animal. "Lay your head down."

Alonzo leaned forward and rested his cheek on the horse's neck.

"Perfect," she whispered from behind.

Warmth flowed from the horse, and Alonzo realized how much the day had cooled. They'd brought sweatshirts, but he knew they'd be useless against the heavy rain looming overhead.

"We should probably get going," he said.

Luz looked around, then up at the threatening sky. "Ooh, I'd love to get some shots of the rain and the river."

"Did you bring a poncho?"

"No."

"It looks like it could get bad."

"It's just water, city boy."

"Sneezing won't enhance the hoop dance tomorrow."

As she glanced around again, Alonzo watched her two loves fight for supremacy.

"I suppose you're right."

He slid down off the horse, taking the blanket with him. Luz continued framing pictures as Alonzo re-saddled the pliant pony.

"This is the most cooperative horse I've ever met," Alonzo said.

"I've been photographing her for so long that she even smiles for me." Luz patted the horse, which nickered and nudged her shoulder. "You like being a star don't you?" She reached into her pocket and pulled out a bag of orange colored chunks. "She loves pumpkin."

While Luz fed the horse treats, Alonzo rolled the blanket and tied it onto his horse's saddle. "Give me some of that pumpkin. The supporting cast deserves a treat, too."

By the time they reached the barn, the rain was falling in solid sheets, and they were both soaked. They unsaddled the horses, rubbed them down, covered them with blankets, and fed them.

Luz was shivering when they finished.

"You need a hot shower," Alonzo told her.

"So do you."

"I'll be fine. My car heater is a giant horno." He put his arms around her. "You sure I can't take you tomorrow?"

"I already told the other dancers I'd go with them."

"What time will you dance?"

"Sometime in the afternoon."

"Can I bring you home?"

When she hesitated, he knew she was considering the explanation she would give the others.

"Let me think about it."

"Okay." He kissed her, their lips cool and damp. "I need to get you home before you get sick."

He cranked up the heat in his car and drove to her house.

She made no move to kiss him goodbye, and he knew better than to do so where her family might see.

"I'll see you tomorrow," she said.

"I'll be there."

As she ran through the rain and pushed open the front door, he noticed the curtain at the front window move aside.

The pueblo had invisible eyes.

*

Rain pounded through the night, and though the morning dawned clear and bright, many of the streets near Alonzo's apartment were flooded. He drove slowly, minding not only the huge puddles, but the beauty of the reflections that sparkled in the standing water.

Two blocks from Starbucks his breath caught sharply. He pulled over and parked, climbed out of the car, and walked back along the sidewalk to the spot he'd just passed. He waded across the flooded street and turned. His feet were drenched, but the scene before him was worth it.

The towering buildings along the street seemed to have tumbled onto their heads and fallen into the water. A stick-bare elm tree at the curb, balanced impossibly upside down on crooked branches.

Alonzo took picture after picture, then stomped in the water and watched the reflection wobble wildly. A car drove by, and the entire picture was erased, like a drawing on a child's Etch-a-Sketch.

It took nearly ten minutes for him to decide which shot to send to Luz, slowly scrolling through the pictures, evaluating and critiquing each one. He tried changing a few to black and white but didn't think that there was any improvement.

In the end, he sent a shot where the bright blue sky appeared to hold up the buildings and save them from crashing onto the pavement. After that, he quickly got coffee and returned to his apartment to change his sopping shoes.

By the time he reached Santa Fe, he still hadn't heard from Luz. He couldn't imagine the photo had disappointed her; he was sure it was one of the best he'd ever taken. He parked in a crowded lot and walked to the plaza.

His phone pinged with a message and his heart lightened, until he saw the name.

"Where are you?" Carlos had texted. "I thought we were going to Indian Market today."

Alonzo had completely forgotten he'd planned to attend the event with his cousin. He was tempted not to answer and tell Carlos later that his phone was dead.

But his cousin deserved better.

"Sorry. I blew it. I'm already in Santa Fe. Where R U?"

"The café in Bernalillo."

"Come on up. I'll meet you."

"Where?"

"At the big statue in the plaza."

"I'll be there in forty-five. Can you remember that long?"

"Yeah."

Alonzo walked slowly around the crowded square, browsing half-heartedly in stores and booths, listening for his phone to ping again. He knew the closer it came to noon, the less likely Luz would respond. The dancers would be changing into their native clothes and preparing for their performances.

"Hey, Dyaami."

Alonzo heard Carlos's voice and turned. "*Kuwe tzi?*"

"I'd be a lot better if you hadn't left me hanging."

"Yeah. Sorry about that." He rubbed his hands together. "I'm cold. Let's get a cup of coffee."

"Whatever." Carlos followed along as Alonzo headed toward a booth with a long line. "Where did you disappear to the other night? One minute you're there; the next, poof."

"I was tired."

"Too tired to say goodbye?"

"I didn't want to get into another discussion with my mom." He felt his cousin's doubting eyes probe his face, and prayed he wouldn't push. Repeating Paolo's words was sure to reopen the raw wound in his heart.

"What time is Luz dancing?" Carlos asked.

Alonzo thanked him silently. "Probably around one."

"Good. Plenty of time to eat first."

Not surprisingly, Luz's group started late. It was nearly two-fifteen before she stepped into the center of the performance area, and laid out more than a dozen hoops in a large circle. She was the final dancer in her group; they'd saved the best for last.

She stood serenely in the center of the hoops before

giving a nearly imperceptible nod to the drummers.

The beat began, but it took a few seconds before Luz responded. At first, only her slight frame seemed touched by the sound. But, gradually, her feet caught the cadence and she came alive. She tipped one hoop after another with a practiced toe, and the hoops were all soon flying around her body as if by magic.

Alonzo watched, his heart nearly bursting. She was beautiful. Her long dark hair hung loose, her face focused but calm. She was so buoyant that her calf-high white moccasins barely seemed to touch the ground. An invisible cord tied her feet to his, and they moved back and forth, mirroring her movements.

Alonzo reached into his jacket and pulled out the pocket-sized digital camera he'd bought after their photo session in Bernalillo.

Carlos glanced over at him as Alonzo, like many in the audience, began taking pictures. "Oh man. This thing is serious," he whispered.

The camera's zoom lens allowed him to narrow in on Luz's nimble feet. He was fascinated at how quickly a slight movement could tip a hoop or bring it magically into her waiting fingers.

He took more than a hundred pictures during the five minute dance, none of her full face, respecting her way of not over-reaching with the camera. The minute the drummer stopped, Alonzo slipped the camera back in his jacket.

Luz ended with a flourish of intertwined hoops, held high, like butterfly wings, and the crowd erupted in applause. Alonzo held back, honoring her with reverent silence. But when Carlos nudged him, Alonzo clapped along with the others, hoping she'd know he was there watching.

"What's next?" Carlos asked as they walked slowly toward the exit.

"Let's get something sweet."

"Sounds good. Are you going to show me the pictures?"

"No."

"Why not?"

"I have to edit them first."

"How long will that take?"

Alonzo shrugged. His phone pinged, and he pulled it from his pocket. Luz had sent a picture of the Memorial in the plaza where he'd met Carlos, with a simple 3:15?

"She wants to meet us at three-fifteen."

"You."

"Me what?"

"She wants to meet you, dummy, not us."

"You came all the way up here. I'm not going to ditch you."

"You're never going to make any headway with that girl if you're always dragging someone else along. Besides, I promised Juan I'd help him fix a busted fence, as long as Neyse made me steak for dinner. I should get back before it gets dark."

"Long drive for a few dances."

"I enjoyed watching her. She's good."

"Yeah, I think so, too."

"Fishing tomorrow?"

Alonzo hesitated.

"Never mind. You have better things to think about. I'll see you at practice."

"Practice?"

"For Christmas dances."

"Oh, yeah."

"You're going, right?"

"Yeah."

"You won't forget?"

"No."

He wouldn't forget.

CHAPTER 17

The sun, which blazed as Luz danced, had retreated behind dull, grey clouds, and a cold wind threatened another rainstorm. Dozens of people hung around the memorial, apparently a popular meeting spot. Alonzo zipped up his jacket and stuffed his hands in his pockets.

Luz appeared out of the crowd, smiling at him as if she hadn't seen him for months. "Hi."

"Hi." He put a tentative arm around her waist. "You were great."

"Thanks."

"Have you eaten?"

"Yes."

"Do you want to look at the booths?"

"Sure. As long as it doesn't rain."

But, the rain god did not listen to the collective prayers that rose from the Winter Market artists, and the two were soon seeking shelter from the downpour.

"What a shame," Luz said. "The artists put so much effort into this show, and the rain spoils everything."

"Maybe it will be quick."

But, half an hour later they were still huddled in the

corner of a coffee shop, finishing their café mochas.

"Is your offer to take me home still good?" Luz asked.

"Of course. You aren't going with the other dancers?"

"I told them I was meeting a friend."

"Are you ready to leave?"

"Yes. It doesn't look like this is going to improve."

They headed south, along with others who had given up on the storm clearing.

"I sure hope the weather is better next weekend," Luz said.

"Are you dancing again?"

"No. It's our Walatowa Winter Arts and Crafts Fair."

"Will you have a booth?"

"Yes."

"Do you want help setting up?"

"My mom and dad usually help me."

He took it as a no.

She smiled shyly. "But, two extra hands wouldn't hurt."

His heart swelled. "What time?"

"Early. We'll start at about seven."

"I'll bring coffee."

"Deal."

They talked little in the car, the rain and the road demanding Alonzo's attention. The storm was moving east, and by the time they reached her pueblo, the skies were washed clean. The sun had barely set, and the evening light glowed iridescent blue behind the red rocks.

She showed him a shortcut to her home, saying, "I'd like you to come in and meet my folks."

"Okay." His heart took an extra few beats. Such a meeting would be meaningful to pueblo parents.

"I'm an only child, so they dote on me. And, since they want nothing more than for me to get married and have kids, they'll be checking you out like a prime piece of potential."

"I didn't realize you were an only child."

"They wanted more kids, but it didn't happen. My mom

has three brothers and four sisters who all have grandchildren. She wants me to hurry up and get started, so I can provide them with half a dozen or so."

"Do you want kids?"

"Of course, don't you?"

"I suppose. Someday." He turned off the ignition.

"If you want to impress them, you should keep the 'someday' part to yourself."

*

"I think that went well," Luz said later as she walked outside to his car with him. "Dad wouldn't have invited you for dinner after the fair next weekend if he didn't approve."

"Were you worried?" he asked, winding his arms around her.

"Maybe a little."

He kissed her gently. "Try not to. I have a few hidden charms."

She kissed him back. "And some not so hidden."

His laugh was a low rumble. "Go back inside. They won't like it much if you catch a cold because of me."

"Will you send me a picture from today?"

"If there's a good one."

She leaned up and whispered, "If I'm as beautiful as you say, they should all be good."

"A seasoned photographer knows it's his skill that makes the picture. As a novice, my shots aren't always the best."

"Nice try. Send me a picture."

He laughed. "Okay." He kissed her again, feeling the now familiar heat rise in his body. "Go inside."

She waved from the doorway as he backed out of the driveway. He'd met her parents, and they seemed to like him. He wondered what they were saying about him right then. Would they pressure Luz to make their relationship more formal?

Was he ready for that?
He surprised himself with his own answer.
He was.

*

When he reached home, he got a beer and settled on the couch. He could see the photos better on his computer, but he was too impatient. He knew Luz would be waiting.

He scrolled through them, stopping to consider several along the way. One caught his attention, and he enlarged it to see if the focus held. Luz had eight hoops already in her hands and was tipping another with the toe of her moccasin. The look on her face was intense concentration without any concern. She knew exactly what she was doing.

Alonzo loved the look.

It probably wasn't the best picture he'd taken that day, but it was his favorite. It was Luz, her inner light shining brightly. He sent it to her.

Half an hour later his phone pinged. He hesitated, knowing how disappointed he'd be if it were a text from Carlos or Felicia.

When he could wait no longer, he took a quick sip of beer and swiped open the message. It was a profile of him, sitting astride Luz's horse, his dark head against the horse's mane. Red rocks and a sliver of blue sky set off his dark hair in stark contrast. It was intimate but not invasive; she'd captured his essence, and his love of horses.

She knew him as no one else ever had.

He wished she were with him. He wanted to wrap his arms around her and tell her he loved her. It wouldn't do to say it over the phone; it had to be in person. Sending their photos back and forth had morphed from sharing pictures to sharing their lives. For him, they had become love letters.

He loved her.

Was it possible she felt the same?

*

Julia called him the next day. "I wanted to talk to you about the planter the other night, but you disappeared."

"Yeah."

"I planted some garlic," she said after he didn't offer any explanation. "I read that it might winter over without dying. I also put in broad beans, and for the fun of it, cabbage and rhubarb. I covered it all with black plastic mulch."

"That sounds like a good experimental field. How is the rose doing?"

"Fine so far."

"Good."

"Thanks again for doing this, Lon."

"If it works, you could have your rose garden, and the pueblo could benefit as well."

"We'll give it our best shot. When do you think you'll start planting in spring?"

"Late February or early March, depending on frost. We'll have to build the screens in Mr. Montoya's field as soon as possible so they're ready."

"I'm happy to help if I can. You know I love gardening."

"Thanks, Auntie. I'm sure I'll need all the help I can get." *Especially with the nay-sayers on the pueblo*, he thought. There were bound to be more than a few.

"Okay. Well, that's it. I just wanted you to know."

"*Hueh.*"

"We'll see you soon."

"Yeah," he said, not sure when that would be.

*

He arrived at Jemez early the following Saturday with four steaming cups of coffee and a heart bursting with love. Luz and her parents had already begun setting up the booth.

Her father took a sip of coffee with an appreciative nod, then started directing Alonzo to help with the heavy lifting.

Once the set-up was complete, Luz began arranging the photographs. Some were framed, but many were printed on stretched canvas, lending a simple, even primitive, look. Alonzo helped as best he could, but Luz obviously knew exactly how she wanted things and moved confidently around the space.

Before long, crowds of both villagers and visitors bustled among the booths, many stopping to compliment Luz on her work. She handled the attention with grace, thanking her admirers and welcoming them to linger as long as they liked. Alonzo was anxious for her to make sales, but Luz appeared unconcerned.

"You're doing well," her mother said, putting money into the simple strongbox. "Six already, and I think that one older couple is coming back."

"Yes. It's been a good day so far," Luz agreed.

Toward the end of the afternoon, several people who had stopped to enjoy the photographs earlier, returned and made purchases. Luz sold out the entire stack of books on Taos Pueblo, and more than half of all the others.

When her father returned to help break down the booth, he beamed with delight at his daughter's successful day. He spoke quietly to Luz in their native tongue, and while Alonzo didn't understand the words, he couldn't miss their meaning. A pueblo woman would not brag about her own accomplishments, but one would be wise to stay out of her father's way if he chose to do so.

"Will you stay for dinner?" Luz asked.

"Sure."

He was disappointed that there was no opportunity to speak to her privately all evening. When her parents retired to bed, her father gave him a look that clearly said it was time for him to leave.

"When can I see you again?" Alonzo asked quietly as the

two stood by the front door.

"When would you like?"

"Tomorrow?"

"It's too cold to go riding."

"What about lunch at Café Pasqual's? They even have a sort of art gallery going there."

"'Sort of' being the operative words."

"No?"

"Sure. I'd like that."

"I'll pick you up around ten."

"For lunch?"

"Indian time."

"Okay."

He wrapped his arms around her, keeping a firm clamp on his words. He'd tell her tomorrow. He'd ask for a table in a quiet corner of the restaurant. It would be perfect.

He kissed her, aware that her parents were only a few feet away behind an easily opened door. The thought that one of them might appear at any moment stole his passion.

"Good night," he said.

"See you tomorrow."

He drove home thinking that tomorrow was an eternity away.

*

The next day, the sky looked like it had been painted by an angry child. A malicious grey was splashed everywhere. Alonzo and Luz walked from the parking lot to Café Pasqual's, one of Santa Fe's most popular restaurants.

"It's going to snow," Luz said. She shivered. "I should have worn my boots."

He wrapped his arm around her shoulders and pulled her close. "Better?"

"Yes."

The café was small and filled with tantalizing aromas and

boisterous laughter. There were three open tables, as well as places available at the large central table.

"Sit anywhere you like," a waitress told them.

"Let's sit at the communal table," Luz said. "That seems like fun."

It was the last thing Alonzo wanted, but he couldn't very well tell her why.

They were immediately drawn into the conversation about the imminent snow storm, and Alonzo's plan for an intimate meal where he could share his feelings, was ruined. By the time they left, the sky was black.

"I hope we get home before it gets bad," Luz said.

But, they were barely out of town when the skies opened up and snow blanketed the road. Alonzo was accustomed to driving in the snow, but a total white-out was more than he cared to cope with.

"I'd rather sit this out by a roaring fire than on the side of the road," he said. Their options were limited. He pulled into a parking lot of a small motel. "What will your parents do to me if I don't get you home until tomorrow?"

"As long as you bring me home alive, I think you're safe."

"Let's see if they have a room with double beds."

"And a fireplace," Luz added.

They stumbled their way into the motel lobby, trying to shake off the snow in the entry.

"I'm so sorry," the woman behind the desk said when they inquired, "but we're completely booked." She looked out at the blizzard and shook her head. "I can't send you back out in that mess. You can make yourselves at home on the couch by the horno. We'll have to hope it clears up soon. If not, I'll serve a family style meal for all our guests at about six and you're welcome to join us."

"Thank you so much," Luz told her.

"The storm was supposed to clear around four, but it doesn't look promising. While we don't have a room, I can bring you pillows and blankets, and you can sleep on the couch. It may not be comfortable, but you'll be safe."

"You're so kind." Luz wiped a tear from her cheek.

"Let's see if you feel the same way in the morning."

"We're happy to pay for a room," Alonzo said.

"Not at all. But, I might ask for your help at dinner. There's no way my employees will be able to get here in this white-out."

"You're in luck," Luz said. "I worked as a waitress all through college."

"And, my mom made sure I knew how to wash dishes," Alonzo said.

"Sometimes things work in the most wonderful ways," the woman said. "My name is Joanna Conrad. My husband, Bruce, and I own the motel. He's the handyman and chef. We live right here on the property."

"The ideal commute," Alonzo said.

Just then, a large, burly man covered in snow, came in toting a cartload of logs.

"We've got two for the couch tonight, dear," Joanna said.

Alonzo rushed forward to help the man unload the wood.

"Thanks," the fellow said, extending a hand. "Bruce Conrad."

Alonzo introduced himself and Luz. "We're your kitchen and wait staff for tonight."

"How fortunate for us," Bruce said.

"And us," Luz agreed.

Much later, when dinner was long over, and the kitchen was as clean as if it were new, Alonzo and Luz sat cuddled together in front of the fire.

"Could this be any more romantic?" Luz asked. "And to think, my parents agreed it was a good idea."

"They might not have been so pleased if the Conrads had had a vacant room."

Luz snuggled against him. "A room couldn't compare with this."

And, Alonzo thought, it certainly would have brought up other issues; issues he didn't think they were quite ready to face.

"Do you want more wine?" he asked. The Conrads had given them a complimentary bottle to thank them for their help.

"No, I've had plenty. Between that and the fire, I'm practically asleep already. I have a feeling this is going to be a perfect night."

It would be a perfect night to tell her he loved her, but before he could settle on the right words, her breathing changed into a gentle rhythm that told him she was asleep.

He was too aware of her body close to his to fall asleep. He was glad that the couple had left the outdoor lights on. He would hate to be out in the storm, but from here, it was beauty in motion. He imagined it might not be so poetic when they were digging the car out in the morning.

He thought briefly of getting up and taking a few pictures, but he didn't want to disturb Luz. She was so peaceful and beautiful. He slipped his phone from his pocket and tried to take a shot of her, but he couldn't do it without inserting himself in the frame.

She stirred when he put his phone back in his pocket. "Are you okay? Do you need more room?"

"I'm fine."

"Good."

"Luz," he said, "have I ever told you how much I like your photographs?"

She turned to look at him. "I don't think you have."

He kissed her lightly. "I think they're wonderful."

She smiled. "Thank you. Some of yours are pretty good. You've come a long way with no training."

"I'm learning from an expert."

"I'm not so sure about that."

"Why so pessimistic?"

"No reason. I keep hoping I'll hear something back from

the Albuquerque Museum."

"About the one-man show?"

"One-woman show."

"Right. And, that's what it's going to be."

"I hope so," she said, and nestled against him again.

Sometime later, Alonzo said, "I have to put more wood on the fire if we want to keep it going." He slipped out from under the blanket and put three of the biggest logs on the bright red coals. "That should do it till morning."

"What time is it?" Luz mumbled, already half asleep again.

"Eleven-fifteen."

"The snow stopped."

"Yes."

He cuddled under the blanket again. "Rest up. You'll need all your strength in the morning."

"To take pictures?"

"No. To dig out the car." He laughed at his own joke, but she said nothing.

He wasn't sure she even heard him. Her soft breath was slow and steady and smelled like strawberries. He held her fast, as if his body alone were protecting her from the cold.

His heart swelled with the love he had still not shared.

*

"It's a winter wonderland," Luz said. She stood at the window, camera in hand, framing shots of the snow-laden landscape. "I want to go out there, but not until we're ready to leave."

"Why?"

"Because my shoes will be soaked."

"Good morning," Joanna said. She came into the room carrying a tray with two steaming cups of coffee and a plate of fragrant muffins. "I see you survived the night."

"Very nicely, thanks to you," Luz said.

Joanna put down the tray. "We're making breakfast. It should be ready in about half an hour."

"Can we help?" Luz asked.

"Maybe after. Fortunately, none of our other guests are scheduled to leave today, so your car is the only one we'll have to excavate."

Alonzo laughed. "Well put. It is buried."

"I heard on the news that this was the biggest storm in the past twenty years. I'm sure the snow plows are already on the highway, clearing the mess."

Luz poured cream into her coffee and took a careful sip. "Ah, perfection."

"There's more in the dining room." Joanna pointed at Luz's camera. "If you want to go outside, I have an extra pair of boots you could use."

"Oh, that would be great. We weren't at all prepared for this."

"I'll get them for you."

"You're so thoughtful. I don't know how we are ever going to repay you."

"There's no need," Joanna said simply.

After breakfast, Alonzo and Bruce shoveled snow off the car and driveway.

"I could help, you know," Luz said.

"We've got it," Alonzo told her. "Take your pictures while the light is still good."

"If you're sure," she said, and began framing shots again.

The sky was a bright, robin-egg blue, and the sun cast long shadows across the pristine snow. The motel sign, which had been nearly invisible in the storm the previous day, was encrusted in ice. Poquito Pueblo, it read, and Alonzo thought its familiar adobe style was like a piece of home in the wilderness.

"She sure is taking a lot of pictures," Bruce said, scraping ice from the car's windshield.

"She's a professional photographer," Alonzo said. "She's

in her element. She has a series of books called *Sunlight and Shadow*. Nothing makes her happier than early morning light."

"Joanna and I would love to see any photos she takes here. We're planning a remodel and are upgrading our website. I think some winter pictures would add exactly the interest and variety we need."

"I know she'll be happy to share them with you. Maybe we could come back in spring, and she could take some in better weather."

"That would be terrific. Thanks."

"We owe you big-time for taking us in."

"It was a pleasure, especially since you did all the dishes! I don't often get to sit with a glass of wine while someone else cleans up my kitchen."

"That was the least we could do."

Joanna had hot chocolate waiting for them when they went back inside.

"Alonzo says Luz is a professional photographer," Bruce told his wife. "They're going to come back soon and show us the pictures she's taken."

"After I've put them on my computer and edited them," Luz said.

Bruce nodded. "I'm hoping we might be able to use a few of them on the website."

"That would be super," Joanna said. "I'm useless with a camera. I cut off people's heads and take unintentional pictures of the floor."

"I hope that some of the ones I took will work," Luz said.

"I have a funny feeling they will," Joanna said. "This meeting was more than an accident. It was meant to be."

After embraces all around and promises of getting together soon, Alonzo and Luz drove onto the highway headed home.

"What an extraordinary experience," Luz said. "I never could have imagined that 'no room at the inn' could have turned out like that. Could it have been any more perfect?"

"No," Alonzo said. *Only if I'd been able to tell you what I'd planned to.* But, the time had never seemed right. Luz had fallen asleep in his arms before he had the right words ready.

Still, thinking of the night, he was filled with contentment. There would be another time, a better time, a time that would be perfect.

The words would wait.

*

Alonzo's phone pinged on Thursday afternoon. The message said, "Dinner tonight? My treat."

He texted back. "Sure. What's the occasion?"

"Tell you later," came the answer. "I'll meet you at Quesadilla Grille at six."

"I'll be there."

He tried to figure out what might have prompted the invitation, but was totally surprised when she told him. After they ordered their meals she said, "I got a call today from the curator at the Albuquerque Museum. I've been chosen for the one-woman show!"

"You got it? Fantastic!"

"It will actually be a three-woman show. They've also invited one potter, Maria Elena Costanza, from your pueblo, and Juanita Peña, a silversmith from Taos."

"Congratulations! I'm so proud of you. I knew you'd do it."

"You did?"

"Absolutely. When is the show?"

"It starts the first Friday in March and runs for a month."

"Will you have enough time to get ready?"

"I hope so. I have to get at least twenty pictures matted and framed, and I want to finish the Laguna book and get copies of it printed."

"Can I help?"

Her smile was slow and sweet. "Yes. Keep sending me photos. They inspire me."

"That's rich. The novice inspires the professional?"

"You inspire me."

"I love you, Luz." The words came out easily, more easily than he possibly could have imagined; more easily, perhaps, than anything he'd ever said to her. He felt none of the heart-racing fear he'd known with Erin, because he knew what Luz was going to reply. At least he thought he did.

She grinned with mischievous pleasure then kissed him. "It took you long enough. I've been wanting to tell you for weeks. I love you, too."

CHAPTER 18

Dinner was a mixture of rich aromas, tastes, and textures. Alonzo had never had a meal so filled with pleasure. Happiness held his heart, more alive than ever, beating with a brand new cadence. His heart had found a home.

"I'd like to go by the museum," Luz said as they left the restaurant. "It's open late on Thursday. We could walk. It's only about five minutes from here."

Alonzo took her hand. "Sure. Let's check it out."

It was crowded and noisy, since Thursday was family night. They walked around, hand in hand, while Luz tried to envision where she would hang various pieces.

Alonzo noticed a poster advertising an upcoming program and stopped to read the details.

"Look at this," he said. "Seed: Climate Change Resistance. An entire day devoted to dialogue about global warming, local food, healthy communities, and the revitalization of indigenous agri-culture practices."

"The way they hyphenated agriculture gives it an entirely different connotation."

"It sure does."

"Sounds like it was designed with you in mind."

"I wish it was sooner. It's not until June."

"Maybe that's a good thing," Luz said.

"Why?"

"You'll have more to offer. By then, you'll have had six months of experience with the planter box."

"You think they'd want to hear about that?"

"I think your ideas are valuable and worth sharing."

"If they work."

"Even if they don't, they're valuable. You'll learn, and the other participants will learn. Maybe someone else there will be working on a similar project."

Alonzo loved her optimism. "Maybe so."

Thoughts of the planter box brought thoughts of his pueblo; thoughts he'd been avoiding; thoughts that brought pain. It would soon be time to practice for the Christmas Dances. Alonzo hadn't danced there since Easter. He missed it and wondered if it was time to go back. Unfortunately, his brother's words still hung in his heart like a torn shirt on barbed wire.

"Are you okay?" Luz asked after a lengthy silence. "All of a sudden you got quiet."

"I was thinking about the winter dances. When are yours?" he asked, unwilling to share his turmoil.

"Guadalupe Feast Day is on the twelfth. They'll be doing the Matachines Dances."

"Oh, yeah? Tell me about those."

"They say that Montezuma brought the Matachines to the pueblos from Mexico. My dad told me that originally it was a European story of a fight between the Christians and the Moors, but I doubt any of our elders would describe it that way. It's funny how so many of our feasts and celebrations came from other cultures."

"From the outside," he mumbled. His heart constricted when it occurred to him that now, Paolo considered him an outsider. According to his brother, Alonzo no longer belonged on the pueblo.

Was it possible that he was right?

*

Alonzo walked Luz to her car, trying to recapture the joy they'd shared earlier in the evening. They were in love and love conquered all.

Or did it?

"I've got the pictures from Poquito Pueblo on my computer. I should have them edited by Saturday. Do you want to see them? I'm pretty sure I can get a room at PICC that night."

"Of course I want to see them. What time?"

"Let's have dinner there. Then we can head into the conference room whenever we're finished. I checked the schedule and nobody has reserved it yet."

"Are you happy with the pictures?"

"Some of them. Snow is tricky; it reflects the light, and the glare can completely ruin a scene."

Alonzo leaned against the side of Luz's car and drew her into his arms. "I bet they're all wonderful...like you."

"I'll only show you the ones that are."

"When will you show them to the Conrads?"

"I thought about calling and asking them about Sunday. Is that okay for you?"

"Whatever works is fine."

"Alright, then I'll call them tomorrow."

He kissed her, feeling like a teenager, huddled below the blaring street light. "I wish you lived in town, so I could take you home."

"I could never live in town, Alonzo."

He nodded. "I know." She'd made it very clear. She knew where her home was.

He kissed her again, her soft lips and sweet mouth arousing him. "You should probably go before I embarrass myself."

She grinned. "We wouldn't want that." She unlocked her car door and slid into the driver's seat. "See you at the center on Saturday. Let's say six, unless I hear otherwise."

"Okay."

"Thanks for dinner. It was supposed to be my treat."

"Next time."

"I'll hold you to that."

He watched her drive off, still smiling with the joy she brought him. He'd finally found his love.

*

They met at the Pueblo Harvest Café on Saturday evening. Luz had made a reservation, which saved them from the wait that was around forty-five minutes.

"I'm glad they put us in the back," Luz said after they'd been seated.

"Why?"

"It's hard to enjoy eating when I can see people standing around waiting. Oh, and by the way, we have a reservation for tomorrow, too."

"For what?"

"Lunch at Poquito Pueblo. I called Joanna last night and told her the pictures were ready. She invited us for lunch. She sounded so excited about the pictures. I hope she won't be disappointed."

"Not possible," Alonzo said.

"You haven't even seen them. What makes you so sure?"

"I saw the look on your face while you were taking them."

"That simple?"

"That simple."

And, he was right.

One shot after another flashed on the screen in the conference room, filling the space with Luz's unique vision.

"Told you," Alonzo said. "Joanna and Bruce are going to

be amazed. And, I can see at least a couple of them included in the museum show."

Luz sighed. "There's so much to do before then. I have to settle on the Laguna shots so I can get that book done, and I've got framing to do on all the ones I'm hanging."

"I can help."

She squeezed his hand. "Just being with you helps. Your confidence in me helps. Knowing you love me helps."

He laughed. "My work here is done."

*

Sunday was overcast and gloomy.

"I hope it doesn't snow again," Luz said as they neared Santa Fe.

"We couldn't find a better place to be stuck," Alonzo said.

"True," she laughed. "But I'm not sure how many times my parents will accept that excuse."

The Conrads welcomed them like long lost relatives.

"We're so pleased you could make it today," Joanna said. "I can't wait to see the photographs! Can we do that before we have lunch?"

"If you'd like," Luz agreed.

"I cleared space in the office so we can all fit in there," Bruce said. "You have them on a thumb drive, right?"

Luz pulled a small packet from her purse. "I've got it right here."

Bruce transferred the files, Joanna brought each of them a cup of coffee, and the show began. By the time it was over, Joanna had used every superlative in the dictionary.

"They're all spectacular!" she gushed. "Just beautiful."

"I'd like to frame one for you as a thank-you for your kindness last weekend."

"That isn't at all necessary," Joanna said.

"Besides," Bruce added, "we got the best of the bargain.

Alonzo did all the dishes that night."

"I'd still like to give you one," Luz insisted.

"I couldn't begin to say which one I like the best," Joanna said. "There are simply too many that I love."

"Maybe you don't have to choose just one," Bruce said.

His wife frowned. "What do you mean?"

"Well, the remodel calls for new art work in all the guest rooms. I don't think we could find anything more appealing or appropriate than Luz's photos. That will make the selection much easier."

"What a brilliant idea," Joanna said. She turned to Luz. "Can we do that? Can you, I mean?"

"Of course. I'd be honored."

"Well then, let's have lunch and after that, we can go through the pictures again and make our choices for the website as well as the rooms."

"I don't think you want all winter shots, do you?"

"No," Bruce said, "but Joanna bought your book on Taos Pueblo and we love several of those as well."

"Maybe you should check out the other books, too," Alonzo said.

"Good idea," Bruce agreed. "And, if you'd like, we could keep half a dozen of each edition of *Sunlight and Shadow* to sell here."

Alonzo looked at Luz, who appeared about to explode with happiness.

"That would be fantastic," Luz said.

"I think some champagne is in order," Bruce said. "Let's have a toast to a new partnership."

Luz was still bubbling later as they drove back toward Albuquerque. "Can you believe it? All this because we were caught in a blizzard and they helped *us*! Eighteen rooms to decorate, plus the dining room, the office, the lounge, and the front desk. And, they're going to sell my books! It's like hitting three jackpots in one day!"

"It's a lot to take on, considering the one-woman show.

Can you handle it all?"

"I'll have to. This is what I've been working toward for years. I'll make out a schedule, and I'll stick to it like my life depends on it."

"I hope you'll schedule some time there for me."

She touched his cheek with soft, warm fingers. "You'll be at the top of the list."

*

Alonzo took off work on Tuesday to attend the Matachines Dances at Jemez. He sat huddled with Luz and her parents as the centuries-old drama was presented to the pueblo. The main characters, El Monarea and La Malinche, were dressed in vibrant costumes. Colorful ribbons streamed down from the back of mitre-shaped headdresses, while fringe dangled in front.

"The clowns are great," Alonzo whispered to Luz, referring to the two men who directed the action and lightened the atmosphere.

"I was afraid of them when I was little," Luz said.

Like the River Men at his pueblo, Alonzo thought. Comic relief that didn't seem quite so funny to a five-year-old.

Along with the principals, two parallel lines of six dancers appeared wearing masks over their eyes and kerchiefs over their faces. They performed nine dances in all, accompanied by drums and a guitar.

Remembering what Luz had told him about the dances, Alonzo wondered how they might have evolved from Montezuma's time, and what other outside influences might have affected them. Maybe outside influence wasn't always a bad thing.

When they'd finished, Luz invited Alonzo for feast at her uncle's house. "He wants to thank you for taking the horses out. I don't think they've been ridden since then."

"We should go again. That was a nice day."

"In our spare time, right? As if I wasn't getting ready for the museum show, decorating the Poquito Pueblo, and preparing for the Christmas Dances."

Carlos had told him that practice was also starting at home. Much as he wanted to dance at his own pueblo again, Alonzo dreaded the idea of facing Paolo.

*

On Thursday morning, Alonzo called Julia. "I was wondering how the plants are doing."

His aunt laughed softly. "They seem to be surviving, though just barely. Would you like to come check them out?" She would not mention practice even though she'd no doubt suspect that was why he'd called. "Come for dinner tonight."

"I'd like that," he said. It would be much easier at his aunt and uncle's house than it would be at his parents', where he'd be questioned about everything, but mostly about Luz.

Julia came out to his car when he arrived. "I wish you could see them in the daytime," she said, pointing her flashlight at the planter box. "They look a little sad at night."

Pathetic, Alonzo thought. The garlic was okay; the beans were wretched, withered and spindly, though still alive. The cabbage and rhubarb were unrecognizable.

"I'm afraid that we'll lose the beans during the next snow, even though I'm covering them whenever it freezes," Julia said.

"What about your rose?"

"I can't tell. I've pruned it back, and I encourage it every day. We have nice long talks."

"That'll be what makes the difference, Auntie."

"That and the fact that after lots of research, I chose the strongest stock I could find."

"This is only the first test. The real test will be whether

they can survive the summer."

Julia put a gentle arm around his shoulder. "There may be many tests before we find the winning combination. The trick is to keep trying."

As it was with most things, Alonzo thought.

After dinner, Alonzo walked to the kiva with his uncle and Carlos. As he expected, Paolo was there, waiting.

"We'll only be a minute," Paolo said to his uncle, then stood silently while Tony and Carlos went inside.

"Why are you here?" Paolo asked, his voice strident.

"Why do you suppose?"

"I have no idea. There's no place for you here, Alonzo. You made your choice, and it wasn't for the pueblo. Go back to town where you belong."

His brother didn't block his way. Alonzo could have pushed past him. But, the schism between them was wide, and would certainly engulf others. Alonzo did not want to cause any turmoil during practice.

He turned on painful heels and walked back to his car. Perhaps Paolo was right. Perhaps he didn't belong there.

*

For the next two weeks, he threw his energy into helping Luz prepare for the upcoming museum show. They reviewed all the pictures for the Laguna Pueblo book, and made the first selections. He doubted he was much help, but Luz insisted that his eye had developed such that she valued his opinion. On some shots, they disagreed. When Alonzo made a convincing case, she listened, and sometimes, though not often, took his advice.

Luz heaved a giant sigh when she finally settled on the cover photo. "That's it then. Now I can send it to the publisher."

"What's next?" Alonzo asked.

"I feel more pressure to decide on the photos for the show

than I do for Joanna and Bruce. Besides, I'll need to get all the permission slips signed for anyone whose face I use in the show." She grinned at him. "That includes you."

"Use whatever you want, I don't care."

"You'll want to see them, to say they're okay."

"Whatever you choose is fine with me."

"You'll still have to sign the permission slip."

"If that's what you want."

"You'll come to the show, right?" Her voice was uncertain, hurt.

"Of course. I wouldn't miss it."

"Then you'll see yourself there."

He laughed, short and sharp. "Yeah, strung up, hanging on a wall."

He couldn't help thinking of the video, when he'd felt like such a fool, a grandstander, a thing most abhorred by his people. Someone full of himself. That was the last thing on earth he wanted.

"Have you thought any more about Christmas?" Luz asked. "I'd like you to come for dinner either Christmas Day or the day after."

"The day after," he said quickly. That way he wouldn't be home alone when everyone else in his family went off to dance. "Can you come to my folks on Christmas Day? Will your parents mind?"

"They'll mind, but it's only fair. Besides, they're getting used to us being together. They like you."

"That's good, because I don't plan on going away."

*

Alonzo picked Luz up at her home Christmas afternoon. The aroma of baking bread was heavy in the air as beehive hornos sent up steam in supplication to the bread god.

"Merry Christmas," she said, letting herself into the car. She leaned over and kissed him.

"You look nice," he said.

Her long, dark hair hung loose over a bright red shawl. "Thank you."

"Did you go to Mass?"

She sighed. "My mom insisted. Sometimes it's easier to go along than to argue."

It was a tactic Alonzo knew well. Taking Luz home shortly after dinner would preclude any long, drawn out discussions about the dances, the grow boxes, and/or moving back to the pueblo. Alonzo still smarted over Paolo's assertion, but he was not about to get into a confrontation with his brother on Christmas. Better to just go along.

Luz found a radio station that played Christmas music, and she sang along as they traveled. The roads were clear, and the late afternoon light cast long, spindly shadows across the landscape. Alonzo wished they were going out to take pictures instead of going to face his family. He hadn't seen them all month, and he knew his mother would be upset with him.

Arriving late, another protective tactic.

Unfortunately, it was Julia's turn to host the holiday, which would leave his mother free to harass him. Hopefully, Luz would serve to deflect the assault.

Alonzo had no sooner turned off the engine when Felicia burst out of Julia's house to greet them.

"You're here!"

"Hey, K'ayama," Alonzo said, sweeping her up off her feet. "Where've you been? I thought you were going to spend Christmas vacation with me."

"Not funny," his sister said with a sour face. "You know Mom said I couldn't." She gave Luz a shy smile. "I'm glad you're here, too. Did you bring your camera? Christmas is the best time for pictures."

"I always bring a camera," Luz whispered, "But not everyone likes their picture taken, so don't say anything."

Everyone was there except Paolo and Erin. When the

couple finally arrived, Alonzo thought Erin looked unhappy. Her voice sounded strange to him, as if the base that held it up had a hole in it. "Are you okay?"

Her smile stopped short of her eyes. "Yes."

He knew something was wrong. She had only spoken one word, but it told him she was not okay. He glanced at Paolo for an explanation, but Paolo was talking to their mother.

Before long, Julia called everyone to the table. The family crowded around, piling plates with turkey, dressing, mashed potatoes, gravy, squash, and her freshly made cranberry sauce.

"Delicious, as always, Julia," Ramon said.

Everyone agreed.

All except Erin.

Alonzo watched her push food around her plate like a child who was being punished. He couldn't hear the whispered words between her and Paolo, and wondered if they'd had an argument before they'd arrived. It wouldn't be unusual, knowing them.

"I can't, Paolo," Erin said suddenly, and stood. "Excuse me." She went into the bathroom and closed the door.

Everyone looked at Paolo.

"She's not feeling well," he said. He turned to Victoria. "We wanted to tell you later. We had a special package for you to open." He glanced toward the bathroom and then said, "This isn't the ideal way to say it but, we're going to have a baby. In fact, we're going to have twins."

"Whooshka!" Victoria cried. "Twins?" She laid her hand over Paolo's and wiped tears from her dark eyes.

Felicia bounced out of her chair and grabbed her brother. "Oh, my gosh. That's fantastic!"

"Yes," Luz said. "It's wonderful!"

Ramon reached out and grasped Paolo's shoulder. "Congratulations, Whooshka. That's great news!"

"Not so much for her," Paolo said. "She's been sick for weeks."

"I thought she seemed peaked at Thanksgiving," Victoria said.

"She wanted to stay home tonight," Paolo told her. "Maybe I should have encouraged her."

"I'll make her some tea," Julia said. "I have some herbs that might help." She looked around the table. "Everyone else, eat. You can't help her by letting dinner get cold."

As bad as he felt for Erin, Alonzo gave his brother silent thanks. Now, their mother would be focused on the upcoming event instead of on Alonzo.

"How will you ever fit into Mr. Montoya's place?" Tony asked Paolo. "Isn't that where you were planning to move?"

"We won't. Neither one of the bedrooms is big enough for two cribs. I've already gone to pueblo housing authority and requested one of the three bedroom houses. Fortunately, there are two available."

"Get the one closest to us," Felicia cried.

"I'm not sure we'll have a choice," Paolo said.

"When is she due?" Neyse asked.

"The middle of May," Paolo said.

"I can't wait," Felicia said. "Can I babysit?"

"We're counting on it," her brother told her. He stood. "I'm going to go check on her."

"So much for spending summer vacation at my house," Alonzo teased.

His mother shot him a warning glance.

"Just kidding," he said.

"Besides," Victoria said, "if Mr. Montoya's house is available, you could move back here. Felicia could see you every day."

"That would be perfect, Lon," Felicia cried. "Will you?"

And just when he thought he was safe. "We'll see," he said, employing the most hated phrase from his childhood. It always sounded like there was a chance, whereas, in fact, there wasn't the slightest possibility.

*

Alonzo expected the day after Christmas to be a quiet affair at Luz's house. She didn't warn him that all of her mother's brothers and sisters and all of their families would be there.

"I was afraid if I told you, you wouldn't come," Luz told him after she'd introduced him to everyone. The house vibrated with talk, laughter, and movement of more than fifty people. The place was so hot that every door and window was wide open.

"Are you hungry?" Luz asked. "Everybody is on their own to find a plate, take what they want, and look for a place to sit. Good luck with that. You're not allowed to push another adult off the couch, but kids are fair game."

Alonzo had always thought that his family's gatherings were crazy, but Luz's family took chaos to a whole new level. And, as the evening went on, it got more and more raucous. Alonzo took refuge in talking to Luz's uncle, who wanted him and Luz to ride his horses more often.

"They don't mind the snow," he told Alonzo.

"The storms these days are pretty nasty. I'd hate to get caught in another white-out," Alonzo said.

Her uncle laughed. "The horses can always find their way home regardless of weather. Food and warmth are great motivators."

"Wait until spring, Uncle," Luz said. "I promise we'll ride more often when it's a little warmer."

A sudden commotion caught Alonzo's attention.

"It's starting to snow again," Luz's mother said as she was closing the windows. "It's supposed to last all night."

Not an ideal time for driving in the dark, Alonzo thought. He looked at Luz. "I should probably get going if I don't want to get caught in the storm."

He thanked her parents, and she walked him out to the front porch.

"Do you have any plans for New Year's Eve?" he asked.

"No. But there's an art film playing at The Royale. It's had good reviews, and the photography is supposed to be fantastic."

"Sounds good. Best of all, I doubt it'll be crowded."

She laughed. "A little too much family for you tonight?"

He kissed her. "They're all nice. There's just so many of them."

"You were a good sport."

He gave her a hug and realized she was shivering. "Get inside. I'll call you tomorrow."

He drove home carefully, thanking the pueblo gods for his own family, no matter how difficult.

*

Every New Year's Day, Alonzo's pueblo celebrated with the Corn Dance, a sacred and spiritual occasion that Alonzo had participated in for as long as he could remember. He'd struggled for days, trying to decide whether it would be less painful to stay away, or to go and be a mere observer. In the end, he decided to go. Since Paolo would be dancing, it was unlikely that there would be any confrontation.

He left his car at Mr. Montoya's and walked the short distance to the plaza. He found a spot near the corner of two adobes, where he'd be protected from the wind. The dances had already started. Alonzo's heart beat in sympathetic rhythm with the drums, and his weight shifted almost imperceptibly from one foot to the other.

"Hello, Dyaami," he heard and he turned. "It's nice to see you here."

"Hi, Aunt Julia. Happy New Year."

"You, too."

Neither of them spoke again as the dancers continued. When they'd finished and had left the plaza, Julia said, "You're not dancing these days."

"No."

"Don't you miss it?"

Julia rarely minced words.

"Yeah."

"What's holding you back?"

Alonzo shrugged.

"This is your home, Alonzo. These are your people. This is your tradition. If you miss it, what's keeping you from participating?" Julia was always honest with the family and she expected honesty in return.

Alonzo swallowed a hard lump. "Paolo says I don't belong here."

Julia paused only a moment before saying, "That isn't Paolo's decision to make. Where you belong is up to you, not him. Don't give your brother your power, Dyaami."

Her words were gentle, her message, uncompromising.

After a long silence, he said, "*Hueh.*"

Sometimes his aunt reminded him of a shaman, seeing before, or behind, or beyond. The family couldn't often argue successfully with her vision.

"The Buffalo Dances are next month," she said. Then, she shivered. "I'm cold. I'm going back to the house." She turned toward home, leaving Alonzo with his thoughts.

The Buffalo Dances.

CHAPTER 19

The weather was bitter cold the next weekend when Alonzo and Carlos danced at PICC, and they wore their heavier winter garb. Julia's words had stuck with Alonzo throughout the week. Dancing that Saturday only served to strengthen his resolve to participate in the Buffalo Dances. Facing down Paolo was the price he had to pay.

Luz was not there that day, and Alonzo missed her quiet presence at the edge of the plaza.

"Where's Luz?" his cousin asked when they'd finished dancing. "I can hardly get through the afternoon without that rocket-sized camera lens following us around."

"She's getting ready for her one-woman show," Alonzo told him as they headed for the parking lot.

"She's getting ready to be famous. I saw Natoma the other day. Patricia Michaels put three of the photographs that Luz took of Natoma on her website."

"No kidding? I wonder if Luz knows."

"She'd have to get her permission to use them. I'm surprised she didn't tell you."

"She's totally overloaded between the show, the books, and the photographs for the motel."

"No time for you?"

"I'm seeing her later."

"Night out on the town?" Carlos teased.

"Something like that."

In fact, he was meeting her at PICC to go through the photo selections she'd made for the Conrads. It wouldn't be much of a night out.

Carlos unlocked his car. "Have fun. I'll see you next weekend."

"I'll be here," Alonzo told him.

He spent the remainder of the afternoon doing his least favorite thing: laundry. But, he'd worn the same undershorts twice that week, and unless he was willing to buy yet another package, washing was mandatory. The only saving grace was going to a laundromat where he could do four loads at the same time.

Instead of reading, as he usually did at the laundromat, he sat thinking about the Buffalo Dance and the best way to confront Paolo. There was no good reason to wait until it was time for practice to start, and yet he was in no hurry to cause what might be another rift in the family.

"You seem preoccupied," Luz told him later that evening. They'd finished going through all Luz's selections, and Alonzo had approved of every one. "Is everything okay?"

"Yeah." He wasn't about ready to tell her the sordid tale of why he'd moved to town, and why his brother thought he should stay there.

"I know I've been completely wrapped up in all these projects. I'm sure this isn't much fun for you."

"It's fine."

"Maybe we could do something fun next weekend. Too bad it's so cold or we could go riding. Eating lunch outside in freezing weather doesn't strike me as a picnic."

"We can't do much on Saturday, since I'm dancing."

"Sunday then. Let's go somewhere. How about Sandia Peak?"

"Do you want to go skiing?"

"No. Let's have lunch at the top. With all the snow we've had, it'd be beautiful up there."

"If you want."

"I want some time with you that doesn't involve photographs or pueblos."

"Does that mean you'll leave your camera at home?"

"No camera, no photos."

"How will we ever know we were there?"

*

Neyse called him in the middle of the week. "Mom is turning fifty this month. We're having a dinner party for her a week from Saturday and we want you to come."

"Fifty?"

"Yes."

"Wow. She sure doesn't look it."

"What does fifty look like?"

"Old, I guess. Not like your mom."

"She does look good, that's for sure. So, you'll come?"

"Sure. I wouldn't miss it, as people like to say."

"Oh, and Lon, bring Luz. Everybody likes her."

Not everybody, Alonzo thought, but didn't say.

Luz was as surprised as he was. "Fifty?" she repeated when he told her about the party. He'd called her right after he'd hung up with Neyse.

"Yeah."

"She looks about thirty. Her skin is beautiful...so creamy. I'll bet she never goes out in the sun."

Luz was right. Alonzo could remember Neyse begging her mom to go with them to the pool at the rec center on the pueblo. He didn't think he'd ever once seen her there.

"You're invited, too. Neyse says everybody likes you." No need to mention Paolo or his mother.

Alonzo could almost hear her smile. "I'm glad. My

214

family feels the same about you."

"So, for this weekend, shall I pick you up on Sunday morning?"

"That's silly. You'll have to turn around and drive back to town. I'll meet you at PICC."

"What time?" he asked.

"How about eight. We could go out to breakfast first."

"Good idea. I've been wanting to check out a place called The Egg and I."

"Sounds good to me. I heard they have a great menu."

Apparently everyone in town had heard. They had to park six blocks away and wait over half an hour to be seated.

"I hope it's worth it," Alonzo said after they'd ordered. "I don't understand why it's so crowded this early; the sun is barely up."

"That's not quite true. The days are getting longer."

"That's what I call optimism. We're barely past the winter solstice."

She smiled. "But we're past it. That's what counts."

When they left, they agreed that it had, indeed, been worth the wait.

The parking lot at the tram to Sandia Peak was jam-packed. They drove around in circles for twenty minutes and finally gave up.

"What's the deal?" Alonzo asked. "What are all these people doing here? It's never like this."

"Oh my gosh, it's Martin Luther King weekend. That's why the restaurant was so crowded. We should have realized. It just shows how distracted I've been."

"That, and this weather is ideal for skiing."

"Or anything else outside for that matter. We should do something indoors and avoid the crowds."

Alonzo thought a moment and then said, "I need to get a gift for my aunt's birthday. Let's go to the mall."

"The mall? Why didn't I think of that?" Luz said. "Do you already know what you want to give her?"

"A book. You can never go wrong with books for Julia."

Happily, Barnes and Noble was not crowded.

"Are you thinking of any particular subject?" Luz asked as they walked into the brightly lit store.

"Gardening. Maybe they'll have something on water harvesting that she'd like."

"As long as we're here," Luz said, "I'm going to check out the books on photography."

"Okay," he said, and squeezed her hand before heading in the opposite direction.

He browsed through the gardening section but didn't find much on water harvesting. However, he found several books on roses, some educational, some coffee table style.

"Hello, Lon."

He would have known the voice anywhere. He turned. "Hi, Erin. What brings you to town?"

"I imagine the same thing that brought you…a gift for Julia."

"I was here first," he teased.

"True."

"You look much better than the last time I saw you."

"I'm feeling much better. Those first three months were awful."

"I'm glad you're better."

"Thanks. How are you doing, Lon?"

"Fine."

"We've missed you."

"Yeah." What else was there to say?

"You haven't danced at the pueblo for a while. Haven't you missed it?"

It took a while, but he finally answered. "I have."

"What keeps you away?"

He could hardly tell her about Paolo's tirade. "It isn't easy for me to be at home, I mean around people there," he said finally. "Everyone knows what a fool I was over you."

Erin shook her head. "Oh, Lon, they don't think you were

a fool, they think *I* was a fool. They think I was a complete idiot not to notice that my boyfriend's brother had a crush on me; that I was so insensitive that I didn't notice all the attention and devotion. So stupid!"

"Don't feel that way, Erin."

Tears caught in the corners of her eyes. "I should have apologized to you long ago."

He put his arms around her. "Don't cry."

He held her, miserable that she felt guilty about something that was entirely his fault.

"I cry about everything these days," she mumbled.

Luz's voice startled him. "Is something wrong?"

Erin pulled away. "I'm being a cry baby," she said. "I can't seem to help myself. How are you, Luz? It's nice to see you." She reached out and hugged her.

"I'm good, thanks. Are you looking for a book for Julia, too?"

"I am. But, as Lon pointed out, he was here first."

"There are plenty of choices," Alonzo said. He felt uncomfortable under the scrutiny of Luz's still questioning eyes. "Did you find anything interesting in photography?"

"A couple of things, but nothing I wanted to buy."

Alonzo took a book on roses from the shelf. "I think I'll get this one." He looked at Erin. "That still leaves you about two hundred options."

Erin grinned. "Maybe I'll get her a cookbook."

"I guess we'll see you Saturday night."

"We'll be there." Erin gave him a brief hug and turned to Luz. "Nice to see you again."

Luz was quiet as Alonzo paid for the book, and he knew she was still questioning the embrace. But Alonzo was unwilling to offer an explanation or an excuse. It was simply too humiliating.

*

On Saturday, a snowstorm covered the pueblo with a fluffy white blanket. By the time Alonzo and Luz arrived at Neyse and Juan's, the village looked like a photograph in one of Luz's books. Alonzo wasn't surprised to find Victoria and Julia already there and helping Neyse in the kitchen.

"Happy Birthday, Auntie," Alonzo said, giving her a warm hug.

"Can I help?" Luz asked after greeting everyone.

"We can't fit another person in this kitchen," Neyse said. "But, thanks. Just make yourselves at home."

Juan got them drinks, and they sat talking in the living room as the rest of the family arrived. Alonzo noticed as each gift was added to the pile, that everyone had had the same idea: every package looked like a book.

By the time the cake was served, Julia had opened the beginnings of a new library. "I'm excited to read every one of them," she said. "Thank you, all."

Felicia squeezed onto the couch next to Alonzo. "Did you dance at PICC today?"

"Yeah."

"Did Luz take pictures?"

"No. She has more than enough pictures of me."

Carlos sat down on the chair by the couch. "Lon is the new star of the show. All the women want their pictures taken with him."

Alonzo shot him a warning glance, but it was too late. Paolo had heard the comment.

"It's the perfect place for Lon," his brother said. "Since he's so into photography, it's only right that he dance somewhere that people can take lots of pictures of him."

Alonzo felt Luz tense beside him.

"I think Dyaami should be dancing right here at home," Victoria said.

"Not as long as he wants to be the star," Paolo said. "Let him stay in town and be a big man there."

Erin leaned close to her husband. "*Heem'e.*"

Alonzo was surprised that she knew the word for enough.

Paolo shrugged and stood. "Anybody want more cake?"

"I do," Carlos said.

"Well, come on then. I'm not going to wait on you," Paolo told him.

The two went into the kitchen, and Alonzo felt himself relax.

"The snow has started again," Tony said, pointing out the front window.

Alonzo was more than happy for an excuse to leave. "I think that's our cue to get going,"

"When will I see you again?" Victoria asked when he hugged her goodbye.

"Soon. I miss your posole. I'll come for dinner one night."

"Alone?" his mother whispered.

He looked hard at her.

"I miss you," she said, her tone defensive and defiant.

"I'll call you," he said, unwilling to make plans without Luz.

"You could bring her," Victoria relented.

"I'll call you," he repeated.

Snow was falling steadily when they drove away. Alonzo was sure that Luz had not heard his mother's words, but she said nothing as they headed toward the highway.

"Is something wrong?" he asked.

"No."

"You're quiet. What are you thinking about?"

After a long pause she said, "I'm trying to figure out why your brother was being so nasty. Is there something between you two that I don't know about?"

Bad blood, he thought. Would a transfusion help? He laughed to himself. There were so many issues between Paolo and him that he wouldn't know where to begin.

"Is it because of me?" Luz asked.

"Paolo's issues are because of Paolo."

"But it has something to do with me, I'm guessing."

Alonzo sighed. It all started with Erin. Did he want to get into it? "It's a long story."

"We've got an hour. Tell me."

He didn't want to share the shame of his adolescent crush: a crush that had lasted far too long; a crush that had caused his estrangement from Paolo and his pueblo.

"I heard somewhere that sharing pain cuts it in half. Why not give it a try? Whatever it is, it shouldn't affect us. Sharing feelings is supposed to strengthen a relationship."

"Paolo is a traditionalist," Alonzo began. "He would have been better off living at Kewa Pueblo with their strict rules and regulations. Anyway, he resents any encroachment from the white world onto the pueblo. He thinks it weakens our life, our traditions, and our integrity."

"Encroachment like photographs?"

"Photographs for profit; photographs for white folks; photographs that change the way our people see themselves."

"So then he sees me as an enemy," she said, her voice solemn.

"More as a threat."

"I'm turning you to the dark side."

"Not the dark side. The outside."

"And Natoma, too, I suppose."

"Yes. Especially Natoma. He sees her agreeing to do the photo shoot as a betrayal."

"Even though it was a pueblo photographer and a pueblo designer."

"Most of our people don't buy expensive designer clothes. So, who is the actual audience?"

"White folks," she said.

"Exactly."

"And that's why you moved to town, because you're a progressive?"

"No." He didn't want to explain about Erin; didn't want

Luz to know what a fool he'd been; didn't want to, once again, taste the bitterness of shame on his tongue.

"I love you, Alonzo. Whatever happened in the past is part of what made you who you are. You're not in jail, so I assume whatever it is wasn't against the law. I can accept anything except being excluded. Tell me the rest."

His gut twisted with effort. "I was fifteen the first summer Erin came to the pueblo. She was beautiful, and unique, and exotic. I fell for her like a blind man off the cliffs at the ancient village. I never had a chance, of course. It was Paolo from the very first day."

"Did Paolo know how you felt?"

"Everyone knew. Everyone except Erin. All she saw was my brother."

"That must have hurt."

"Yeah."

"So then, what happened?"

"Last spring, Erin got the idea of helping Aunt Julia create a rose garden in her yard. She asked me a ton of questions about water harvesting, most of which I couldn't answer. But, I did a bunch of research and started meeting her at the university twice a week, where she'd enrolled in a water resource class."

"And Paolo found out."

"Yes. It was completely innocent, not to mention completely one-sided. Erin didn't know how I felt. I never told her. So when Paolo flipped out, she was shocked. No matter how much we reassured him that nothing had happened, he was furious. It got so uncomfortable being anywhere near him that I moved into town."

"But, you're back on good terms again, aren't you?"

"It was better for a while. But then this thing with Natoma came up. He thinks I encouraged her to sell out. At Thanksgiving he told me I didn't belong on the pueblo…that I should stay in town."

"And you thought he was right?"

"I didn't want a fight. It was easier to stay where I was."

"You gave up a lot."

"Yeah. Too much."

"Are you going to move back?"

"I don't know. But, I am going to dance next month, at the Buffalo Dances. He won't like it, but I won't let him stop me. Not anymore."

"You're ready for a fight?"

"If that's what it takes."

"Good for you." She reached over and stroked his face. "It's up to you to decide where you belong."

She sounded exactly like Julia. But, they weren't the ones who had to confront Paolo. Alonzo had spent most of his life deferring to his brother. Much as he dreaded it, the time had come for that to end.

*

A week later they were on their way to Santa Fe to deliver the first framed photo to Joanna and Bruce.

"I hope they like it," Luz said as they pulled into the parking lot at Poquito Pueblo.

"Are you kidding?" Alonzo said. "They'll love it. They loved all the pictures you took."

"Yes, but I chose this one without their input."

"Have a little faith. Not only is this your business, it's your passion. You know what you're doing."

The couple greeted them enthusiastically and led them into the dining room, where a table was laid with coffee and freshly baked coffee cake.

"I'm so excited," Joanna said. "I was sure when you said you had a surprise for us that it was a photograph."

"We were hoping, anyway," Bruce added.

Luz handed Joanna the package, wrapped in crisp brown paper and tied with twine.

"Can I open it?" Joanna asked.

"Of course," Luz told her.

Joanna pulled the tape from the paper and unwrapped the photo. It featured the motel sign, backlit by the early morning sun and loaded with snow from the night of the storm. A bright blue sky promised a beautiful day to come.

"I thought it might work in the lounge," Luz said.

"It could work anywhere," Joanna said. "It's wonderful."

"It sure is," Bruce agreed. "I can imagine it behind the welcome desk, where we can enjoy it every day. Thank you, Luz. It's a special gift, and one we'll always treasure."

"Something like the gift you gave us when you saved us from the storm," Luz said. "That's a memory we'll never forget, either."

"Yeah," Alonzo added. "You guys probably saved us from freezing to death."

Joanna poured four cups of coffee. "Let's drink to our mutual appreciation."

Alonzo leaned back in his chair. "How is the remodel coming along?"

"Very slowly," Bruce said. "We decided to enlarge the dining room while we're at it, and that means all sorts of extra permits and engineering considerations."

"Thanks to Bruce, the restaurant has become a popular spot for locals to dine," Joanna said. "Truth be told, he'd rather have a huge restaurant and no motel. I'm the opposite, which makes us either a good match or a nightmare of opposing opinions."

Bruce reached out and squeezed his wife's hand. "We're the perfect combination, darling. Nobody else would put up with either one of us."

"Enough about us," Joanna said. "How are you doing with preparation for your show at the museum?" she asked Luz. "It's only about a month away now, isn't it?"

"Five weeks," Luz said, "and I could easily use ten. There are so many decisions to make, not to mention all the prints to frame."

"I trust you brought your books for us to sell," Joanna said. "I've already figured a place for them on the sideboard in the lounge."

"Yes, I brought them. Six of each to start. And, I want to thank you again. It's so kind of you to feature my work here."

"If you have flyers for the show, we could put them out as well," Joanna told her.

"I actually brought some along," Luz said. "It was Alonzo's idea."

"I had a feeling you'd offer," Alonzo said.

"We're planning to go on opening night," Bruce told them. "We've already made arrangements with a chef friend to take over the kitchen that night. We'll plan a limited menu and cap reservations. It works out fine at this time of the year, since getting fresh local produce is all but impossible."

"We try to use only locally grown fruits and vegetables, but in winter, it's tough," he wife added.

"Alonzo is interested in year-round gardening," Luz said. She nudged him. "Tell them about the planter box."

They spent the next hour discussing water harvesting and Alonzo's dream of increasing the production of produce on the pueblo.

"It's a brilliant idea, Alonzo," Bruce said. "And if you can pull it off, I'll be your first customer."

"Geez, that would be amazing," Alonzo told him. "Of course, it will be months before we know if I can make it work."

"No worries," Bruce said. "We're not going anywhere."

CHAPTER 20

As Alonzo expected, his mother wanted to have a big family dinner to celebrate his birthday. He would have been happy with a card and a kiss.

"You can bring your friend," Victoria said when she called to make the arrangements.

"Her name is Luz, Mom."

"Yes. You should bring her."

"You don't make it easy, Mom. You obviously don't like her."

"She's too old for you, Dyaami. You're wasting your time *and* hers."

"Try to be nice to her, please." He could never tell his mother he was in love. She'd have to figure it out.

When he invited her, Luz was delighted.

Alonzo couldn't imagine that she hadn't picked up on Victoria's disapproval, but she gave no hint of it.

"Is there anything I can do to help?" she asked. "Maybe I could bring dessert."

"I'll ask," Alonzo said, but he already knew the answer.

"I've got a surprise planned for you next Saturday night, so don't make any plans," Luz told him.

"What kind of surprise?"

"The birthday kind. The kind I don't tell you about in advance."

"Give me a hint."

She thought only a moment and then said, "You're going to love it."

He laughed. "That narrows it down. Not."

*

The dinner party at his parents' was less painful than Alonzo had anticipated. His mother was pleasant to Luz, Paolo was pleasant to him, and Felicia was pleasant to everyone.

After he'd opened his gifts, Felicia said, "There wasn't anything from Luz."

"Don't be rude," Victoria said quietly.

"My gift is a surprise," Luz told the girl.

"I love surprises!" Felicia said. "Give us a hint."

"I'm afraid if I did, your brother would figure it out. You'll have to wait."

"When will you give it to him?" Felicia pressed.

"Next Saturday."

"Does it have to do with photography?"

Luz gave her a smile that matched the mystery of the Mona Lisa's. "I'm not saying."

"Well," Felicia said to her brother, "I'm going to call you next Sunday morning to find out what it is. I can hardly wait, can you?"

Alonzo ruffled her hair. "Hardly."

*

They agreed to meet late Saturday afternoon at PICC. Luz suggested picking him up at his apartment, but he vetoed that without a second thought. It was enough of a concession that she insisted on driving.

He had no idea where she was taking him, although he thought she was making too big a deal about it for it to be a movie. She drove around town for a bit, and at first, Alonzo thought she might be lost.

"You're messing with me, aren't you?" he asked.

She laughed. "Just trying to get the timing right."

At last they pulled into a huge public parking lot where a giant sign blared, *Cavalia Odysseo*.

"The horse show? No kidding?" Alonzo asked.

"No kidding. Have you seen it? Carlos didn't think so."

Carlos, the convenient middle man. "No. But I've been curious about it."

"I thought maybe you'd like it."

"I'm sure I will."

According to the program they were given, it was the biggest touring show in the world, which, of course included the biggest tents. It looked like a white canvas town.

"I thought it was owned by Cirque du Soleil," Luz said, "but they're not even affiliated."

Their seats were in the second row. Alonzo felt like they were almost a part of the show. More than once he caught his breath as horses pounded directly toward them, and it felt like the performers would ride right into the audience.

During intermission, Luz asked, "What do you think?"

"It's fantastic! The riders are amazing, and the horses are phenomenal. I wish I could watch them train."

"Wouldn't that be something?" Luz agreed. "Sixty-seven horses. That's a lot of training."

When the lights dimmed for the second half, Alonzo squeezed Luz's hand. "Thank you."

"For what?"

"For knowing me this well," he whispered.

They followed the crowd out to the parking lot when the performance was over.

"I think that was the best show I've ever seen," Alonzo

said. "The way they used the film in the background and changed the scene to places all around the world was ingenious. I wonder who dreamed up that idea."

"And combining horsemanship with gymnastics was so unexpected. Those performers are multi-talented. I wonder if they learned gymnastics or riding first."

"Too bad we can't ask them." He tightened his arm around her waist. "It was the perfect birthday present, Luz. Thank you, again."

"I'm glad you liked it. When I saw the ad on TV, I knew we had to go."

"Say, when is your birthday?"

She laughed. "July fourth, can you believe it?"

"Wow. The whole country celebrates."

"I didn't like it when I was little. The fireworks scared me. When I got older, it was fun. And then there were all the concerts on TV. But, it was tricky to have a party because it's such a family oriented holiday, and everybody always had other plans."

"That must have been disappointing."

"My folks always planned my party the weekend before. Eventually, it was like having two parties."

"It won't be easy for me to top tonight."

"Well, you've got five months to figure something out."

"After *Cavalia*, I'll need it."

*

As time grew closer to the Buffalo Dances, Alonzo found himself more determined than ever to participate in the celebration.

Carlos called him when he found out the date of the first practice. "Meet us at the rec center. We'll walk to the kiva with you."

Alonzo's laugh was quick. "Are you planning to protect me from Paolo?"

"Heck no. But if there's a fight, I don't want to miss it."

"Funny."

"I thought so," Carlos said.

The night of the first practice, Alonzo stood in the bitter cold at the rec center, waiting for Carlos. He knew the dancing would warm him, but at that moment, he wished he'd worn a heavier jacket.

Carlos arrived along with Tony and Juan.

"Cold enough for you?" Carlos asked quietly.

"Yeah," Alonzo said.

They walked to the kiva in silence, so as not to draw any unwanted attention to themselves.

Paolo was already there when they entered the kiva. He gave Alonzo a look of absolute disdain. Alonzo thought it was possibly the first time he had ever gone against his brother's demands. He knew Paolo wouldn't say anything during practice, but he had no doubt there would be words afterward.

His stomach tightened in expectation as practice drew to a close. One of the elders asked to speak to Tony and Carlos, so Alonzo left alone. As expected, Paolo was waiting outside.

"I'm surprised to see you here, brother," Paolo said, his voice friendly, in contrast to his face.

"Why?"

"I told you before, you don't belong here."

"So you said."

"I said it, and I meant it. Our traditions obviously mean nothing to you. Dancing here when you have so little regard for the pueblo is a travesty."

"My regard, or lack of it, is none of your concern, Paolo. I'm a man. I'll make my own decision about whether or not I should dance."

"You're not welcome here, brother."

"I'm sorry you feel that way, Paolo. But, unless the elders tell me I can't dance, I'm coming." There was nothing more to say, so he turned to leave. He heard his brother's footsteps on the gravel behind him and wondered if Paolo would jump him. But, at the fork in the road, to his relief, his brother turned in the other direction.

His heart beat heavily until he reached his car, where he sat while the heater warmed him. It hadn't been as bad as he'd imagined. The worst part was not Paolo's anger, but his disapproval. Disappointing his brother made him feel like a failure. He'd spent years doing all he could to please Paolo; defying him lay far outside his comfort zone.

He pulled away from the rec center, sure his relationship with his brother would never be the same. Sadness overcame him and pressed like a boulder on his chest. Was this misery a necessary part of becoming a man?

*

Alonzo had noticed the racks of Valentine cards when he chose Julia's birthday card, but he hadn't thought much of it. The only Valentine card he'd ever given anyone was the handmade variety first and second graders made for their mothers.

But on February 12th, it occurred to him that he needed a card, or maybe even a gift, for Luz. Candy and flowers were too predictable, but what would she like? He went straight to the mall after work and found a dozen other last minute buyers crowding the greeting card section at Barnes and Noble.

He read through nearly every card in the display, but not one captured his feelings for Luz. He went to three other shops in the mall with the same result.

Nothing fit.

Nothing was good enough.

Nothing said what he wanted to say.

He had to do it with a picture. One he'd take himself. One that would be meaningful to them both.

But what?

And why had he waited so long to figure it out?

He was completely distracted at practice that night and felt guilty that Paolo might be right. Perhaps he didn't belong there. Perhaps he'd lived in town so long that his pueblo roots couldn't sustain him.

He saw his brother there, of course, but they didn't speak. They'd said all there was to say the week before.

On his way home, he came up with the idea he'd been searching for. When he reached his apartment, he looked up sunrise times on his computer. Six forty-five. He'd have to leave early. He set his alarm for five o'clock and went to bed anticipating his perfect solution.

Sandia Heights was about an hour's drive from his apartment, and he knew a spot there where he'd have a perfect shot of the mountain. By six-thirty he'd parked and was drinking his coffee, waiting for the magical moment.

The morning was cloudy, not at all what he'd imagined. But as the rising sun lit the sky, the clouds turned a bright orange-pink, and Alonzo was thrilled. It was a heaven-sent Valentine.

He spent ten minutes taking one shot after another, each special, each unique, each a possibility. The sun peeked over the mountain and peered through the clouds, asking no more of life than to warm another day.

Choosing a single photo to send Luz took forever. He wanted it to be perfect, and none of them were. He finally settled on one where the rays of the sun fanned out like golden spikes and the clouds glowed iridescent orange.

He sent it with a single line: "You are the light of my life."

Her response was nearly instantaneous. It was a picture of her smile, radiant, and remarkable, and needing no words.

He'd pleased her.

*

On Saturday, he danced with Carlos at PICC. Luz was there, working in the gift shop. It felt to Alonzo like he hadn't seen her in forever, even though it had only been a week. He hung around after the dances, waiting for the last customer to leave.

"I've missed you," he told her when they were finally alone.

"Me, too," she said. "I loved your Valentine's card."

"I'm glad. It took me a while to figure it out."

"We're on for tomorrow, right?"

He nodded. She had suggested celebrating on the weekend in order to avoid the inevitable crowds on the holiday. Besides, although he hadn't mentioned it, she knew he had practice. "Early dinner. I made a reservation, although I doubt we need it."

"You never know. Maybe half of Albuquerque had the same idea."

He'd chosen Farm and Table, where he could order beef, and she could have the vegetarian meal she often preferred.

"Shall I pick you up at about four?"

"Let's meet here," she said. "It'll make it easier for you later."

He knew she meant because he'd be driving to the pueblo for practice. He loved that she understood him without words. It was absolutely one of the best things about their relationship. He wondered if all couples evolved that way or if their affinity was unique.

She'd never once mentioned the viral video of him, a fact for which he was grateful. There was still the occasional mention of it at work, and of course, Carlos had to tease him about it now and again. But, not Luz. She'd seemed to know that it wasn't a topic for discussion. He was glad. Nothing sounded worse to him that the obnoxious nickname, "horseman hero".

*

Paolo ignored him at practice that night. On one hand, it was a relief not to have to argue with him. On the other, he despaired as sadness took up residence in his heart. Alonzo hated the notion that Paolo was disappointed in him, even when he believed his brother's opinion unreasonable.

The worst thing was discovering that he missed his brother; missed talking to him, and hanging out with him. He often found himself wondering how Paolo felt about being a father. Alonzo worried that even if they mended their relationship, they might never again be close.

*

"You seem down tonight," Luz said to him over supper the next afternoon. "Is anything wrong?"

"No," he told her. Luz knowing him well was not always an advantage. "How are you doing with the show? Do you have all your prints framed?"

"All but two. And, did I tell you, the Laguna books finally shipped? I should get them Tuesday or Wednesday."

"That's good. When do we set up?"

"Next Wednesday. Can you come right after work?"

"Of course. I could take the day off if you want."

"No. They won't let me start until after closing."

"Are you excited?"

"Absolutely. And nervous. What if nobody comes? What if the people come, but they don't like it? What if I get bad reviews? That could ruin the show for the entire run."

"Not possible. It's going to be a smash hit. I predict that all your books are going to sell out."

"Wouldn't that be wonderful? I'd be happy if I could sell half a dozen."

"Don't set your sights so low."

"I don't want to be disappointed."

"Now who's sounding down? You were chosen because you're a talented artist. Remember that."

"I'll try."

He drove her back to her car at PICC where they stood hugging like a couple of teenagers.

"I'll be glad when we're back to seeing each other more often," he said.

"It'll only be a couple more weeks," she told him.

"I wish we could get snowed in somewhere again."

"I'd go for that, but I'm not too sure about my parents."

"We'll make it on a feast night. There will be so many people at your house that they won't even notice you're not there." He kissed her. "I love you."

"You make me so happy," she said. "So happy."

*

He went to practice every night that week. Paolo continued to ignore him. It hurt, but he wasn't going to let it dissuade him. Dancing was too important.

Julia invited Luz to sit with her during the dance, and while Alonzo didn't imagine his mother appreciated the gesture, like Paolo, she'd have to live with it. He was done giving up what he loved because someone else didn't approve.

As he stood in line waiting to enter the plaza, Carlos asked quietly, "Nervous?"

He shook his head. "No."

"Are you coming for feast afterwards?"

"Yeah."

It all seemed normal again.

Almost.

Luz was helping Julia in the kitchen when Alonzo got to their house late that afternoon. He greeted his aunt and gave Luz a brief kiss.

"Hungry?" Luz asked.

"Starving," he told her.

The rest of the family straggled in after having changed out of their traditional dress. Most of them greeted Luz warmly; Paolo merely nodded. Victoria said hello, but her tone sounded to Alonzo more like "go away".

The couple served themselves from the buffet of dishes Julia had prepared and went into the living room.

"There's room here," Felicia said, patting the couch beside her.

Alonzo guided Luz to the spot next to his sister and then sat on her other side.

"What did you think of the dances?" Felicia asked.

"They were great. Similar to ours but not the same," Luz said.

"What about feast? Is the food the same, too?" Felicia asked, taking a bite of her aunt's green chili.

"Very close. My mom's posole tastes almost exactly like this."

Alonzo felt grateful to his sister for her unqualified acceptance of Luz. All Felicia seemed to require was that she was Alonzo's choice. Life would be so much easier if his mother and brother were as welcoming.

He shouldn't take Felicia so much for granted. He'd have to invite her to spend another weekend.

They'd barely finished their meal when Victoria asked, "Who wants pie?"

Carlos and Luis were on their feet before she'd completed the question.

"I'm too full," Luz complained.

"That won't win you any points," Alonzo whispered.

Luz sat up straighter. "Is it peach?" she asked.

Victoria smiled. "One is. I also made berry and apple."

"I can't say no to your peach pie," Luz said.

"Well done," Alonzo said, as his mother turned back to the kitchen.

The rest of the family was divided on their favorites, but

all agreed that Victoria's pies were the best in the village.

Alonzo was relieved when Paolo and Erin said their goodnights.

"I'm no fun anymore," Erin said. "I'm tired all the time."

"You have good reason to be," Victoria told her. "You're creating two new lives."

"I never imagined being pregnant would take so much energy," Erin said.

"Don't forget you're still working full time," Victoria said. She gave her daughter-in-law an affectionate hug. "Things will be better once you're on maternity leave."

"Yes," Erin said. "One more month."

"Meanwhile," Victoria told her, "if you need help with anything, call me."

"*Nachra*," Erin said, the pueblo thanks spoken easily.

Alonzo remembered a time not so long before, when his mother was as unhappy with Paolo's choice as she was now with his. He hoped that soon, something would happen to soften his mother's objections to Luz.

"We should probably get going, too," Luz said. "I have a big week coming up."

"That's right," Julia said. "Your show opens on Friday, doesn't it?"

"It does. I feel a little like Erin, tired before I get there."

Alonzo didn't expect any sympathy for Luz from his mother, and he was right. Victoria offered no words of comfort.

"Well," Julia said, "we'll be there next weekend to check it out. I'm sure it will be a huge success."

"I hope so," Luz said. "It's been a lot of work."

Julia put an arm around her waist. "My guess is that most things worth doing are a lot of work. And creative things, even more so."

Alonzo said a silent prayer of thanks for his aunt.

They said goodnight to everyone and started toward town. Luz had met Alonzo at PICC early that morning and had left her car there.

"I loved watching you dance today," Luz said.

"You've seen me dance a dozen times."

"It was different today."

He knew exactly what she meant. Dancing at the center was movement without meaning. Dancing at the pueblo meant a mystical connection to the past. For him, it meant giving new life to his roots, which had grown dry and brittle. He vowed to himself that he would never let that happen again.

They stood beside Luz's car saying goodnight.

"Let's do something together tomorrow," Alonzo said.

Luz frowned. "I have no time."

"You have to eat. We could go to lunch."

"It's an hour each way for me to come into town, Alonzo. I don't see how I can do that and get done all I have planned."

"I could help you."

She kissed him. "I appreciate the offer, but they're all things I have to do myself."

"Like what?"

"Like autographing the books."

"Nobody would know if it was your handwriting or mine."

"I'd know."

"So, I won't see you until Wednesday?"

"I'm afraid not."

He shifted, feeling frustrated.

"I thought you were with me on this," she said.

"I am. I just didn't realize how much of your time it would take."

"It's only one more week, Alonzo. Please be patient."

"I'm trying."

"I want the show to be as good as I can make it. This is my big chance to get noticed. If the press isn't positive in the first two or three days, I might as well not have bothered."

"Okay, I get it."

"Thank you."

He kissed her, and she shivered. "Are you cold?"

"Freezing."

"It's time for you to go. If you don't have time to have lunch with me, you certainly don't have time to be sick."

"I'll see you Wednesday," she said.

"Right after work."

He watched her drive away from the center, feeling the nearly forgotten sense of rejection that had tormented him the year before. Realistically he knew it wasn't the same. Luz loved him; Erin hadn't. Yet here he was, alone on a Saturday night because his girlfriend had no use for him.

He got back into his car and started toward his apartment. It would only be another week.

CHAPTER 21

Wednesday night was a hectic study in logistics. Luz was already at the museum with her parents when Alonzo arrived. Two museum employees were also there to help hang the photographs. They all had to work around the potter and jewelry maker in a coordinated effort to get the three-woman show set up.

Alonzo could feel the tension in Luz's every movement; her voice was tight and her temper quick. He felt like nothing he offered to do was helpful and wondered why he was even there.

"Is this where you want the books?" he asked, nodding toward the top of a black cabinet.

"No," Luz said "People won't see them sitting there. They don't show up that well against the black."

"We usually feature books in the gift shop," one of the employees said.

"Of course," Luz agreed. "Just leave them in the box," she told Alonzo.

He put the books back where he'd found them, feeling as useful as an English saddle on a pack mule. He'd be glad when the whole thing was over.

"Could you take that box into the gift shop?" Luz asked, sounding as if she were strangling her annoyance.

"Sure," he said, happy to be doing something. He'd be happy to be doing *anything*.

Luz arranged the books much the same as she had at PICC, making sure each copy was signed.

"Are we done?" Alonzo asked when she'd finished.

"I'm not sure," Luz said. "I have an awful feeling I've forgotten something."

"You've got all day tomorrow to think about it," her mother said.

"More like to worry about it," her father mumbled.

"I want it to be perfect," Luz said, her voice tight and defensive. "I may never get another chance like this."

"Trying to be perfect is like trying to outwit the gods," her mother warned.

Luz sighed, her entire body screaming, "You don't understand."

"Let's go get some dinner," her father said. "It's late, and these people would like to go home," he added, nodding toward the museum workers.

Luz put on her jacket, but Alonzo could tell she was reluctant. "Where should we go?"

"The Frontier is open late," Alonzo said. A restaurant near the university, he'd spent many late nights studying there. "It's not fancy but they have Mexican food, burgers, sandwiches, and salads."

"That sounds like what we need," Luz's father said.

"Do you want to ride with me?" Alonzo asked Luz.

"No. I'll take my car. That way we don't have to come back by here."

Another rejection. He knew he was being unreasonable, but it stung all the same. He drove himself to The Frontier feeling expendable.

Dinner was quiet. It was obvious to Alonzo that Luz was going through the museum in her head, trying to second-guess all the decisions she'd made earlier. He thought that the best option was for him to let her be. With luck, the old Luz would be back after the show.

Their goodnight kiss was brief. Luz had parked right next to her parents, who sat waiting as the couple parted.

"I'll talk to you tomorrow," Alonzo said when Luz got into the driver's seat.

"Don't forget that the reception starts at six Friday night."

"I won't forget," he assured her. How could he? She'd told him a dozen times.

"I don't want you to be late."

"I won't be late."

When he called her the next day she was completely distracted.

"I'm signing twenty-five more books tonight, just in case," she told him. "Do you think that's enough?"

"I guess." What did he know?

"I'm worried about tomorrow night. The forecasters are predicting rain."

"A little water never hurt anybody."

"Lots of people won't go out at night if it's raining."

"If they don't go tomorrow, they'll go on Saturday." The silence that followed told him he'd said the wrong thing.

"I wish you'd understand, Alonzo. The first weekend of any show is the most important. The reception sets the stage for the entire exhibit."

"Your folks will be there. I'll be there."

"That's not very comforting, Alonzo." She paused. "Did you post the flyers I gave you at your office?"

"Of course."

"Do you think anyone is interested?"

"I don't know." If only Kate were still there. She knew how to organize a crowd.

"Will you remind everyone tomorrow?"

"Sure." He wasn't sure that it would make much of a difference. Only three people had mentioned going.

"And you'll be there before six, right?"

"Whenever you want me, I'll be there. Try not to worry, Luz. I'm sure it's going to be a great opening."

*

Rain started the next morning and didn't let up all day. Alonzo texted Luz a picture of an umbrella, but didn't get anything back from her.

His colleague, Simon, who had expressed the most interest in attending the show, meant to go the next day.

"My girlfriend has plans with the family tonight," Simon told him. "But we're going tomorrow."

That wouldn't help with the reception.

"Are there a lot of pictures of you, Lon? You know, the video king and all."

Alonzo took a deep breath. "One or two."

There were actually three. Luz had insisted that he sign permission forms for her to display each one. There was one of Natoma as well. Aside from that, all the photos were of the pueblos.

"Who knows," Simon said, "you may end up a rock star."

Alonzo's clenched jaw mirrored his clenched stomach. "Just what I need."

At quarter of six, Alonzo parked his car in a lot near the museum. The rain was falling in great blustery gusts, and the streets ran heavy with water. He hadn't thought to buy an umbrella even after texting one to Luz. Instead, he ran down the street, brushing water from his jacket before entering the museum.

Luz was pacing back and forth near the door. "Finally!"

"It isn't six yet."

"I know. I'm just nervous. The other two artists are too, by the way."

"Are your folks here?"

"Yes. They're sitting in the exhibit room." She frowned.

"Joanna texted me. They're not coming tonight. Remember the chef who was going to help them out? He got sick."

Alonzo put his arm around her. "I'm sorry. I'm sure they are, too."

"She said she was. But, that doesn't help much now."

He hugged her. "Try not to let it get you down. You look terrific, if that helps."

"Thanks."

She was wearing a long black skirt with a red sweater and a chunky turquoise necklace. Her long hair hung loosely down her back, emphasizing her pueblo heritage. She was beautiful, and Alonzo felt suddenly protective.

"I'm sure that things are going to turn out fine."

"I hope so," she said, glancing toward the door, which had not opened again since Alonzo came in.

It opened only a few times that night.

*

"Don't be discouraged," Luz's mother said as the museum was ready to close. "People will come over the weekend."

"It's all because of the rain," her father added. "Tomorrow will be sunny, and folks will come out of hiding."

"All that food gone to waste," Luz said.

"You sold four books," Alonzo told her. "That's more than the jewelry maker can say."

"Did she have books?"

"No," he admitted. "All I meant was…"

Luz pulled on her hooded jacket. "I appreciate all the optimism, but let's face it, this was a disaster."

"One night won't make or break your show," her mother said. "Tomorrow there will be all sorts of tourists visiting Old Town. Some of them are bound to come by."

"I don't want people to come by accident," Luz said.

"What difference does it make?" her father asked. "The more people who see your work, the better."

"He's right," Alonzo said. "It doesn't matter why or how they come as long as they come." He opened the front door and held it for Luz and her parents.

"I want people to come because they've heard about me or they like my work. I should have done more advertising."

The rain had finally stopped, and the sky shone with a brilliant full moon as Alonzo walked them to their car.

"Will you come again tomorrow?" Luz asked him.

"If you want me to."

"I do. I can't stand the thought of being here alone."

"You don't have to be here at all," her father said.

Luz shook her head in frustration. "But I do, Dad. The other two artists plan to spend the entire weekend here. It's what you do when your work is being featured."

"What time?" Alonzo asked.

"I'll be here at nine when they open."

He helped her into the car. "I'll meet you then."

"Thank you."

He squeezed her hand. "Tomorrow will be better, I'm sure."

"I certainly hope so."

He watched them drive down the street, Luz's sad face imprinted in his mind. He hated seeing her disappointment and wished he could think of a way to increase attendance. He knew Julia and Erin and Felicia would be coming, and maybe, Simon and his girlfriend.

He walked to his car, discouraged that he'd let her down on this all-important night.

Saturday morning was no better; even though it was sunny; even though the museum had special signs out; even though Alonzo had asked Mother Earth to help. By noon, only a handful of visitors had stopped to see the exhibit.

"Maybe we should walk over to Old Town and offer to pay people to come," Luz said.

"Maybe we should walk over to Old Town and get some lunch," Alonzo suggested.

Luz grimaced. "I'm not hungry. You go."

"I can wait," he told her. "Maybe you'll feel more like it a little later."

But waiting did nothing to improve her appetite or her mood. By two o'clock, Alonzo was starving.

"Are you sure you don't want me to bring you something?" he asked. "You should probably eat a little, at least."

She lowered her voice. "I can't eat. I feel sick. You go. And, eat there. Please, don't bring any food back here. I don't think I could stand the smell."

"If you're sure," he said.

"I'm sure."

"I guess I'll go to Backstreet Grill. It's only a couple of blocks away. I have my phone. Call me if you change your mind about eating."

"I will. But, I won't."

He gave her a quick kiss. "See you in a bit."

Unlike the museum, the restaurant was busy. Alonzo had to wait forty-five minutes before he was finally seated, and the chili verde he ordered took nearly half an hour. It was almost four-thirty by the time he got back to the museum.

"You missed your aunt," Luz told him. "She brought Erin and your sister. They got here right after you left."

"You should have called me. I would have come back."

"You were so hungry, I thought it was better not to."

"The meal was good, but took way too long. So, did Julia like the exhibit?"

"Yes. They all did. Erin bought all three of my books!"

That will go over big at home, he thought. "See, I told you things would be better today."

She smiled at him. "I think three books are as good as it's going to get. It's almost closing time."

"Are you coming tomorrow?"

"Yes. For a while. I'm working at PICC. I couldn't find anyone willing to take my hours."

"What time are you working?"

"Nine to twelve."

"Do you want me to be here then?"

"That's sweet. No. I don't think so. I'll come by after work, but I doubt if I'll stay. It's too depressing to sit here doing nothing." She looked about to cry.

"How about going for dinner tomorrow night?"

She hesitated and then said, "Sure. Why not? Feeling sorry for myself certainly isn't helping."

He put his arm around her. "You have a right to be disappointed. You put a lot of work into this, and it hasn't turned out the way you wanted."

"It certainly hasn't."

"If you're not too tired, we could go to a movie tonight."

"I'd like that," she said. "Something light, like a comedy. None of that heavy foreign stuff you always insist on."

He laughed. "Right." Luz was on her way back.

They went to the Century Downtown theaters, ate hotdogs and popcorn, and watched a romantic comedy. Alonzo was sure that Luz was worrying about the show, but she didn't mention it, and neither did he. The evening ended like so many others they'd shared recently, standing next to her car, kissing goodnight.

"Shall I meet you at PICC tomorrow?" he asked.

"That works. What time?"

"Five-thirty? That gives you a chance to stay at the museum until closing, in case it gets busy."

"Where should we go for dinner?"

"I don't care. Why don't you make a reservation and surprise me," he said.

"I can do that."

He kissed her, his entire body responding to hers. "I wish you'd move here so I could take you home."

"You know that's not going to happen."

"Yes."

She'd never leave the pueblo. She'd made that clear.

"You could take me to your apartment."

He thought of his dingy and depressing room. "No."

"Why not?"

"Because."

She kissed him again and then opened her car door.

"Drive carefully, okay?" he said.

"I will. I'll see you tomorrow night."

*

Alonzo was waiting at PICC for nearly fifteen minutes before he got a text from Luz. "Be there in driving time."

When she arrived, she was wearing a grin as wide as the Rio Grande. "You'll never believe it; the museum was packed today! There were so many people they had to stand in line to go through the exhibit. It was fantastic! I sold out of the books. I'll have to take more to them first thing tomorrow, although I can't imagine they'll be busy on a week day."

"That's great, Luz. Congratulations. What do you suppose happened?"

"I have no idea. But whatever it was, I'm grateful."

Delight oozed from her skin and touched his heart. He loved seeing her so happy. "Me, too. So, where did you choose to go to celebrate?"

"Someplace we've never been before. Well, I've never been before. Indigo Crow."

"Never heard of it."

"It's in Corrales. It's supposed to be really good. Their specialty is pairing locally grown produce with wine, but I'm sure you could get a beer if you'd rather."

"Locally grown?"

"Yes. They make a big deal about it."

"Sounds interesting."

"It's sort of expensive, but it's my treat."

"How can I say no to that?"

"Shall I drive?" she asked.

"Uh, no. I'll drive." He was surprised she still even asked.

They were barely on time for their reservation at six. The menu was fancy and, as Luz had said, expensive.

"Get whatever you want," she whispered. "I knew that it was going to cost me."

"Good thing, because nothing here is cheap."

"I'm a famous photographer now. I can afford it," she teased.

He ordered a steak with gorgonzola fingerling potatoes and fresh squash; she chose a duck breast with herbed risotto and Brussels sprouts. The meals were delicious, but Alonzo wasn't sure they were worth the fuss or the money.

He offered to pay, but she insisted. "I already told you it was my treat."

"You'd think a meal with produce from the area would be cheaper."

"It goes to show how valuable your self-watering system would be if it increases production."

He hadn't thought about Julia's plants in a while. He needed to call and ask how they were doing. He'd been so focused on the recent dance and Luz's show that everything else had been lost in the mix.

"You're still working on it, right?" Luz asked.

"Yeah."

"You haven't said much about it lately."

"I've been thinking about other stuff."

"It's too important to let go."

"I won't let it go." Not after all the trouble it had caused.

They walked out to the parking lot and got into the car.

"What else would you like to do to celebrate?"

"Something crazy."

"Like what?"

"Like…going swimming."

He stared at her. "Swimming?"

"Not that exactly, but something like it. Something unexpected. Something to remember."

"Like swimming."

"Yes. Because it's freezing cold, and it's actually the last thing you'd want to do."

"So, you want to do something you don't want to do?"

She hit him. "You know what I mean."

"Not really," he said.

"Think of something we'd do in the middle of summer."

"Like eating ice cream cones?"

"Yes."

"Outside."

"In our bare feet," she said.

"We can do that, I guess."

"No. Let's make banana splits!"

He shrugged. "Okay."

"You have a patio at your apartment, right?"

"Yes."

"Perfect. Banana splits on the patio."

"We'll freeze."

"That's the whole point. It's crazy. We'll remember it forever."

"Only if we survive."

Much later they sat together on his living room couch.

"My teeth hurt," Luz said.

"No complaints. Banana splits were your idea."

"I didn't realize it was so cold tonight."

"I could get you a blanket."

She snuggled closer to him. "I don't need a blanket. I just need you."

CHAPTER 22

Alonzo found the Arts and Entertainment section of the Sunday newspaper on his desk when he arrived at work on Monday morning. His hands balled into fists when he read the headline, "Horseman Hero Rides Again," set over a picture of him in one of Luz's photographs.

He wadded it up and threw it in the trash, blood pounding in his head. How could anyone have recognized him?

They couldn't.

None of the photos showed his full face.

He pulled the paper out of the trash and read the brief article to see who would have told the reporter his identity. The only quotes were from Luz.

Luz?

He threw the paper back into the trash.

His head buzzed. How could that be? Why would she do that? Thoughts spun circles in his brain, turning this way and that, careening into each other, making no sense.

It had to be Luz. Nobody at the museum knew him.

Nobody.

Not a single person.

Only Luz.

Sadness wrapped around him, as heavy as a buffalo robe, pressing down, crushing his lungs and stealing his breath.

Why?

Why? Maybe for the publicity; to entice more people to attend the show. Was it possible she sold him out for the *publicity*? If so, it had worked. She'd had her crowd.

As the day wore on, several of his coworkers mentioned reading the article and said they intended to go to the show.

Simon came by his desk at lunch time. "We really liked Luz's photographs," he said. "We went to the museum on Saturday afternoon, but you weren't there."

Alonzo pulled himself out of a mental morass. "Must have been when I went for lunch."

"You made the news again."

"Yeah, I saw."

"Once a hero, always a hero, eh buddy?"

"I guess."

He felt so sick he could scarcely talk.

The specter of betrayal spiraled. Knowing Luz could hurt him like this was overwhelming. How could he face her? How could he even talk to her?

After two texts and three phone messages from her, he turned his phone off. There was nothing to say.

"I love you" obviously meant nothing.

He couldn't think: anguish assaulted his mind. He couldn't eat: bitterness soured his mouth. He couldn't rest: despair invaded his dreams.

He'd been a fool. Again! He'd believed her when she'd said she loved him. Idiot. If she had truly loved him, she never could have hurt him this way. Loser. He thought she'd understood. Moron. He should have been more careful with his heart. Dolt.

He dragged himself to work the next day, unable to concentrate. A profound sense of loss constricted his chest, and made each breath a burden.

He knew he should call her. Confront her. Challenge her.

But what was the point?

She'd done what she'd done. It couldn't be undone, it couldn't be forgotten, and it certainly couldn't be forgiven.

It was over.

Each day was a new torture: waking up, remembering, hauling himself from the bed, forcing himself to go to work.

Breathing.

Living.

Her betrayal haunted every moment.

By Saturday, his pants hung loose at his waist. He'd barely eaten all week. He was existing on coffee and beer.

A knock on his front door startled him that afternoon. There wasn't anyone in the world he wanted to talk to. He ignored it.

"Lon! Answer the door!"

It was Carlos.

He heaved himself up off the couch and opened the door.

"Well," Carlos said, pushing in, "at least you're alive."

Alonzo closed the door.

"What the heck is wrong with you?" Carlos demanded.

"Not a thing."

"Luz called me. She's been trying to get hold of you all week. She says you haven't answered your phone, and you haven't replied to her texts. She's worried like crazy. She begged me to come check on you."

"Do you want a beer?" Alonzo asked.

"No, I don't want a beer! I want to know what the hell is going on."

Alonzo went into the kitchen. "I need a beer."

"I swear, Lon, if you don't tell me what's happening, I'll wail on you."

"Did you see Sunday's paper?" he asked, opening the beer.

"Everybody at the pueblo saw it."

"That's what's going on."

"What does that mean?"

"Luz talked to the reporter. She told him it was me. The show wasn't doing well, and she wanted more traffic."

"She told you that?"

"She didn't have to. She's the only person he quoted."

"Somehow it doesn't sound like Luz. Why don't you call and ask her?"

"And listen to some flaky excuse? No thanks."

"So you're going to ignore her? After going out with her all this time? That stinks."

"Are you kidding me? What *she* did stinks. I can't imagine anything worse. She doesn't deserve a phone call. She doesn't deserve another thought."

Carlos stood. "You're wrong. You don't know what happened if you don't ask her. She deserves that much." He walked to the front door. "I'll call her and tell her you're not dead. The rest is up to you."

His cousin's words hung in the air long after he left.

Could there be another explanation?

*

Late in the afternoon he drove downtown and parked near the museum. He knew it closed at five and wanted to see her as soon as she came out. He was sure that she'd be there on a Saturday, especially now that the show was such a success.

He wasn't exactly certain what he was going to say to her other than "What made you do it?" He located her car near the park, where he found a bench and sat down to wait.

Fifteen minutes later he saw her. He stood and walked toward her, his heart racing. How had it come to this? Only the week before they'd been in his apartment...

She recognized him before he had time to speak, her eyes heavy and sad. She waited.

"Carlos came by," he said.

"I asked him to."

"I couldn't talk to you."

"Why not, Alonzo?"

"Because of the paper. Because of what you told the reporter."

"I told the reporter about my work."

"You told him about me."

"Do you seriously believe I'd do that?"

"Who else?"

She looked at him, her dark eyes a deep pool of pain. "You must have no idea who I am." She turned toward her car, then whipped around. "Have I ever once mentioned that video? Have I ever said those words to you? Ever? Don't you think I know how you feel?"

"Then who?"

"Not me," she said, and got in her car.

Her taillights blazed in the dusk like two bloodshot eyes.

Not her?

Then who?

On Sunday he was so exhausted that he slept most of the day. He went out that night just long enough to buy a burger and a soda. Hunger was now the only thing he felt beside pain: both were deep and pervasive. Both were numbing. Both left him weak in body and spirit.

Work brought his only solace. Something else to think about was a relief. At noon, Simon stopped at his desk. "A bunch of us are going to Howie's later. Want to come?"

"Not today."

"You're not hiding out, are you?"

"Hiding out?"

"You know, horseman hero and all."

The hair on his neck bristled. His brain shifted gear. "By any chance, did you talk to a reporter at the museum?"

Simon smiled, but his eyes shifted. "I did. Probably said too much, eh?"

"Why would you do that?"

He shrugged. "To impress my girlfriend. Sorry, buddy."

Alonzo shook his head. It was Simon.

Not Luz.

"No hard feelings, I hope," Simon said, patting his back.

What could he say? Alonzo paused, then mumbled, "No."

Simon had turned his world upside down and he didn't want hard feelings? The man walked away, trailing the remains of Alonzo's life behind him.

It wasn't Luz.

*

She didn't answer his calls.

She didn't respond to his texts.

She didn't intend to make it easy.

He'd accused her of betrayal, and she was innocent. Would she accept his apology? Could he make it up to her? The sick feeling that had plagued him for a week ramped up.

Short of driving out to her pueblo, which he didn't intend to do, he had to wait until the following weekend to find her at the museum. Approaching her at her home, in front of her parents, was impossible. He couldn't bear the shame.

So, he waited.

The following Saturday he found her car in the lot near the downtown park. He waited on the bench. Daylight savings had started, so it was still light when she appeared.

He approached her, his heart beating so hard he wasn't sure he could speak. "Can we talk?" he managed.

Her eyes were as flat and cold as the night desert. "Why?"

"I need to apologize. It wasn't you. I know that now. It was Simon. He was there on Saturday. He told the reporter."

"So, you believe Simon, but you didn't believe me?"

"I'm sorry, Luz. I'm so sorry. It's no excuse, but it made me crazy. You were the only one quoted in the article." His voice trailed. What else could he say? "I'm so sorry."

She stared at him for a long moment. "What hurts the most isn't that you wouldn't even talk to me, it's that you thought I could do it. You thought I would betray you to get a few visitors for my show."

"Can you forgive me?" he croaked, his voice nearly unrecognizable.

"I don't know. Could you, if I'd treated you that way?"

He thought about it. "I don't know."

She seemed to soften after that. "At least you're honest."

They stood silently, looking at each other with a collective pain that threatened to destroy them both.

"I should go," she said finally.

"Will you call me?" He hadn't intended to beg, but he couldn't simply let her walk away.

"Will I get your voicemail?"

He winced.

"I have to think about it," she said.

"I'll wait."

His body ached as he watched her drive off. He wanted to hold her and kiss her and tell her again and again how sorry he was. He wanted to make up for the pain he'd caused her.

But, it was impossible unless she could forgive him and allow his love to help heal the wound he'd inflicted.

The next week dragged like draft horses slogging through quicksand. Alonzo knew that Luz needed time to think, but he kept checking his phone, wondering if he'd missed a call.

Carlos called him on Friday night. "Just checking in," he said. "Did you talk to Luz?"

"Yeah. She didn't do it. It was a guy from work."

"And that surprised you?"

"I was stupid."

"You can say that again."

"Yeah."

"Did she forgive you?"

"No. Not yet, anyway."

"I don't blame her."

"I don't either," he admitted.

"Want to go fishing?"

"No."

"You're going to sit around your apartment and wait for her to call?"

"Pretty much."

"Okay. Well, let me know if you change your mind."

"Yeah, I will."

*

The next afternoon his phone buzzed with a text. It was a single photo from Luz. No message, just a photo of Rodin's statue, The Thinker.

At least she was letting him know. It was way more than he had done for her. He took it as a sign of hope. She cared enough to tell him she was still thinking. He didn't need three beers that night to put himself to sleep.

Practice for the spring dances started the next week. Alonzo was glad, since it would take up his evenings and, perhaps, lighten his spirit. The annual feast to ask for rain was one of his favorites. He doubted he'd get much resistance from Paolo since he'd danced in the Buffalo celebration the month before.

On Friday afternoon he got another text from Luz. It was a picture of a plate with bacon, eggs, hash browns, and toast.

He immediately texted back, "When?"

"Tomorrow."

"Where?"

"The Egg and I," she texted back. "8:30."

"I'll be there," he told her.

Had she decided? Did he have a chance? Could she forgive? Forget? Would they be a couple again? A hundred questions pinged through his brain. He said a special prayer at practice that night, that Luz would give him another chance.

*

Alonzo was there early. He sat in his car drinking a cup of coffee from Starbucks, trying to sooth his anxious heart. He'd been on a crazy emotional roller coaster ever since Luz's text, high one minute, plummeting the next, fearing what their meeting would bring.

When she stepped out of her car, his breath caught in his chest. Her beauty still stunned him.

"Good morning," he said, handing her a cup of coffee.

"Thanks." She smiled, not the intimate smile he knew so well, but a cautious, tentative smile that said she was wary.

They were seated in a high-back booth that afforded them the perfect degree of privacy. After the waitress took their order, Luz sat forward and folded her hands on the table.

She looked at him with eyes so filled with pain that his insides trembled. "This has been a nightmare. An absolute nightmare. What you did turned my entire life upside down."

Alonzo shook his head. "I'm so sorry, Luz."

"That's what you keep saying. I am, too. Because it was completely unnecessary. The answer was simple. All you had to do was ask me, Alonzo. Ask me, and believe me."

"I know. I know. It's all my fault. I was a total jerk."

"It made me question our whole relationship, question you and question me. I kept thinking of everything we've done together, wondering where it might have gone off track. What had happened to make you doubt me? I thought we'd created something stronger than that."

"It wasn't you," he insisted.

The sadness in her eyes sliced into his heart. "I thought you knew me." She sighed. "I thought I knew you."

He forced himself to take a breath.

"For the life of me, I couldn't figure out why you didn't just ask me."

"I was stupid," he whispered.

"The thing is," she began, then paused.

His hope tumbled into the abyss.

"...the thing is, Alonzo, I love you. I guess part of loving someone is being willing to forgive them when they mess up." She shook her head. "This certainly qualifies as that."

"It certainly does," he said, his voice remorseful. He reached out and took hold of her hands. "It'll never happen again. I promise."

"I'll have to trust you on that. Just so we're clear, if it does, there won't be another chance. If you have a question about something I've done, you need to ask me."

"I get it." He heaved a giant sigh. "I get it, truly." His heart swelled. "Geez, I've missed you so much! My life is miserable without you."

She smiled her old smile. "Good."

Joy enveloped him. Joy and relief. Would anything ever be as sweet as her forgiveness? He doubted it. He could breathe again, after days of struggling to survive.

They sat holding hands until the server brought their meals. Luz took a bite of her waffle and moaned. "This is delicious. I haven't been hungry for days."

"Me either," he admitted.

He ate like a starved man, savoring every bite, noticing the temperature and the taste and the texture. He felt fully alive for the first time in forever.

Later, they walked out of the restaurant holding hands, neither one willing to let go of the other.

"What now?" Luz asked.

"Something surprising?"

She laughed. "We did that already."

He hugged her. "And it was memorable."

"No banana splits. Something else."

"Swimming?"

"Uh, no. But, the Rio Grande Arts and Crafts Festival is at the fairgrounds. That could be fun."

"It's fine with me."

Alonzo didn't care what they did. Doing it together was the only thing that mattered.

CHAPTER 23

On Sunday, Alonzo drove to the pueblo, where he was meeting with his aunt and uncle about the spring planting. He purposely didn't have breakfast, since he knew Julia would expect him to eat as soon as he stepped in the door.

Before he left his apartment, he'd texted Luz a picture of the sunrise. No reply. It didn't worry him. She'd been with him until very late, so she was probably still sleeping.

"Did you take a look at the planter before you came in?" Julia asked, handing him a plate loaded with pancakes, bacon, and scrambled eggs.

He gave her a sly grin. "No. I was distracted by the smell of the bacon."

"The cabbage and rhubarb are toast. Some of the broad beans are gone, but a few are hanging on. The garlic survived pretty well."

"That's not as bad as it could have been," he said, taking a bite of eggs. "What about your rose?"

"Believe it or not, I think I see some new growth on it."

Tony patted his wife's hand. "I think you're dreaming." When she pulled away, he added, "That's okay. You keep believing. But, I'm afraid we'll need more than that for you to have a rose garden."

"We're going to do our best," Alonzo told her.

"I cleared a bit of Mr. Montoya's field yesterday," Tony said. "It's a real mess. There's a lot of work to do before we'll be ready for planting."

"You didn't need to do that, Uncle. I told you I was planning to clear it."

"It was no problem. Our field is ready, and I had some free time. Today I have to go into town, so you're on your own."

After Alonzo finished eating, he walked to the fields where he found several other villagers preparing the soil for the upcoming season. Tony's field looked pristine, the dark, rich earth ready to receive the seeds he'd select.

Mr. Montoya's field was another thing altogether. Even though Tony had worked there, it was obvious it had been neglected for many months. The law of the pueblo mandated that an abandoned field revert to the pueblo for someone else's use. But, since their family was caring for Mr. Montoya's horses, Tony assumed they could work his field as well.

"We haven't seen much of you lately, Dyaami," one of the elders called over from where he was tilling his own soil. "What brings you here?"

"Uncle Tony and I are going to plant Mr. Montoya's field," Alonzo told him.

The elder stopped working and said, "Tony has enough work keeping up his own field."

"Then I'll work it," Alonzo said.

The old man's eyes narrowed, and he grunted something that Alonzo didn't understand.

He understood the look, though.

He kept working, edgy under the man's disapproving glare. This might not be as easy as he had hoped.

At the end of the day, he was exhausted, but pleased with his progress. He sat on the ground, leaned against a fence post and finished the bottle of water that Julia had brought him. One more day, he figured, and the field would be ready.

He walked back to Julia and Tony's, got the clean clothes he'd brought out of his car, and went to his parents' house. News of him being in the village would have reached them, and his mother would be expecting him for dinner.

"You look tired, Dyaami," she said when he greeted her.

He nodded. "Mr. Montoya's field was a mess."

"Are you sure about this planting idea?" she asked.

"Yes, I'm sure."

"Some people aren't going to like it."

He put an arm gently around her shoulders. "That's their problem, not mine."

She looked at him with loving eyes. "They'll make it your problem, Dyaami."

"It's going to be fine, Mom. Don't worry, okay?"

But, in the back of his mind he saw the disgruntled face of the elder. Problems were definitely possible.

When the family had all finished eating dinner, Victoria put on her jacket. "Erin hasn't been feeling well. I told Paolo I'd stay with her this evening."

"How much longer before the babies are due?" Alonzo asked.

"Eight weeks," his mother said.

Felicia clapped her hands. "I can hardly wait!"

"When are they moving back here?" Alonzo asked.

"In two weeks," Victoria said. "Paolo still has to paint."

"You'll be able to help us, right?" Ramon asked.

Alonzo nodded. "Yes." He wasn't entirely sure Paolo would want him there, but he'd be there.

His mother kissed his cheek. "Good. Will I see you tomorrow?"

"Yeah." There would be a practice every night that week. He intended to take full advantage of his mother's cooking while he had the chance.

"I'll make posole," she told him before she left.

Felicia nudged him. "She always makes your favorites."

"That's because I *am* her favorite," he teased.

"You keep telling yourself that," Luis said with a laugh. "We all know the truth."

The truth, Alonzo knew, was that Paolo was her favorite. He'd made his peace with that long ago.

After darkness had fallen, Alonzo walked to practice with his family. Paolo arrived shortly after they did, and gave him a dismissive nod. The elder who'd spoken to him at the fields gave him a similar cold greeting. It hurt his heart, but he'd decided to dance, and he would not let their disapproval convince him otherwise.

Driving home later, he called Luz. "I miss you."

"Me, too," she said.

She wouldn't ask him about practice, and he wouldn't mention it.

"Is there any chance you could help us take down my exhibit?" she asked.

"When?"

"Friday afternoon."

"Sure. I'll come over after lunch."

"Thanks, Alonzo. They won't miss you?"

"Not after all the overtime I worked last month. Maybe we could squeeze in a quick dinner afterwards."

"Yes. I'd like that."

"Are you sad about the show ending?"

She was quiet for a moment and then said, "Maybe a little. Having all the attention and accolades has helped sales. But, I'm looking forward to starting my new book, and working on both has been nearly impossible."

"Which pueblo is next?"

"Tesuque."

"Home of Camel Rock."

"Yes."

"I've heard that's one of the most photographed landmarks in the state of New Mexico."

"That's what they say."

"Do you think you can find a new angle?"

"If I can't, I'm in trouble."

"Can I go with you?"

"As long as you don't distract me, sure."

He laughed, a slow rumble that started in his chest and rose to break free. "I like distracting you."

"Yes, I know."

"I'd like to do some more distracting."

"Soon," she said.

It couldn't be soon enough for him.

*

On Friday afternoon, Alonzo met Luz and her parents at the museum, where they spent three hours taking down her show.

"Why is it so much easier to take it down than it was to put it up?" Alonzo asked.

"No decisions," Luz told him. "Also, I sold four pieces, so there aren't as many photos to pack."

"That's great," he said, giving her a quick hug. He still wasn't comfortable showing affection in front of her parents. "How did the books do?"

"Really well. And, they want to continue to sell them in the gift shop. Not only that, they said to bring in the new ones as I complete them."

"That's terrific, Luz. I'm so proud of you."

She flashed a shy smile that went straight to his heart.

He gave a quiet thanks to Mother Earth for the happiness Luz had brought him. His life had changed so much since he'd met her. Things would be perfect, if only he could figure out where he belonged.

*

The next day, Alonzo and Tony worked together in Mr. Montoya's field, digging holes for the water-catching nets, under the scrutiny of the elder who had spoken to Alonzo the week before. Although the man said nothing, he watched them with obvious concern.

That night after practice, Ramon took Alonzo aside. "It seems like there's some sort of problem. The elder from the field stopped me when I got here earlier. He says the Tribal Council wants to speak to you."

"Me?"

"Yes."

"Why?"

"I assume it's something about the field. He didn't say. They're meeting on Tuesday night, week after next."

"And they want me there?"

"Yes."

His stomach clenched. "There must have been more objections than we counted on."

"Maybe it's just a formality."

"Maybe," Alonzo said, but his stomach said otherwise.

*

Paolo was not at the kiva before the dance on Easter morning. At first, Alonzo thought he was merely late, but when their clan entered the plaza to dance, Paolo was still not with them. Alonzo briefly wondered if it was because of him, but quickly dismissed the notion. Paolo's frustration with him would not keep his brother from dancing.

The entire family went to Julia and Tony's for the midday break, and learned the reason for Paolo's absence.

"Paolo called after you'd all left this morning," Julia told them. "Erin was in labor. They were on their way to the hospital."

"It's way too early," Victoria said. Her normally calm voice sounded like her vocal cords had been stretched tight.

"She's not due for another seven weeks."

Felicia began to cry. "What's going to happen?"

Julia put an arm around her niece. "They have medicines that can stop labor, sweetheart. Don't cry. This isn't uncommon with twins. Erin's doctor is a specialist. He's handled preterm labor before, and he knows exactly what to do. She is going to be fine, I'm sure."

Alonzo was comforted by his aunt's explanation but he could see that his mother wasn't.

"Do you think I should go to the hospital?" Victoria asked.

"No," Julia said. "I think you should dance."

"And pray," Neyse added.

"Yes," Julia agreed, "we should all do that. But for now, let's eat. You all need nourishment for this afternoon."

Alonzo ate without appetite.

Victoria didn't eat at all.

Ramon tried to encourage her, but she pushed him away.

"You need food if you're going to dance this afternoon," he insisted.

"Then I won't dance," she said.

Ramon leaned close to his wife. "That won't help."

"I want to go to the hospital," Victoria said.

"Me, too," Felicia said.

"That's the last thing they need," Ramon said. "Let's wait for Paolo to call. He'll know what's best for Erin."

Alonzo could feel his mother's frustration, but he agreed with his father. "Paolo will let you know if he wants you there, Mom," he said gently. "Come back to the dance. I think that's the best thing for everyone."

Victoria let her son's words persuade her when her husband's did not.

Late in the afternoon, when the dance was over, everyone gathered again at Julia and Tony's. When Paolo finally called, Victoria switched the phone to speaker.

"They've stopped her labor," Paolo said, his voice weary.

"She's exhausted, and they want her to sleep now."

"Do you want me to come?" Victoria asked. "I can bring you some dinner."

"No, Mom. But thanks. I'm going to grab a sandwich and coffee and then sit with her. They want to keep her overnight. I'll stay. We'll be fine."

"I'd like to do something to help," Victoria said.

"You'll be able to," Paolo told her. "The doctor is putting her on bed rest. We'll need someone to help every day. Her mother is coming to stay for a while after the twins are born, but she can't come now."

Alonzo watched his mother's small frame straighten. "I can do that. Whatever you need and whenever you need me, Paolo, I can do that."

"Thanks, Mom."

"I can help, too," Julia said.

Felicia leaned toward the phone. "We can all help."

Paolo was quiet for a bit and then, in a trembling voice said, "Thank you."

After they'd hung up, Ramon said, "That's going to make next weekend complicated. How are we going to move them to the new house if Erin has to stay in bed?"

"That's easy," Julia said. "We'll bring her here. That way she won't be tempted to get up and run the show."

"Yes," Victoria agreed, "it would be best if she was completely out of the picture."

"I'll find some more help," Ramon said. "We can get the move done in one day."

"I'm not sure we'll need anyone else," Tony said. "Between Paolo, you, Alonzo, Luis, Juan, Carlos and me, we should be able to get things moved easily."

"I was thinking that four trucks would be better than two," Ramon said.

"Don't forget about Felicia and me," Neyse said. "We're both pretty strong."

"You two can help me put things away in the new

house," Victoria said. "It may not be the way Erin wants it in the long run, but if we can unpack most of the boxes, she won't have to climb over or search through things. That'll make it much easier after the babies are born."

Alonzo loved the way the family pulled together, put all else aside, and took care of each other. When one member was in need, the rest stepped in. That was the power of the pueblo.

"I can help, too," Luz said when Alonzo called and told her the news later that night. "If there's one thing I'm good at, it's packing."

Alonzo thought of all the things she'd transported to and from the museum for her exhibit. "Yes, you are. And I'm sure they'd appreciate that."

"Poor Erin. I bet she was scared."

"Yeah." He hadn't allowed himself to think about that.

"I'm sure they're going to be fine," Luz added after a long silence.

"There's one other thing," Alonzo said. "I've been called before the Tribal Council. I guess somebody's not happy about me working Mr. Montoya's field."

"Why should anyone care? You said there were several abandoned fields."

"You know how it is on the pueblo. We never actually asked if we could work it, we just assumed nobody would mind."

"Maybe it's only a formality."

"Maybe."

But, Alonzo still had an uneasy feeling it was more than a formality.

"I've missed you," he said. "Let's have dinner tomorrow night."

"I'd like that. Where?"

"I don't care. What sounds good to you?"

"Someplace small and quiet. Things have been so hectic lately. If it weren't so cold, we could go on a picnic."

"Tired of banana splits on the patio?"

She laughed. "It was fun, once. But once was enough, I think."

"What about The Cellar? We could get a booth."

"That sounds perfect. Shall I call for a reservation?"

"Do you think we need one?"

"Maybe, if we want a booth."

"Should I meet you there?"

"Sure," she agreed. "How's six o'clock?"

"That's fine. Do you want to go to a movie afterwards? I know a place that's small and quiet."

"Where's that?"

He chuckled. "My apartment."

*

When he got home from work the next afternoon, he called his mother. "Any news about Erin?"

"She's home," Victoria whispered. "She's sleeping. I'm at their house packing up the kitchen."

He wanted to ask how Paolo was doing, but it felt too awkward. "Is there anything I can do?"

"Not right now," his mother said. "We'll need you this weekend, of course."

"I'll be there. Luz wants to help, too. She says she's good at packing."

"We'll take all the help we can get," she said.

Did he hear a softening in his mother's voice, or was it his imagination?

"Let me know if things change," he told her. "I can come after work any night this week."

"Thank you, Dyaami. For right now, we're fine. Paolo wants to keep it as quiet as possible here this week. He doesn't want Erin to be tempted to get up."

"Okay, then we'll see you on Saturday."

He met Luz at the restaurant, where they were seated in a

small comfortable booth. They ordered drinks and then sat reading the menu, which featured a tempting selection of tapas.

"I want to try *everything*," Luz said. "It all sounds delicious."

Alonzo glanced up at her. "I think we should narrow it down a little more than that."

She nodded. "You're right. You order half, and I'll order the other half."

"Did you miss lunch today?"

"Yes. I was out at Tesuque Pueblo longer than I'd expected."

"Let's order two or three things to start and see how it goes."

"Okay. What about the risotto croquettes, the stuffed mushrooms, and the shrimp skewers?"

"Sounds good to me."

She feigned surprise. "You mean I have to share?"

He grinned. "Never mind. I'll get the flamed cheese, whatever that is, the sautéed clams, and the Spanish chorizo."

After they'd ordered Luz asked, "How is Erin?"

"She's home resting. My mom was at their house packing when I called."

"I bet she's happy to be out of the hospital."

"I'm sure. The thing is, she won't be happy about the resting part. Erin isn't one to sit around and do nothing."

"We'll have to get her some things to keep her occupied."

"Like what?"

"Magazines. Books. Movies. Stuff she can do in bed." She thought a moment and then said, "Does she know how to knit?"

"I have no idea."

"If she doesn't, this might be the time to learn. I could teach her the basics. My grandmother taught me when I was in about the fourth grade."

"Is it hard?"

"Not at all. I could get her a simple instruction book and a pattern for a baby blanket. She could make one for each of the twins."

"That might be even better than you helping us pack."

"Oh wait. Here's an even better idea. I can make one blanket while she makes the other one."

"If she's a beginner, hers might look a little rough compared to yours."

"No need for comparisons. Besides, I'll be right there to make sure she gets it right." She picked up a mushroom from the plate the server had put down. "This is going to be fun."

"We can go to the mall when we finish eating."

"I need to go to a specialty shop for good quality yarn. We won't find that at the mall. There are a couple of places in town, but I doubt if they'd be open late."

"Will you have time to get everything you need by Saturday?"

"No problem," she said. "I'm working a half day at PICC tomorrow. I'll go shopping after I finish there."

"Do you think we should ask her if she wants to learn to knit first?"

"We could, I suppose. Or, we could surprise her. You know how much I like surprises. Does she?"

"I have no idea," he admitted.

Strange, he thought. After all those years of mooning over Erin, he hardly knew her at all.

*

He still had no idea on Saturday morning as they watched Erin open the bag of yarn, tears streaming down her face.

"It's so soft," she said, pulling a skein of pale green yarn from its nest and rubbing it against her cheek.

"Do you know how to knit?" Luz asked.

"Sort of. My friend, Taylor, and I took a class when we

were in high school. I actually finished the project, a scarf. It wasn't fancy, but I loved it."

"It'll come back to you," Luz said. "It's like riding a horse: once you learn, you never forget."

"Thank you, guys."

"If you're up to it, we can start this morning," Luz said.

"I'm fine. Yes, please. Let's do that."

Julia came in from the kitchen carrying a cup of tea. "Here you go," she said, handing it to Erin. "What can I get you two?" she asked Luz and Alonzo. "Have you eaten?"

"Yes," Alonzo said. "And I have to get over to Paolo's, so nothing for me."

"Wait a second, and Carlos can go with you."

Carlos joined them in the living room, looking blurry-eyed and tousled. "I'm ready."

"You haven't eaten," his mother said. "How about a piece of prune pie to go?"

"It's too early to eat," he said.

"Not for me," Alonzo told her.

Julia wrapped several slices of prune pie and handed them to Carlos. "I'll bring sandwiches over around noon."

"Thanks, Mom," Carlos said, kissing her cheek.

"Have fun, you two," Alonzo said to Luz and Erin. "We'll see you later."

Luz walked out to the car with him and Carlos. "I'll come help this afternoon when Erin is napping."

Alonzo gave her a quick kiss. "Okay."

As they drove out of the yard, Alonzo noticed the new growth on his aunt's rose bush, and he thought about the upcoming meeting with the Tribal Council. Was it about him working the field, or the new system he wanted to install?

"Drop me at the new house," Carlos told him. "Paolo separated us into two teams. You're at the old place."

"Do you think we can finish in one day?" Alonzo asked.

"We can empty the old house. That's easy. Getting everything put away in the new house will be harder."

"Who else is at the new place?"

"Your mom, Neyse, Tony, and Paolo. Neyse insisted that since she helped Erin set up the old house when she rented it, she knows where Erin would want things."

"Sounds reasonable to me."

Alonzo dropped his cousin in front of Erin and Paolo's new house and then drove to the lakeside development where Erin had moved when she came to the pueblo nearly two years before.

His father and Juan were loading boxes into the back of a truck when he pulled up in front.

"What do you want me to do first?" he asked his father.

"There are boxes in the garage," Ramon said. "You can start there."

Felicia came out of the house. "Hi, Lon. Did you bring lunch?"

"We just had breakfast," Ramon said.

"That was hours ago," Felicia said. "I'm starving."

"How about some prune pie," Alonzo said, remembering the package Julia had wrapped. He got it out of the backseat, opened it, and offered it to his sister.

"You're a lifesaver," she said. "This moving business is hard work!"

Luis struggled out of the house with a huge box. "Lunch time already?"

"Just a short break," Ramon said. "We want to finish this job today."

"We'll be done by noon," Luis said.

That was fine with Alonzo. He didn't relish spending any more time around Paolo than he absolutely had to.

CHAPTER 24

Alonzo faced the Tribal Council alone.

They were an imposing group of men, all older than he in both age and experience. They carried the weight of the pueblo with them wherever they went; their decisions were final and followed with few questions.

"Tell us your plan for Mr. Montoya's field," one said.

He'd expected the question and had his answer ready. "I've been studying techniques for harvesting water. Uncle Tony and I built a planter box by their house to see how it would work. The plan is to try it on a larger scale at the field. If we're successful, it could increase crop production for the entire pueblo."

"What makes you think the pueblo wants to increase production?" another asked.

He hadn't expected that. "Why wouldn't they?"

"Why would they?" the old man challenged.

Alonzo thought for a minute and then said, "Increased production of produce would mean more food for here and greater revenue on the open market."

"So, your motivation is money?" the first man asked.

He made the word sound dirty.

Alonzo considered his response. "My motivation is improving the lives of our people."

"Which happens when you have more money?" the head councilman challenged.

"I believe so, yes. I don't see any advantage in being poor."

"Living simply is our way, Dyaami. You've been gone too long. You think like an outsider," another said.

The rest nodded silently.

"Influence from the outside is not always in the best interest of the pueblo," the head of the council said. "If you want to make changes here, you need to live here. You're either part of the pueblo or you're not. You must decide where you belong. Mr. Montoya's house is available, if you choose to come back." He paused and then fastened hard eyes on Alonzo's face. "We will talk again in one month. Until then, do not work the field."

There it was, the thing he'd dreaded.

An ultimatum.

He couldn't have it both ways: he couldn't live as an outsider and an insider at the same time. He had to decide where he belonged.

He walked to his aunt and uncle's house, where they were waiting with his parents to hear the outcome of his meeting. Light spilled from the front window and threw shadows across the planter box. The garlic now grew with renewed vigor.

"How did it go?" his father asked.

"About the way I figured," Alonzo said. "They said I can't build the water-harvesting system here unless I'm living here."

"You should move home," Victoria said.

He gave her a gentle smile. "I can't, Mom. That time is gone."

His mother's face twisted in pain. "Then where would you go?"

"If that's what I decide, they offered me Mr. Montoya's house."

Alonzo watched his mother recalculate and then smile. "That's right around the corner from us. You could still come for dinner every night. It's perfect."

A perfect disaster, he thought; moving back to the pueblo where people thought him a fool, and his brother thought he didn't belong.

"I'll have to think about it," he said.

"When do they want to see you again?" Tony asked.

"Next month."

"That gives you plenty of time to consider the pros and cons," Julia said.

"I can't work the field until I decide," he told them.

"Maybe that will encourage you to decide sooner," Victoria said.

But Alonzo knew the decision would not come quickly.

He called Luz on the way to his apartment. The mere sound of her voice soothed his soul. She'd brought him so much contentment, he couldn't imagine his life without her.

"I'm not sure what to do," he said after telling her about the council's mandate. "I honestly believe that the water system could benefit the pueblo, and I want to build it. But, I'm not sure I could handle the negativity there."

"From your brother?"

"Yes." The contentment he'd felt collided with Paolo's condemnation.

"You can't let his opinion be the deciding factor. You have to do what's best for you, Alonzo."

"Yeah."

She was right. It was simple. But the big question remained: what *was* best for him?

*

On Saturday, Alonzo drove to Jemez and met Luz at her

uncle's barn. His horses hadn't been exercised for weeks, and they'd agreed to take them out for a ride.

Alonzo's phone rang as they were saddling the horses.

"Hi, Mom. What's up?"

"*Kuwe tzi*," she said. "I thought you'd want to know that Erin went into labor again last night. One of the babies is having trouble this morning, so they have to do a C-section. She'll be going into surgery as soon as they get the delivery room ready."

"Are you at the hospital?"

"Yes."

"Do you need me to come?"

"No. I just didn't want you to be the only one in the family who didn't know."

"Thanks, Mom. Call me if things change."

"I will."

When he'd hung up, he told Luz what his mother had said.

"We don't have to go riding if you'd rather be at the hospital," she said.

There was a time when he wouldn't have considered being anywhere else. He would have been there to support Paolo.

Now? Now, Paolo didn't want his support.

"That's okay. There's nothing I can do there to help."

They rode out to the Red Rock Trail and, when the sun was fully overhead, stopped for lunch.

Alonzo checked his phone for a message from his mother, but being so close to the mountains, there was no service.

Luz laid out the simple meal she'd prepared. Alonzo had no appetite. He ate half of a sandwich and then rewrapped the rest. "It tastes good. I'm just not hungry."

She nodded. "Maybe we should go back."

"Yeah."

They rode back in silence. Words he might have spoken

withered without a voice. Alonzo tried to keep his mind a blank, but thoughts of Erin in distress sat in his brain, and he could not banish them. He knew she would be devastated if something were to happen to either of the twins. He knew Paolo would be destroyed if anything happened to Erin.

Once they reached the barn, he found a text from Victoria. "Fernando and Victorio are here!"

He called her immediately. "Are they all okay?"

"Erin is fine. She's resting. Victorio is fine, too. He's the biggest. He weighs four pounds and fourteen ounces. Fernando is smaller, only three pounds and fifteen ounces. They're concerned about him."

"Why?"

"Because of his weight. And, lots of times, premature babies, especially the smaller ones, get jaundice."

"What's that?"

"The doctor says it happens when the liver isn't working right, and there's a build-up of something called bilirubin. He said it's common in twins."

Alonzo's stomach clenched. "Is it serious?"

"Not as long as it's treated. The pediatrician thinks he might have to stay in the hospital for a week or so."

Alonzo asked to talk to his brother.

"Paolo is with the babies."

"Will you tell him congratulations for me? Erin too, when you see her."

"Of course."

As soon as they hung up, Alonzo told Luz what his mother said, and then, did a search for jaundice on his phone.

"Oh geez," he said. "It says here that jaundice can cause brain damage."

Luz wrapped an arm around his waist and looked down at the phone. "It's easily treated with phototherapy," she read. "It usually clears up in two to three weeks."

"Yeah. Usually." A sharp pain in his chest felt like his

heart had splintered.

"You should go and see them. It'll make you feel better. I can take care of the horses."

Her words were a soothing balm. Alonzo pulled her into his arms. "No. We'll go together after we're finished here. There's nothing I can do to help, so there's no rush. But, thank you for offering."

He kissed her, touched by her goodness and generosity. "I love you, Luz," he said, thinking again how bleak his life would be without her.

He'd known her for less than a year, and yet he knew, at that moment, he wanted her in his life forever.

The realization took his breath away. He struggled to speak. "I'll always love you," he told her at last. "Always."

*

Visiting hours at the hospital were from noon until eight in the evening. When Alonzo and Luz arrived they met the entire family in the waiting room.

Felicia jumped up to greet them. "You should see the babies. They're so cute!"

"They're so little," Luis added.

"How is Fernando doing?" Alonzo asked.

"They're treating him for jaundice," Ramon said. "The doctor said he should be fine."

"Can we see them?" Alonzo asked.

"Erin can only have two visitors at a time," Ramon said. "Paolo and your mom are with her right now."

"Fernando is in the nursery," Julia said. "They've got him under a special light to treat the jaundice. I can take you there so you can see him, if you want."

"Yes," Alonzo said. He took Luz's hand.

Julia led them into the corridor and down the hall to the nursery, where several babies were in view through a large window. Toward one side, a tiny form lay in a small opaque bassinette with a bright, blue light overhead. A shock of black hair covered his head and a blindfold covered his eyes.

"Wow," Luz said. "He *is* little."

"Yes," Julia agreed, "but he's completely fine, except for the jaundice."

As they stood at the window, the baby turned toward them and waved a scrawny arm in the air.

Alonzo felt his heart reach out, and an unfamiliar longing, one that he'd never known before, came over him. "Does anyone ever hold him?"

"Of course," Julia said. "They'll take him to Erin so she can hold him and start bonding. They'll pick him up to feed him. The doctor said he'll need more frequent feedings to help get rid of the excess bilirubin. He'll be held a lot."

"He looks so alone," Alonzo said.

Luz squeezed his hand. "I'm sure he's going to be fine. The doctors have treated babies like him before. They know what's best for him."

But, Fernando began to cry, and Alonzo's heart broke. He felt a nearly uncontrollable impulse to go into the nursery and gather him into his arms.

"Sort of little, isn't he?" Victoria had joined them and stood looking at the baby.

"He sure is," Alonzo agreed.

"You can go in and see Erin and Victorio if you want," she told them. "Only two visitors at a time. And don't stay long," she warned. "Erin needs to rest."

"Thanks, Mom," Alonzo said. "We'll say hello really fast. Where's Paolo?"

"In the waiting room."

"We'll see him after. What room is Erin in?"

"Three–seventeen."

Alonzo and Luz found the room and entered quietly. Erin lay in the bed looking pale and tired. Her eyes fluttered open when Alonzo said, "Hello, Mama."

She smiled. "That sounds so strange."

Luz kissed her cheek. "It won't take long." She bent over the bassinette that stood next to the bed and gently patted the baby. "Hello, Victorio. Welcome to the world."

"Did you see Fernando?" Erin asked.

"We did," Alonzo said, his heart twisting at the thought of his tiny nephew.

Erin's smile disappeared. "They think he's got jaundice."

"Mom told us," Alonzo said.

Luz patted Erin's hand. "They're already treating him with the blue lights. You mustn't worry. That won't help you or him."

Erin wiped a tear that had stolen down her cheek. "I know you're right, but it's hard. He seems so vulnerable."

Alonzo was afraid she was going to start crying, which clearly wasn't good for her. "We should probably get going. There is a bunch of others who want to visit."

"I hope you'll come again," Erin said. "There's not that much to do here, and I'll have to stay for three or four days."

"Of course we will," Luz assured her. She gave Erin a careful hug and stepped back so Alonzo could do the same. "Let us know if there's anything we can bring you."

"Thanks for coming," Erin said as Alonzo hugged her.

"I'll come tomorrow if you want," he told her.

"Yes, please. That would be wonderful."

"Try to get some rest," Luz said. "You have a big job ahead of you."

Erin reached over and patted the baby. "That's for sure."

Luz started down the hall toward the exit, but Alonzo stopped her. "Let's say goodbye to Fernando."

They walked back to the nursery and stood for a while, looking at the infant.

"See you tomorrow, little man," Alonzo told him finally.

Luz blew him a kiss. "Be strong."

"I'd like to see Paolo before we leave," Alonzo said.

They headed to the waiting room where Paolo sat talking with Ramon and Luis. Alonzo approached his brother and extended his hand. "Congratulations."

Paolo stood. "Thanks."

Alonzo wanted to hug him the way he would have in the past, but the emotional distance between them pressed down on him and tethered his arms to his side. Instead, he reached out to his father. "You too, Grandpa."

Ramon laughed. "I'm too young to be a grandfather."

Paolo sat down next to him. "You're going to have to get used to it, Dad."

"Is Mom with Erin?" Alonzo asked.

"Yes," Paolo said. "She and Felicia are saying goodbye. Even though she won't admit it, Erin's exhausted. I'm afraid all the company is making it worse."

"Then we won't go back. Tell them bye for us," Alonzo said.

"Thanks for coming," Paolo said, and Alonzo thought he heard genuine appreciation in his voice.

He felt a sudden connection to his brother that had been missing for months. "Of course," he said simply.

Alonzo and Luz walked out to his car. "Are you hungry?" he asked, starting the engine. "I'm starved."

"A little. I ate more lunch than you did."

"Let's get take-out and go over to my apartment. We can watch a movie."

"Fine with me."

Much later, they sat together watching an old Kurosawa film and talking quietly about the twins. Alonzo could not get the image of Fernando's frail form out of his mind. He felt an inexplicable attachment to the baby and a strange yearning to see him again.

"What time should I meet you tomorrow?" Luz asked.

"Meet me?" He felt like she'd pulled him out of a cave.

"Yes. We're going on the Georgia O'Keeffe tour, right?"

"Yeah. Sorry. I wasn't thinking. When does it start?"

"One–thirty."

"How about around eleven–thirty at the center? We could

go somewhere and have lunch first."

"That would be nice," she said, and he drifted back into thoughts about the baby.

After a bit, she asked, "Is something wrong?"

"No. I'm just tired."

"It's been a long day. I suppose I should get on the road."

He held her for a long time, not wanting to let her go. "I love you, Luz."

Her smile thrilled him. "I love you, too."

His lips lingered on hers, wishing she could stay.

When they parted she said, "I know you're worried about Fernando. He's going to be fine, Alonzo. I can feel it."

He let her calm confidence lull him. Her quiet strength pushed away his fears and he held her fast.

Finally, he took her back to PICC where they'd left her car.

"Get some sleep," she said. "I'll see you tomorrow."

As he watched her drive off into the dark night, he felt a sad emptiness, as if she were taking a vital part of him away with her.

This was not what he wanted.

He wanted to be with Luz. He loved her. She made him feel whole.

He belonged with her.

He jumped into his car, ready to chase her down, and ask her to marry him. But, as he headed out of the driveway, he stopped. Luz deserved something better than a rushed proposal at the side of the road.

She deserved a time and place that had special meaning to them both.

*

Alonzo couldn't focus on the Georgia O'Keeffe tour they took the next day; his mind was buzzing with ways he might propose to Luz. Sending her a photo of an engagement ring was the first idea he vetoed; it was barely better than chasing her down on the highway.

There were several possibilities that appealed to him: the top of Sandia Peak; a horseback riding adventure; dinner at her favorite restaurant; a picnic by the Rio Grande. Ideas swirled in his head like leaves caught in a windstorm.

"Are you thinking about Fernando?" Luz asked as they finished the tour. "You're so quiet."

"I was," he lied.

"Let's go visit. It'll make you feel better."

Paolo was in the room with Erin, and Alonzo didn't want to interrupt, so they went directly to the nursery. He took Luz's hand as they stood at the window.

A nurse was bending over the bassinette, changing the diaper on the baby, whose tiny hands clenched, while his mouth was stretched open wide. Alonzo could hear Fernando's plaintive wail in his constricted heart.

"Who are you visiting?" someone asked.

They turned to a nurse, who had her hand on the knob of the nursery door.

"Fernando Herrera."

"Our littlest guy. I'll bring him over."

She went inside, and spoke to the other woman, who wheeled the blue-light-covered crib over to the window.

"Hello, little man," Alonzo said, placing his palm on the window. "How are you?"

As if the baby sensed Alonzo was there, he turned toward the window and stopped crying.

"He heard you," Luz whispered.

Alonzo couldn't imagine that he had, and yet the baby now looked peaceful and content.

They stood at the window for the next ten minutes.

Alonzo spoke softly to the baby. "You have to get strong, little man, so you can be with your brother."

"Do you think he knows he has a brother?" Luz asked.

Alonzo didn't have to think. "He knows."

They walked to Erin's room where they found her, Victorio, and Paolo all sleeping.

Alonzo put his finger to his lips and stepped away from the room. "They need all the rest they can get."

They spent a quiet evening together. A proposal was in Alonzo's heart, but he wasn't yet ready. The right circumstance eluded him. So, he waited.

*

Alonzo visited Fernando the next two days, standing outside the nursery window, talking quietly to the baby. Erin and Victorio were discharged and went home on Wednesday, and when Alonzo arrived at the nursery after work, Fernando was screaming.

A nurse held him, trying to feed him a bottle, but he twisted back and forth, refusing.

Alonzo put his hand on the nursery window. "You're okay, little man. It's time to eat, so you can grow big and strong like your brother."

The baby stilled. Moments later, he took hold of the nipple and began sucking. The nurse looked up at Alonzo and smiled. He stood and watched as Fernando finished the bottle. Then, the nurse placed him back in the blue-light crib and wheeled it over to the window.

"Hello, little man," Alonzo said, his palm pressed toward him. "You did a good job there. You look stronger to me. You'll be able to hold that bottle by yourself pretty soon."

He stood talking quietly to Fernando until his own stomach began to growl. "I need to go get some dinner now. I'll see you tomorrow."

Julia was at the hospital nursery the next evening when Alonzo arrived. "Your brother is sick. He's staying at your parents' house. Your mom is taking care of Erin and the baby, so I'll be visiting Fernando until Paolo is well."

"How is Fernando doing?"

"He's been fussy since I've been here. Erin says he hasn't been nursing the way they'd like him to."

The nurse Alonzo had seen several times waved at him. Then, she prepared a bottle, and brought the baby over to the nursery window.

Alonzo put his hand on the window. "Hello, little man."

The baby stretched his tiny body and then latched onto the bottle.

The nurse looked up. "Thank you," she mouthed.

"Seems like all he needed was Uncle Alonzo to visit," Julia said.

"Yeah. We're pals."

When Fernando had finished his bottle, the nurse put him back in his bassinette and came out to the hallway.

"I know you're not his father. Are you related?" she asked Alonzo.

"I'm his uncle."

"It's strange, but he seems to sense when you're here."

"How could he when his eyes are covered?" Julia asked.

"I've seen it a few times," the nurse told them. "We're trying so hard to put weight on him. I was wondering, since he always eats so well whenever you're here, is there any chance you could come by in the morning as well as the evening?"

"Sure," Alonzo said without hesitation.

"I think it might make a big difference for Fernando."

Alonzo was up early the next morning and arrived at the hospital just as a nurse was changing Fernando's diaper. "Hello, little man," he said, and the baby turned toward him.

The nurse's frown turned to a smile when Alonzo put his hand on the window. She nodded and went to prepare a bottle. Once again, Fernando downed the entire thing as Alonzo stood watching.

"You know I'm here, don't you?" Alonzo whispered. "I'll be here every day for you. The truth is, little man, I'll be here for you whenever you need me."

CHAPTER 25

Alonzo visited the hospital twice a day for the next week, and watched the tiny boy gain weight and lose his yellow tinge. When the child was almost two weeks old, the nurse told Alonzo that Fernando was finally ready to go home.

Alonzo was at the nursery that Saturday afternoon when Erin and Paolo arrived.

Erin hugged him. "I didn't expect to see you here."

"This is my home away from home," he said. "How are you doing?"

"Stronger every day," she said.

Paolo extended his hand, which Alonzo shook.

"I'm glad you're better," Alonzo told him.

"Me, too. I thought I'd never ditch that miserable cold."

The nurse waved them into the nursery. When Alonzo waited outside, the nurse waved again.

Tentatively, he opened the door.

"You, too," she said. "It's only fair."

She took the car seat from Paolo and carefully tucked Fernando into it.

The baby looked like a doll in the huge contraption.

The nurse handed Erin a sheaf of papers. "Those should

answer most of your questions. And, if you ever have any trouble feeding him, just call his uncle."

"His uncle?" Paolo asked.

"Yes. Your brother has a mystical connection to this baby."

"How did that happen?" Erin asked.

"Don't you know?" the nurse asked. "Your brother-in-law has been here visiting every day. Twice a day, in fact. Fernando seems to sense whenever he's here, and that's when he eats the best. I doubt if Fernando would be going home this soon if it weren't for his uncle."

Tears brimmed in Erin's eyes. "I had no idea. Thank you, Lon."

Paolo put a once-familiar arm around Alonzo's shoulder. "*Hueh*," he said in a broken voice.

Alonzo softened at his brother's touch. "No problem."

The three walked together out to the parking lot, where Paolo fastened the car seat into its cradle.

Alonzo put his hand gently on Fernando's head. "Goodbye, little man. I'll see you soon."

The baby turned his head toward the voice. His eyes flickered open, and a tiny smile quivered on his lips.

"Come see us," Erin said, hugging Alonzo fiercely.

"I will," he promised.

Paolo looked at him with loving eyes. "Thanks, Lon."

"Any time," Alonzo said.

His heart clenched as he watched them drive off. He'd miss seeing Fernando every day. Alonzo couldn't explain it, but they did have a special connection.

His phone buzzed with a text. Luz had sent a picture of Poquito Pueblo with the word, "Dinner?"

"Yes," he texted back. "I'll come get you."

"I'll meet you," she messaged.

"I'll come get you," he repeated. "Be there in an hour."

Joanna greeted them with hugs and kisses when they arrived at the restaurant. "It's so good to see you guys again.

It's been way too long."

"We've missed you, too," Luz said. "It's nice to be here again. Each time I walk in the front door I feel like we're coming in out of the storm. I'll never forget the wonderful night we spent by the fireplace."

"I won't either," Alonzo agreed.

"You're welcome to hang out there after you eat," Joanna said. "It's been so cold today that Bruce built a fire."

"That sounds heavenly," Luz said.

When they finished dinner, they sat together on the couch where they'd slept during the snowstorm. The fireplace blazed with a new log Joanna had recently added. Alonzo's heart felt full and complete. He'd never been more content.

Luz sighed and laid her head on Alonzo's shoulder. "I could stay here forever."

Her simple words set the stage.

"Could you stay with me forever?" Alonzo asked, knowing this was the moment he'd been waiting for.

"Here?"

"Wherever. I want to be with you forever, Luz. Will you marry me?"

She sat up, tears springing to her eyes. "Seriously?"

He grinned. "Do I sound like I'm kidding?"

"No." She laughed. "I mean yes. Yes! Of course I'll marry you."

He kissed her, long and lovingly, then pulled away when he heard footsteps in the room.

"Sorry," Joanna said. "I didn't mean to interrupt. I was wondering if you'd like a cup of coffee or a glass of wine?"

"Do you have any champagne?" Luz asked.

"Of course. Are we celebrating something?"

"We are," Luz said. "Alonzo just proposed."

"Oh, my gosh!" Joanna said. She leaned over and gave Luz a quick hug. "That's wonderful! Congratulations!" she said to Alonzo. "I'll get the champagne."

He put his arm around Luz again. "I don't have a ring."

She chuckled. "Why not? Did you think I'd say no?"

"You did say no," he teased.

"That wasn't my final answer."

Joanna and Bruce joined them with a tray of glasses filled with champagne.

"I hear congratulations are in order," Bruce said. He offered a hand to Alonzo.

When they each held a glass of champagne, Joanna said, "I hope you will be very happy together. And, if you'd like, you can spend your honeymoon here."

"That would be perfect," Luz said. "I can't think of anywhere I'd rather go."

Alonzo looked around the room. "It's really nice, but I think we could use a little more privacy."

*

As the day of the tribal council meeting neared, Alonzo thought more and more about his future. He'd soon have a wife to consider. Did he want to live at Jemez? Would it be better to find a small house in the country? Or, was he ready to defy Paolo's edict?

"You know how I feel about it," Luz told him the night before the meeting. "But, you don't have to be on the pueblo to build a watering system. I bet you could get a plot at a community garden in town."

They'd had dinner at a small diner, and were sitting in his car in the parking lot outside PICC, where they'd met earlier.

"The whole idea is to help the pueblo. If I can't do that, what's the point?"

She had no answer.

Neither did he.

*

His mother had insisted he have supper with the family

before he went to the meeting. She'd made his favorite green chili, but he had no appetite. He pushed the food around his plate, trying to make it look like he'd eaten.

"I'll pack up the leftovers for you to take with you," Victoria said, clearing his plate from the table.

Neither she nor his father had asked him about his decision, and he was relieved. He still hadn't made one.

When the time came, he left for the meeting on foot. As he reached the end of the street, a figure came out of the shadows and fell in beside him.

"*Kuwe tzi*," Paolo said quietly.

Alonzo said nothing.

"You should come and see the twins, Dyaami. Fernando is growing so fast."

"That's good."

"You made a big difference, Lon, when he was in the hospital."

"Yeah?"

"Yeah. A huge difference. I didn't thank you enough."

The emotion in his brother's voice tore a hole in Alonzo's reserve. "It's fine."

Paolo's voice dropped. "I've missed you."

Alonzo slowed, uncertain where this was going.

"I was wrong, Lon. About the water harvesting. I was stupid. Maybe I was jealous. I don't know. But I do know that I was completely wrong. Increasing crop production *would* be an advantage to the pueblo. You should move home, Lon. You belong here."

Alonzo stopped and turned to look at his brother. He could barely make out his features in the dark night.

"I was a jerk," Paolo said. "I'm sorry."

Alonzo didn't know how to respond to the abrupt about-face.

"Tell the council you're moving back. You'll have Mr. Montoya's place. And Lon, I'll help you with the field. It really is a good idea."

"What about Natoma?"

Paolo shrugged. "She'll decide what she wants to do, I guess. It's not up to me."

"But you don't approve."

"No."

"You still blame me."

"No. I was wrong about that, too."

"What changed?"

Paolo looked away and then back at his brother. "I became a father. Seeing Fernando so helpless and vulnerable…" He choked. "Nothing is more important than family, Lon. Come home, please."

Alonzo put a reassuring arm around his brother. The request was all he needed. "Okay."

After their embrace, Alonzo said, "I've gotta go."

Paolo put a hand on Alonzo's arm. "There's one more thing. Erin and I want you to be Fernando's godfather."

A lump rose is Alonzo's throat. He thought of all the time he'd spent at the hospital encouraging his tiny nephew. "I'd like that."

"We're having the naming ceremony Sunday morning at dawn. Will you come?"

"Yes."

"Bring Luz."

"I will."

*

Traditionally, the naming ceremony took place at sunrise, which would be five-thirty the following Sunday. Alonzo and Luz agreed to meet at the Starbucks in Bernalillo and then drive to the pueblo together. The sky was clear that morning, the stars glittering in the blackness like jewels jettisoned into space.

Luz got into his car and handed him one of the cups of coffee she was holding. "Good morning."

"Thanks. Have you been waiting long?"

"Long enough for the coffee to be drinkable."

They were the last to arrive at Erin and Paolo's house. Alonzo noticed how warmly his mother greeted Luz now that he'd announced they would marry.

"It won't be long before we're having another celebration," Victoria said, kissing Luz's cheek.

"Where are the boys?" Alonzo asked.

"They're both asleep," Erin said.

"I hope they won't sleep through the ceremony," Felicia said.

She and Luis had been asked to be Victorio's godparents.

"It will be easier if they do," Erin said.

Felicia frowned. "That won't be any fun. I want Victorio to be awake and know we're naming him."

"Be careful what you wish for," Paolo said. He looked at his watch, then put his arms around Alonzo and Luis. "It's almost dawn. Are you guys ready?"

The brothers looked at each other and nodded.

Paolo and Erin went into the nursery and carried out the sleeping babies. Paolo handed Victorio to Luis, and Erin gave Fernando to Alonzo. Then, accompanied by Felicia and Luz, the two godfathers carried the boys outside for the ritual. In the age-old tradition of the pueblo, only the godparents would participate.

Once outside, they walked to the side of the yard where the rising sun would hit them full on. Alonzo and Luis handed the swaddled babies to the women. As the brilliance of the light split the morning open, Luz and Felicia held the babies up toward the far horizon.

"Mother Sun," Alonzo said, "you who are coming up in the east this day, now give these newborn babies health, growth, and happiness. That is our prayer." He put his hand on Fernando's head. "Shaasrk'a. This is his name."

Luz held the baby up even higher and repeated, "Shaasrk'a."

He nodded at Luis, who put his hand on Victorio's head. "Ch'iidiga. This is his name."

Felicia lifted the baby. "Ch'iidiga," she said.

Alonzo continued. "As in all life, even the plants in the field, these two want health and growth and old age. That is our prayer."

Victorio woke and began to cry.

Fernando's eyes fluttered open upon hearing his brother. He squinted in the bright light, turning his head toward his uncle. Alonzo put his arm around Luz's shoulder and leaned toward the baby. "Good morning, little man."

Fernando stuffed his tiny fist in his mouth and began sucking.

"He's hungry," Luz said.

"He's not the only one," Luis said. "Let's go eat."

While Erin nursed the infants, Victoria and Felicia set out the food. Julia and Tony arrived, along with Carlos, who looked barely awake.

"What are the new names?" Julia asked.

"Fernando is Shaasrk'a, and Victorio is Ch'iidiga," Alonzo said.

"Road Runner and Sparrow Hawk," Tony said. "Good choices."

Paolo sat down on the couch next to Alonzo. "When are you moving home?"

"Next month," Alonzo said. "I gave my landlord notice yesterday."

"We can start work at the field whenever you're ready."

"I'm ready."

Erin came into the room carrying one of the twins. "Victorio is conked out, but this one is wide awake." She handed the baby to Paolo. "Your turn, Daddy."

Fernando's bright eyes fixed on Alonzo.

"That's your godfather," Paolo said quietly.

The baby reached out a tiny arm as if trying to touch his uncle.

Alonzo leaned over and took the baby. "We already know each other, don't we, little man?"

"I'm going to get another cup of coffee," Paolo said, and he went into the kitchen.

"Is there room for me?" Luz asked, sitting down beside Alonzo.

Summer light streamed through the living room window and glistened in her dark hair.

"You two look pretty comfortable," Luz said.

"There's something about him that makes me feel at home, like this is where I'm supposed to be."

"I think that's because this *is* where you're supposed to be."

"On the pueblo?"

"Yes. With your family."

"And with you," Alonzo said.

"Yes," Luz agreed.

Alonzo put an arm around her shoulders. "I never thought I could be so happy."

Luz smiled with contentment. "Me, either. And, this is just the beginning."

THE END

GLOSSARY

The Pueblo language, Keres, is an oral and not a written language. The following words are spelled phonetically to approximate their pronunciation in English.

Dawaa'e: thank you
Dyaami: eagle
Dzah: no
Dz'i qwii gudeii kwih: what's up?
Ha'a: yes
Haakoh kaama: goodbye; can I leave?
Haawe: snow
Hatzi shkuwitahwa: I don't understand
Heem'e: enough
Henateetz: cloud
Hin'a: okay
Hueh: thank you (male)
K'akana: wolf
K'ayama: chipmunk
Kiva: ceremonial building
Kotra auksi: mean
Kuwe tzi: hello; how are you?
Ma'a: stop
Ma'aku: quiet
Maasr'a: light
Manta: shawl
Nachra: thank you (female)
Pakowtza: cookies
Saucha: child
Shro tzima: I love you
Tiya: dog
Tzanawani: grump, grouchy
Tuu'ma: just kidding
Tzitzi: water
Whooshka: robin

Also by Linda McGinnis

Cloud Dancer series:
A California girl spends three summers on a
Pueblo and falls in love with a handsome, enigmatic
young Pueblo Indian.

Pueblo Summer
Second Summer
Summer Ghost
Summer Vows

Sweet Refrain series:
Six young women, roommates at Willette
College in the late fifties, spend four years learning
about friendship, life, tragedy, and love.

Till I Kissed You
Devoted to You
Let It Be Me
Love Of My Life

Dreams of Home
Chronicles the struggles of two Japanese families
in Hawaii during World War II.

The Bridal Ball series:
Love, friendship, and dreams come true.

The Bridal Ball
The Bridesmaid's Waltz

When not writing,
Linda enjoys traveling, photography,
knitting, and quilting.

Visit her on the web at:
LindaMcGinnis.com